TOUCHED

By Darlene Campbell

Martin Sisters Publishing

Published by

Martin Sisters Publishing, LLC

www. martinsisterspublishing. com

Copyright © 2012 Darlene Campbell

All rights reserved. Published in the United States by
Martin Sisters Publishing, LLC, Kentucky.
ISBN: 978-1-937273-92-7
Editor: Kathleen Papajohn
Literary
Printed in the United States of America
Martin Sisters Publishing, LLC

DEDICATION

Gerald and Laverne Reliford,
my spiritual parents & my dear friends
whose lives teach me to see through eternal eyes.

ACKNOWLEDGEMENTS

I would like to say thank you to Carolyn Townsend, Daniel Haggerty and Kay Williams for their initial input and to Joyce Coomer for her editor's hat and friendship. Also, I want to say a special thank you to the Casey County Book Club and to the Edmonton Red Writer's Group. Thank you, Lori Perkins, for the car rides and the literature talks. And as always, thank you Connie, Ann, Julie, Aunt Dot & Phillip, my first readers, my confidants, my family and Rachel, my heart. Also, Pastor Jerry, thank you for your Sunday stories that inspired me to write about a boy like Frankie.

Chapter One

Upper Cumberland, Kentucky, 1960

The sun hadn't been up long, but the morning was already hot when I got to Crooked Springs School. My thin shirt clung to me in the humidity and I could tell that our first day back was going to be a scorcher. As I approached the schoolyard I saw a group of younger boys gathered by the fence. Sandy Coltrain, a dusty-haired seventh grader, seemed to be the center of attention. He was every bit of fifteen, but he wasn't as big as a fly speck and couldn't even read from a first grade book.

"Hey, fellas," I hollered. They all looked up.

"Fr…Frankie…have you heard?" Sandy said. "It's bad, real bad."

"What is?" I asked

Sandy was all wide-eyed and wired. "My…my…daddy…he found a dead person."

"What?" I said. "He did not. You're making that up."

"I…ain't making it up." I could count to ten between every one of Sandy's words. "My daddy, he was slopping the hogs when he see'd it. B…bones."

"Oh, it's probably an old dead cow." I said, "You ought not to be telling such tales."

"Ain't no tale," Scooter Jones, a redhead boy with more freckles than a bird dog said. "It's all over the ridge. I'm surprised your folks ain't done heard about it."

"For real?" I said. "Sandy's daddy found a body?"

"Yessiree, Frankie, for real," Sandy said. "Ain't no cow. Got a p-people head. Daddy, he went up the hog pen the back way and st-stumbled over something in the leaves. He come just to raking em back and there it was, a dead p-person. So Daddy, he come to the house and got me and Mommy. He showed it to us, Frankie, and I see'd it, that dead person with a people head. Then Mommy said to tell somebody so Daddy, he ran down to McAllister's place and called the sh-sheriff."

I knew that the Coltrains didn't have a phone. Many families on the ridge didn't have phones yet, just as many still didn't have indoor plumbing, but the McAllisters had everything. "The sheriff, he come with some men and they took it out of there."

"Who was it?" I asked.

"Nobody knows," Scooter said. "She wasn't from around here."

"It was a woman? I thought you said it was just bones."

"It was," Sandy said. "But them bones was wearing a rotted d-dress." Then he jerked his head around at the sound of approaching steps. "Better quit talking about it. Here comes Li-Liddie Grace. G-girls don't need to know."

Sandy wouldn't talk in front of girls, especially not Liddie Grace McAllister.

Liddie Grace walked right up to me, popped a big old pink bubble with her gum then said, "I'm glad you're back for one more year, Frankie Keilman." Then she turned, her black ponytail swishing, and walked toward the school house.

I looked up and noticed that almost all the students were there now. I could see my cousin, Harlan, coming across the field, along with Elmer Page and Idy Jo Darling. Miss Mays came out and rang the bell. The year had begun.

6

When recess came, all of us fellers went down to the field like we were going to play a game of ball, but we got to talking about the skeleton again, until Liddie Grace McAllister and her little gang of girls meandered up to us.

"You boys gonna play ball today or just stand there looking at the fence like a horse a'fixin to jump?" she said.

"Now, Liddie Grace," I said, "we're gonna do what we're gonna do and if I wanted to I'd just jump the fence, I would, and it wouldn't be any of your business."

"Now that's something I'd like to see. Frankie jumping a fence. I'll bet you can't do it. You can't jump that high," Liddie Grace said, then she let loose a giggling. That girl was always giggling and her giggles sounded like the bells on my daddy's work horse harness, all light and tinkling.

I stared at Liddie Grace, who tied her black hair back with red ribbons and wore little white socks and pretty brown shoes with a shiny penny tucked in them. She smelled like flowers and wore long store-bought skirts that swished when she walked. I suppose her teeth were the first thing a boy would notice, because they were big, whiter than biscuit flour, and always showing on account of how she was always giggling. I was as nervous as a sinner at a baptizing every time Liddie Grace talked to me.

Cousin Eugene had once told me that women had the power to destroy a man's whole self. He said they were like flypaper, sweet and pretty until a fellow landed, and then they up and turned into a death trap. He had convinced me that marriage was not for a man like me, a man who wanted to see the world.

If I married there would be no hope of me ever going to Rome and seeing the works of Michelangelo, and I would never see the Great Wall of China or get to hike through the jungles of Africa, all of which were big dreams of mine. Sometimes when I was in the outhouse behind the school I could hear Liddie Grace and her little gang of girls talking from where they liked to hang out, down over the hill. She talked all the time about getting married and having babies. I wanted no part of that stuff.

Still, I lost my senses around girls, especially her, and almost always ended up doing or saying something stupid. Truth be told, Lidie Grace was like a lodestone and I was like a magnet. No matter how much I didn't want to think about such terrible frightening things as settling down and giving up on my traveling dreams, I couldn't manage to stay away from that girl.

I stuck my hands in my pockets and stared at that fence. It couldn't have been more than four feet tall. I was slender and lanky, a real fast runner and kind of wiry. I had fairly long legs. I could do it. I'd show her that I really could jump just about anything if I set my mind to it.

Tiny Elmer interrupted my thoughts. "My legs are twice as long as yours, Blondie, and you don't see me bragging that I can jump that fence." He smiled at Idy Jo Darling. He was sweet on her, even if she did stand only a little taller than his elbow.

His name wasn't really Tiny Elmer. We called him that because he was a foot taller than anybody else. "You don't have to jump, you big Goliath," I said. "All you have to do is step over it." I stretched my arms and rolled my head. "Gotta loosen up." I could hear all our classmates yakking in the distance.

Then I noticed Ellie McThacker, a toothpick of a girl, standing under the oak tree next to the building. Our gang called her a leper, because she always kept to herself. She spent most of her recess time reading while the rest of the high school girls giggled and gathered in little huddles. I hadn't realized I was staring at her until Liddie Grace hollered at me.

"Hey, Frankie," she said. "What's the matter? You about to chicken out?"

"I never chickened out of anything in my life," I said. That wasn't entirely true, but it was close enough.

"Oh, I'd like to see you jump it then," Liddie Grace said.

8

Several of Liddie's friends chimed in, "Yeah, come on, Frankie. Do it for Liddie Grace."

"Ha," Cousin Harlan said. "Frankie's all talk. He ain't gonna jump no fence."

Liddie Grace winked at me. I felt my face get hot. I wished she wouldn't do that in front of people. She was dead set on making sure everybody knew we were courting.

"You ain't scared, are ye?" Harlan said.

"Course he ain't scared," Elmer piped up. "Frankie ain't scared of nothing."

"Ya'll just stand back." I looked over at Ellie McThacker once more. A breeze carried a strand of light brown hair across her face. I don't know what came over me, but I hollered out, "What about you, Ellie McThacker? You think I can jump this here fence?"

She nodded.

"What are you grinning at, Frankie?" Liddie Grace said, "Talkin' to the leper ain't gonna make you jump any higher. Better stay away from her, you might catch something."

I took off running and as I neared the fence, I bounded, spread my legs and was airborne. "Woo who!" I hollered. A second later my right foot cleared the fence, but it wasn't followed by the other. My left foot was momentarily snagged by the top strand of barbed wire. I hit the ground on the other side of the fence and rolled down a slope. For a second I lay there, addled. As soon as I realized I was still in one piece I stood. That's when I heard Liddie Grace giggling. She was giggling her dad-blame head off and hollering bloody murder.

I turned around and my gang was standing by the fence. A bunch of the little kids had stopped what they were doing and were running toward us, yelling, "Funny Frankie."

"Frankie," Harlan said, "you've ripped the whole rear end out of your britches. We can see your drawers."

I bent back and twisted around to see my behind. Sure enough, I could see my own underwear. Liddie Grace's legs folded up under her and she fell to her knees, laughing. They were all laughing. Tiny Elmer slapped himself on the leg and howled like a hound dog. Then Harlan spat a wad of chewing tobacco on the ground and grinned at me. "You're a mess."

I looked over at Ellie McThacker who never laughed at anything, and I could have sworn that the little leper was grinning.

Something came over me. I just turned around and wagged my behind at the whole lot of them, letting them see my underpants real good.

"Franklin Delano Keilman, what on earth do you think you're doing?"

I stopped my butt dance and turned around. There stood Miss Mays and she was not happy.

Chapter Two

"I asked you what you think you're doing," Miss Mays said.

My mind told my mouth to speak, but no words would come out. "I...I...I..."

"He's been telling us he could jump that fence for three years," Liddie said. "And today, well, he jumped the fence."

Miss Mays crossed her arms, "So he did, did he? What is he then, a horse?"

Miss Mays was about five feet two and had to look up at me, but she had eyes like a copperhead snake and a stare that could make a grown man cower in fear. I knew it was in my best interest to look away but nothing doing; I couldn't break from her Medusa glare.

"You stay late today," she said, her voice as soft as a kitten's paw and as stern as hellfire preacher's.

I knew what that meant. Sentences. Lots and lots of sentences.

"Recess is over," she said then turned and headed back toward the building. All the little kids ran after her. I stood there watching as my friends and Liddie's group of followers turned and headed inside. That's when I realized that my shin was hurting and for the first time I noticed that the bottom of my pant leg was torn. I pulled it up. There was a six inch scratch on my leg, just deep enough to bleed. I was dabbing at it with dry grass when a peanut butter-colored hand offered me a handkerchief.

I looked up and there stood Ellie McThacker, reaching out to me. I hadn't heard her approach, had no idea she was still outside, but there she was. I hesitated to take her handkerchief. My momma would turn seventeen shades of purple if she knew I was receiving help from a McThacker.

"Well, it ain't dirty," she said. "If you don't want my help..."

I grabbed the handkerchief. "Thank you."

I held the handkerchief tight against my leg. Then I looked up and noticed something about Ellie McThacker. Her eyes, so pale blue that they were nearly white, sparkled like jewels. Maybe it was the light or the way she was standing, but I couldn't help but stare at them. I had never been close to her long enough to notice her eyes before, but they were like sunlight on winter ice.

"Miss Mays is gonna get us if we don't get back inside," she said, "So you better hurry up." She turned and ran back toward the school.

I looked after her until she disappeared inside the school house, then I pulled my pant leg down and followed, more stunned by Ellie's help than either my ripped pants or the cut on my leg. I took off my shirt and tied it around my waist to cover the seat of my pants. Momma would have a fit that I was running around school in my undershirt, but she would also have a fit that all those womenfolk (meaning the girls in my class) had seen my drawers. Either way, Momma wasn't going to be happy.

Back in the school Miss Mays told me to finish a report I was writing on the Count of Monte Cristo. I headed my paper, sat there for a moment, trying to think how I should start. What if Ellie McThacker wasn't really who we thought she was? What if she was really some nobleman's daughter who'd been stranded down in Swamp Holler? Then I wondered what her life was like? Was her daddy really a moonshiner? Did he really kill her momma? The suspense was eating at my guts. Then a ruler came down on my paper, hard.

I looked up. Miss Mays' eyes seemed to be shooting little darts at me. "Sorry, Miss Mays, I'm just trying to find the right way to start it."

"How about you finish writing your name on it first?" she said, then moved on to help some younger students.

It was a long afternoon. I couldn't stop thinking about Ellie McThacker, about her eyes and her brown hand that held that white handkerchief out to me or the way she came to school in boy shoes. I kept staring at her. She kept her nose in that book she was reading. I knew she had a report to do, too, and I knew she would make a top grade on it. What on earth was wrong with me? Before this day, I had not noticed Ellie any more than I would have noticed a particular blade of grass, but now the blade had sunlight on the ice for eyes and soft brown hair that blew like wild grass in the wind.

At two o'clock Miss Mays sent Tiny Elmer out to ring the dismissal bell. I watched as all of the other kids left. Altogether, there were thirty in our school, give or take a few. Sometimes, when it was tobacco stripping time or crop planting time, there would be a lot less. Often kids stayed home to help with the crops.

There were dozens of one room schools scattered around, usually there was one every five to ten miles or so and most of them were a lot like Crooked Springs School with one teacher and about twenty-five or thirty kids, ranging in ages from seven to seventeen. I happened to be the oldest one at Crooked Springs. I had spent two years in fourth grade because of long division and a failed tobacco crop.

As soon as the room had cleared out, Miss Mays called me up to her desk and told me to sit in the chair across from her.

"What got into you today, Frankie?"

I shrugged. "I don't know, Miss Mays. I guess I just wanted to prove to that Liddie Grace that I wasn't a coward."

"Now why would Liddie Grace think you're a coward?"

I studied Miss Mays before I answered. Sometimes she still talked to me like I was a fourth grade boy, struggling with long division, what could I say to her? That I was a man? That I was almost as old as my dad had been when he married my mom? Or that I was too old to be sitting at the teacher's desk or writing after school sentences because I decided to pull a harmless daredevil stunt?

"Miss Mays," I said, "I don't mean any disrespect, but I'm too old for this. I'm too old to even be here with all of these little kids. Most men my age have a job and are supporting a family."

She smiled then said, "My point exactly. You're old enough to go to college next year."

"Yes and weren't you already teaching by the time you were my age?"

Miss Mays glared at me for a moment then she smiled. "Didn't you tell me that you want to be a minister?"

I shrugged. "My momma wants me to be a preacher. I don't know what I wanna be just yet. I think maybe she's just afraid I'll get drafted into the army or something and there won't be anybody to take care of her when she gets old."

"Frankie," Miss Mays said, "that's disrespectful to your mother."

"I didn't mean it that way. I just heard her say that on the phone to Aunt Ima Jean here while back is all, so I figured that might have something to do with it."

"You're intelligent," she said, "and gifted. Gifted enough to become whatever you set your heart to becoming. Frankie, I want to see you go to college. I was shocked by your actions today. The choice you made was not the type of choice one would expect of a young man, yes…man…of your character and intelligence.

"Those children look up to you and they're going to imitate you. I just wanted to remind you to make sure that your actions are worthy of their admiration. Being popular has its curse. People are always looking at you and judging you. The name you make for yourself is something that you'll live with for the rest of your life. I just wanted to remind you of that."

"Then no sentences?"

"No sentences," she said. "But there is one thing."

"What?"

"Ellie McThacker is waiting outside. She stays late, every day. I usually walk with her until we get past the Jackson place, on account of their dog. Ellie's terrified of dogs. I really have a lot of paper work to catch up on and wondered if you'd walk with Ellie, just until she gets past the Jackson's?"

"You want me to walk Ellie home? As punishment?"

"Not punishment," she said. "Discipline. And not all the way, just to the head of Swamp Holler. I'm not going to force you, but since you showed us all your underwear today, I figured the least you could do is to put some of that gregarious energy into helping a classmate."

"My parents wouldn't want me walking with her."

"Why's that?"

I took a deep breath. What was I supposed to say? That they thought the McThackers were white trash? No, I couldn't say that to my teacher who obviously didn't know how local folks felt about the McThackers or that Ellie was the school leper. If my teacher said I needed to walk Ellie McThacker to the head of Swamp Holler, well then, far be it from me to disobey my teacher.

I stood. "Yes, ma'am."

Miss Mays nodded. "Thank you, Frankie."

Ellie was sitting at a picnic table near the oak tree when I came out of the school.

I hollered, "Ellie McThacker, teacher says for me to walk with you past the Jackson place. So, are you ready?"

She scooped up her stack of books and meandered over toward me. "Miss Mays ain't walking me home today?"

"No. She has too much work to do. She told me to do it. So are you ready?"

Ellie nodded. We walked in silence across the school yard.

"Why do you always carry so many books?" I said just to break the uncomfortable silence as we neared the dirt road in front of the school.

"I like to read," Ellie said.

"What do you read?"

"Lots of things."

I took one of the books from her stack. "Call of the Wild." No wonder you're afraid of dogs. Hey, isn't that a guy's book? Why would you want to read a book about dogs in Alaska?"

She hung her head. "I'm not afraid of dogs."

"But Miss Mays said..."

"I'm not afraid of dogs," she said.

"Then why does she walk you home?"

Ellie shrugged. "We talk."

"You talk? To the teacher?"

"She's my friend."

"Miss Mays, the teacher, is your friend?"

She nodded. "She's not always a teacher you know. Sometimes she's just a regular person. She's only two years older than my brother."

I looked back toward the school where Miss Mays was probably still sitting behind that wooden desk, grading papers. She wasn't from the ridge, but her great aunt, Edna Holt Burns, was suffering from dementia, and so rumor had it that Miss Mays had moved from Lexington to take care of her great aunt. I suppose that was what saved Miss Mays from the gossip that other outsiders would have had to endure. She was an outsider, but she was blood kin, on her momma's side, to one of Briar Ridge's most loved and respected citizens. Besides, Miss Mays had an instinct about her that allowed her to fit in and win over even the most critical busybodies on the ridge. She wore her blond hair done up on her head like an old lady and wore dresses plumb near down to her ankles all of the time. I suppose she was younger than I thought. Still, I had a hard time imagining our teacher as just a regular person.

"Well, what do you talk about?"

"Just stuff."

"What kind of stuff?"

She shrugged again.

"Fine, don't tell me then."

"You wouldn't understand."

"What do you mean I wouldn't understand?"

"Girl stuff. We talk about girl stuff."

"You mean like books?"

"Yeah, and other things."

"Does she let you borrow all of these books?"

Ellie nodded. "I always take care of them."

"Don't get me wrong, but why would a girl like you need to read so much anyway?"

"What do you mean a girl like me?"

I knew I had said something wrong. I took a step back as if Ellie really could give me leprosy. "I…I…I…" no words would come out of my mouth.

"What could you possibly know about a girl like me? You don't know anything. I thought you were different than Liddie Grace and the others. I thought you..." she turned and started walking.

"Wait," I said. I had to know what she thought. It shouldn't have mattered. I mean who knew that she ever thought anything about anyone, but it did matter. All of a sudden, it mattered a lot. I caught up to her. "You thought what?"

She picked up her pace.

"Ellie McThacker if you don't talk to me I'm gonna follow you all the way home. I didn't mean to hurt your feelings. I was just trying to make conversation." She kept walking.

"Ellie, I'm sorry."

She stopped and looked at me, her arms still full of books. "I thought maybe you wanted to be my friend, but you're just making fun of me like all of the others."

"All the others? Making fun of you? Why would you think..."

"Y'all think I'm too stupid to hear the things you say about me?" she said. "Think I don't care that you all call me a leper? I know that Liddie Grace is afraid she'll catch something if she sits next to me. I know that Idy Jo feels sorry for me, that she thinks I'm a little orphan. I know that the little kids won't come near me because their parents tell them that my daddy's the devil, but you, Frankie, I thought...I thought... I guess I was wrong." She started walking again.

"Wait!" I yelled. "You just wait a minute. Miss Mays told me to walk you all the way past the Jackson place and that's what I aim to do. I don't care if you are mad at me."

She picked up her pace. "Go home, Frankie," she called over her shoulder. "Go back to your comfortable little life where empty head giggling girls like Liddie Grace McAllister chase after pretty little perfect boys like you and you'll end up in your sweet little lives, with your little farms and your little clicks and..."

I stepped in front of her, causing her to run into me and drop a couple of books. I bent down and picked them up for her. "I'm sorry, Ellie McThacker. Don't be so mad at me. Maybe I would like to get to know you, if you'll let me."

Then she just stood there, staring at me, her lips half parted, her shoulders straight, the wind blowing her hair across her tanned face and a streak of light filtering through the trees, falling upon her back, making a halo around her.

In that moment, I wished I had a pencil and paper in my hand. I would have drawn that girl. She looked as elegant as the statues of Michelangelo. Her little flour sack dress stuck to her body, and I could see that even though she was probably twenty pounds lighter than Liddie, she was all curvy and girlie under that thin little dress. Why had I never realized it before? I couldn't stop staring at Ellie McThacker because she was pretty, not in the way that Liddie Grace was pretty in stylish clothes, shiny shoes and red ribbons but in the way that a red-wing hawk is pretty when the sun catches on its white belly as it comes out of nowhere, lets out its cry and circles above your head, catching you off guard and amazing you, because you wonder how long it's been watching and why it suddenly decided to cross your path.

"You ought not to have said that," she said.

I gulped. "I only meant that you're smart. I didn't think you needed to read all of those books."

She looked down, "I thought you were making fun of me. I'm sorry I said that you were just gonna end up married to Liddie Grace with a house full of kids, all with big white teeth. I shouldn't have said you were just like the others."

We were quiet for a long uncomfortable few seconds then I up and said, "You didn't say anything about big white teeth."

Ellie smiled. She really smiled. Her smile was like walking into an unexpected patch of sunlight in the middle of the woods. I smiled too, then I laughed and she laughed. I felt like climbing trees or doing some other ridiculous stunts, but I didn't. I was supposed to walk this girl to the bottom of Briar Ridge and that's what I aimed to do.

I took the books from Ellie and started walking. And for some reason unbeknown to me, I told Ellie McThacker every thought in my head that afternoon.

Chapter Three

My family's house was white with a large front porch and a rock walkway. It was surrounded by a picket fence and seven hickory trees. It sat across the field and down the holler just about a quarter of a mile from my cousin Eugene's place and was surrounded by fields and forests on all sides. A gravel road led from the main highway to our driveway. Daddy and Eugene together owned over a hundred acres. The farm had been in the family for two hundred years, ever since our ancestors came over from the highlands of Scotland to preach the gospel to the ignorant heathens of southern Kentucky.

The name, Keilman, came from Germany because my paternal grandmother had married the son of a German shopkeeper whose great-niece was Merideth Goodin. She ran Goodin's store, two miles up the main highway.

"Where have you been, Frankie?" Momma asked the minute I walked in the door.

She was sitting on the rust-colored couch in the living room, smoking a cigarette and drinking coffee, her auburn hair in curlers while she watched her 'stories', which is what she called the soap operas that she never missed.

"I stayed late and helped Miss Mays with something." I wasn't lying, not really.

She never even looked at me, "Well, that was a nice thing of you to do," she said. "Your daddy and Cousin Eugene are in the back field, down by the little barn, unloading some hay for the cattle. He said tell you to get on down there as soon as you got home from school." She took a draw off her cigarette and crossed her foot. She gave off the air that she was queen of the world, or at least the living room.

"All right," I said and started out the door.

"Change your clothes first," she said.

I turned around at the door. "Momma, I was showing out in front of Liddie Grace McAllister today. I jumped the fence at school just to prove to her that I could do it and I have ripped my new pants. I'm so sorry, Mo..."

She glared at the television, "So you ripped your pants showing out in front of Liddie Grace?"

I was scared she was about to have a conniption fit then turn right around and nag me until I wished that I have cut my head off instead of just scratching up my leg. My momma could nag the flies off a horse and cause a hog to just give up and die before it ever reached the slaughter house.

"Do you have any idea how much a pair of store bought pants cost now-a-days?"

"I'll pay for them," I said. "I'll cut grass for people on the ridge and pay for them."

"Yes, you will," she said. "Leave them on the sewing machine and I'll mend them in the morning while you're at school. Still, I'm not mad at you. That Liddie Grace is a fine girl, from a fine family. I understand why you would want to show out in front of her."

"Did you hear about that skeleton Sandy Coltrain's daddy found down below his hog pen?" I asked.

"The whole ridge has heard," she said. "Alice McAllister says that it was somebody from off from here. Sheriff told her that most likely somebody was passing through, killed her and hid her body down below that hog pen back off the road. She says that the body was covered in leaves and what not. Most likely the hot summer smell of that hog pen drowned out any smell that seeped through." She shook her head. "It's an awful thing, Frankie, to think that somebody would just kill a person like that. Reckon she was a bad woman?"

I shrugged. "I don't figure anybody could be bad enough to earn an end like hers. You think they'll ever find out who did it?"

Momma shook her head. "Likely as not. The one that did it's probably long gone from here now." She shuddered. "I hope so anyway. I hate to think that some killer might be lurking around out yonder in the woods somewhere. You be careful, Frankie. Lord knows I'd die if something was to happen to you. I don't know what I'd do." She took a puff off her cigarette. "Get on up there and change your britches."

I went upstairs to my room. I heard the phone ring, went to the top of the stairs and listened.

"How sweet," my mother said. "Yes, showing out to win her affection." She waited for the person on the other end of the line to finish. "Oh, yes, they're going to end up together...uh, huh, a fine couple. That's right. Oh yes, such an honest boy."

I knew who she was talking to, Liddie Grace's mother. I felt an awful pit in my stomach, worse than if Momma had nagged at me. Store-bought clothes, lipstick and a whole host of other new-fangled oddities had turned up at our house since Alice McAllister had started talking to Momma.

Up in my room, I stood before the dresser mirror and turned around to survey the damage. Sure enough, every time I took a step my underwear showed. After I'd changed into my work clothes I went downstairs and headed out to what we called the little barn, which meant that it was really just a large shed. Besides the little barn, our farm included the corn crib, a tobacco barn and a hay barn with a back lot where we kept a couple of milk cows. Off to the side of the hay barn we had a hog pen where we always had at least one hog to kill for winter.

I heard my dad hollering at Eugene before I reached the field. Neither one of them spoke as I approached. It sounded like Eugene was mad enough to bite nails and poop horse shoes.

"You never put things back where they go," Eugene said. "You got no respect for a man or his tools."

My cousin Eugene was at least two decades older than I, and he was almost as tall as Tiny Elmer. I had never in my life seen him in anything other than bibbed overalls and a straw gangster style hat. He was thin and lanky and had never moved faster than a box turtle. Nine out of ten times when I saw him, he either had a pipe or a piece of straw in his mouth. He lived alone and ate a steady diet of pinto beans, cornbread, cabbage and strong coffee that he boiled on his wood stove. If there was anything that ticked him off, it was doing things differently or somebody who would not put something back where he felt it belonged. He and my dad could not have been more opposite.

My dad was short, maybe five and a half feet. He had been bald since he was twenty-four and was like a little spider, always running and moving and fixing things. He had more projects going than he could finish, misplaced things he had just laid down and couldn't remember a person's name to save his life. He never did anything the same way twice and did well to get a tool back in the shed, much less hang it on the proper hook.

"I put it back," my dad said.

"Well," Eugene grumbled. "Where in the Sam Hill did you put it?"

"Right yonder," my dad said. "Right yonder in that dag blasted shed."

"Ancil, I done checked and it ain't there. Don't you be asking me to borrow nary other thing."

"Frankie," my dad said. So, he did know I had showed up. "You run on over to the house and find this son of a biscuit eater's pitch fork, then bring it back here and stick him in the as…"

"Don't know what you're so cussin mad about," Eugene said. "You're the one what lost my pitchfork." He turned and shuffled back toward his house, a simple white A-frame with a sand bucket well and a wringer washing machine in the back yard.

My dad flew into cussing and kicking the hay wagon.

"Do you still want me to go look for the pitchfork, Daddy?"

"You blamed little greenhorn, of course I do. We can't load this hay without it."

I scurried off across the field and down the road toward our house. When I reached the front yard, I kept going until I had rounded the back corner. We had a chicken coop behind our house, a woodshed, an outhouse and a couple of overstuffed out buildings chock full of Daddy's junk. He never threw anything away, and he often ended up with duplicates of everything and lots of broken or rusted things. It took me a good half hour to find that pitchfork. I finally spotted it lying on a hillside down behind the woodshed, in some tall weeds. I thought about how that if I hadn't found it Momma would be on her way to the garden and maybe step on it and get hurt.

I headed back to where I'd left Daddy. When I got there I found him sitting on the hay wagon, with a hand rolled cigarette hanging from his lips, smoking like a stove full of water-soaked wood. I thought how easy it would be for him to drop a spark and catch the whole wagon on fire.

As I approached him, he took a long draw off that cigarette, put it out on the wooden wagon frame, then jumped down and went to pitching hay. We took turns and I decided it was a good time to talk to him about some things that bothered me.

"Daddy," I said. "Will you tell me again about the McThackers?"

"No good."

"How well do you know them?"

"Old Mooney McThacker's a thief and a murderer. And that boy of his, they say he's a ridge runner. They go way back around here. My grandpa had a run in with them in his day. One of them stole a sheep right offen his farm. Came walking up the road one day with a sack on his shoulder. Now that old Grady McThacker, he couldn't talk plain and people said he wouldn't right in the head. Anyway, Grandpa said, 'Hey, old man McThacker, what you got in that sack?' And old McThacker just looked at him and said, 'mutton'. Now Grandpa thought he was saying 'nuttin' on account of him not talking plain, but he was plain old telling my grandpa that he was walking off with one of his sheep in that sack. Then Old Grady said he had to go cause the weather was getting heavy. Grandpa thought he meant that he had to hurry on home on account of it was real foggy out."

I didn't tell my dad but I was pretty sure that was a just an old joke somebody had handed down and I didn't think that had really happened. "Well, what else do you know about them?" I asked.

"They used to sell shine right out from under the church house steps, back in the day. They say old Elsie McThacker had a still set up down on George Creek in Swamp Holler. She'd make the stuff then her old man would haul it up to that empty lot between Meredith's store and the church house. Why I reckon he'd set up shop and sell liquor to the sinners while meeting was going on."

"Whatever happened to him?"

"Came up a storm one day and they say he was drunk as a bare butt monkey, ran outside and started hollering up to heaven that he wouldn't afraid of no storm and that he dared anybody to do anything about it. Sure enough, a lightning bolt split that sky and fried him right there on the spot, cooked him like a pig on a stick."

"What'd you reckon made him do it, Daddy?"

"Just born to it, I reckon. Bad blood tends to run in families like that."

"But couldn't a person go against it? I mean what if a McThacker decided to be different? You know, go to school and get an education?"

My dad grunted. "What's got you to asking such foolish questions anyway?"

"I don't know. I guess I was thinking about when I get to be a preacher one day. What if a McThacker needs help or wants to come to my church? Then what? Do I not let them in my church because of their last name?"

"That's foolish talk. Ain't no McThacker ever set foot in a church unless he was up to something wicked. I don't want to hear no more about it."

"All right," I said.

After supper that night I sat out on the porch, listening to the crickets chirp. I whittled at a cedar stick, my mind wandering to first one place then another. Mostly it kept wandering back to the way Ellie McThacker looked with the wind plastering her dress to her body when she had told me not to walk her home.

I put my whittling away and went up to my room. I guess by most folk's standards on Briar Ridge we were fairly well-off. Of course, we weren't in any league with the Dawsons or the McAllisters, but I was one of the few boys on the ridge whose parents were bound and determined that I was going to get an education, mainly because that was an opportunity that neither of them had ever had and they wanted me to keep up our family name, above all else.

"Keilmans have always been respected and if you ruin your name you got nothing to fall back on," my dad had said that to me more times than I could remember. That's why I was still in school, instead of working full time on the farm like most fellas my age.

In my room I took out my Bible and read the story of Jesus and the woman at the well. This woman had been what Eugene would call a bad woman. She had been with five men and was shacking up with one who wasn't even married to her and yet Jesus himself talked to her and offered her living water. I could picture the story in my mind and lo and behold, that woman had a face just like Ellie McThacker's. If Jesus cared about the wayward woman at the well wouldn't he also care about Ellie? As far as I knew she hadn't been married five times and she wasn't shacking up with anybody. She had somehow just managed to come into the world as a motherless McThacker.

I closed the Bible and put it back in my drawer. No matter how hard I tried to think about other things, I couldn't stop thinking about Ellie. I kept thinking about her peanut butter colored hand, holding that handkerchief out to me and her sparkling eyes. Then I would see those same eyes all angry and full of hurt and I could hear her breezy little voice scolding me, scolding Liddie Grace. In the next second I would see her standing there in that halo of light. And I thought about her lips, how they were full and shaped as perfect as a pair of human lips could be shaped. She had lips like the models in Momma's wish books, which is what she called her stylish clothing catalogs. I reached under my bed, took out my sketching papers and drew her, standing with the light on her back and the wind in her hair. I worked on that sketch way into the night, worked on it until it looked just like Ellie.

It was late when I finished the drawing and my parents were already in bed. I studied it for a long time by low lamp light then placed it in the box and went to bed, with pencil smudges still on my hands. That night I dreamed about a man getting struck by lightning and about a roasting pig.

Chapter Four

It was four-thirty in the morning when I got up and helped Daddy with the milking, and then I put on my second best pair of pants, a checkered shirt with button down collars, and my good boots. Then I went down for a bite of breakfast.

Momma and Daddy were in the kitchen. Our kitchen looked like a page from a catalog or the set of a television show. A sink and adjoining counter top with cabinets below and cupboards above, sat under a long row of windows, dressed in ruffled red and white curtains. Although we didn't have running water yet, Momma had insisted that the sink be put in because she was planning on getting it soon. There was a butter churn in the corner between the gas range stove and the refrigerator, the top of which contained a bread box and a cookie jar. We also had a wash table and a wood cook stove in the corner. A small brown shelf set beside the door which led into the living room. This was where Momma kept the AM radio, a brown wooden box with a white station indicator in the middle and gold knobs for tuning on each side. In the center of the room we had a big wooden table with matching wooden chairs.

I gobbled down a couple of biscuits and four strips of bacon, guzzled a glass of milk, grabbed the lunch Momma had packed for me and headed out the back screen door. The walk was a little over a mile and a half, not bad considering how far some kids walked to school. I yawned all the way there. My staying up late was already catching up to me.

The school was a white weatherboard building that sat on the side of the road, separated from a cattle field on three sides by the barbed wire fence that I had tried to jump. An American flag hung on a pole near the door and there was a bell situated to the right of the door lentil. A great long string dangled low enough so that even the youngest child could ring the bell.

When I entered, Miss Mays was seated at her desk with a group of six and seven year olds gathered around her. Liddie Grace was going over spelling words with some nine and ten year olds and a group of middle grade kids were doing math on the board behind Miss Mays.

Harlan wasn't there and probably wouldn't be for several days. His daddy needed him to haul in hay. Tiny Elmer and Idy Jo were doing some kind of a book report. I heard footsteps and turned around. There stood Ellie in the door, her head down. She never looked up nor spoke a word. As usual, she slid into her seat in the back, opened her books and got to work.

Things went on as usual until lunch time when Miss Mays sent us all outside to eat. It was a hot September day and I was thankful for the shady yard behind the school where my gang always sat.

I parked myself on the bench at the picnic table my dad and I had built for the school and commenced to taking out my sausage and biscuits that Momma had packed me when Liddie Grace pounced over there and wiggled her tail right in beside me. I scooted all the way to the other end.

"What's the matter, Frankie? Afraid you'll get girl cooties?"

"No, I just need space when I eat. That's all."

Tiny Elmer laughed. "Is that right? You're as skinny as one of them fence posts out yonder. How much room do you think you need?"

"He ain't skinny," Liddie said. "He's just a tad on the thin side. Don't worry, he'll get plenty of muscle when he gets a little older. Momma said Frankie's gonna be really handsome by the time he's in his twenties. She says he's got good bone structure."

I didn't care much for the notion that Liddie and her momma talked about my bone structure.

I looked up and saw Ellie, sitting on the back steps, alone as usual. Something came over me, and all at once, I was plum mad at Liddie Grace and her momma. I was mad at my momma, too. My bone structure was none of their business. I stood up. "Ellie McThacker, you come over here and sit with us. My momma has put enough food in here for three people. Get over here and help me eat it. There ain't no sense you eating by yourself all of the time."

I thought Tiny Elmer was going to wet his britches and Liddie Grace got strangled on her water. Then Idy Jo stood up and waved her over. "Yeah, Ellie. Come eat with us." I smiled at Idy Jo, and remembered how Ellie had said Idy Jo was nice to her out of pity. I understood how that could make Ellie feel angry. I suppose somebody being sugar sweet to me out of pity would make me feel mad, too.

Ellie came over and of course I saw right off that she didn't have a thing to eat and I wondered how many times Ellie had done without in her life. I wondered if she had food at home and if her daddy cared whether she ate or not.

I patted the space between Liddie Grace and myself and as Ellie sat down, I noticed Liddie Grace inching toward the far edge of the bench, like she thought she might catch some disease off Ellie.

The table was quiet for a couple of minutes then Idy Jo up and said. "I really did like that poem we read in class this morning, the one about the girl dying by the seashore. How about y'all?"

Tiny Elmer crammed a piece of cornbread in his mouth. "You know I don't go for all that old mushy stuff, Idy Jo. I'm just here til next month anyway. Soon as I have my birthday, I'm quitting. Pap done said it'd be okay."

"School won't be the same without you," I said.

"I got to quit," he said. "Tommy got his leg shot up and ain't nobody to help Pap when it comes backer stripping time."

Tommy was Elmer's older brother. He had been squirrel hunting a couple of weeks earlier and had accidentally shot his own foot. Well, the truth was that it was more an act of stupidity than an accident. His boot heel had worked loose and wouldn't quit flapping. He wasn't having any luck finding a squirrel and said he thought the noisy boot heel was scaring them off, so he got mad. He got so mad that he stuck his foot up and tried to shoot that heel off. He missed and hit his foot. The wound had set up an infection and the boy plum near lost his foot over the ordeal.

I suspected that if Elmer quit school, Idy Jo would soon follow. Besides, Elmer was so big and so old that maybe high school wasn't the right course of action for him anyway. There were three third grade kids in the school and they could all read better than he could. The only person further behind that Elmer was Sandy Coltrain and he was afflicted.

I imagined Elmer would go to work on his daddy's farm, then when his daddy passed on, the farm would be Elmer's and he would marry Idy Jo and there they'd be, just like everybody else on the ridge, for the rest of their natural born lives. I looked at Ellie. She had been right about people on the ridge. Getting married, raising babies, chopping tobacco, raising hogs or sheep or cattle, that was our life and to tell the truth, I didn't know anybody who had ever done much of anything different.

I handed Ellie a homemade raisin cookie.

"Thank you," she whispered and she ate it like she was a little mouse, taking tiny bites, making it last as long as she could.

That afternoon, I pretended I had work to do for Miss Mays and let Elmer, Idy Jo and Liddie Grace get out of sight before I went back inside where Miss Mays was gathering her stuff to leave. Getting away from Liddie Grace was like getting rid of bed bugs. I finally told her I was still in trouble.

Ellie was in her seat, reading that book about Alaska.

I stood in the doorway and cleared my throat. "Miss Mays."

She looked up. "Yes, Frankie."

"If you're busy, I can walk Ellie past the Jackson's for you."

"Well, I don't know," she said. "Your parents might be…"

"They won't be worried," I said. I thought to myself that they wouldn't know I was walking with Ellie.

"Well, all right," she said.

I turned around. "Ellie, I'm walking you today. Come on. Let's go." I went back to her seat and helped her get her stuff together. She started to pick up her heap of books.

I stepped in front of her. "I'll carry them for you."

"Frankie, I can carry my own..."

"I want to," I said.

"But why?"

"Just because."

She smiled. "Thank you, Frankie."

We walked for a couple hundred feet from school then she up and said, "I did like that poem Idy Jo was talking about. I liked it a lot. It was sad how they both died because they loved each other."

"I think it's spooky," I said. "I think that other poem he wrote, "The Raven," is spooky, too. I don't care much for his work."

"Well, that's because you don't understand it," she said.

"Oh, I understand it all right, Ellie. I just think that man had downed a jug or two of liquor when he wrote those things."

"What do you like to read about?" she said.

I shrugged. "I don't know. I like that book, My Side of the Mountain. Sometimes I wish I could be like Sam Greely and hide out in the mountains for a year."

"Yeah, me, too," Ellie said. "I'd make my own candle out of a turtle shell just like he did."

"And I'd kill myself a deer and wear its hide for a suit of clothes," I said.

"You'd stink if you didn't tan the hide right."

"Well, you could tan the hide and I could catch the fish," I said.

"Oh, and then we could eat turtle soup," she added.

"Turtle soup is good," I said. "My Uncle Lester makes it sometimes."

"If we had to go anywhere at night, we could use the stars to guide us," Ellie said. "I know all about stars and constellations. I can find my way to any place so long as I can see the North Star, just like ancient sailors could."

"Really?" I asked.

"Really," she said.

"But how did you learn all of this stuff?"

"Mickey taught me. He's real smart you know. He knows all about stuff like following the stars and what you can eat in the woods. Also, he takes me to a big library up in Lexington sometimes."

"Your brother has a car?"

She nodded. "Yeah, but it's not as great as you think. He uses it for his work and he's not home a lot of times, especially at night. Anyway, they have books on everything you can imagine at that library, even astronomy."

"Astronomy, huh? Now, Ellie, what do you need to know about the stars for? I mean really, what good will it do a person?"

"Well, Frankie, haven't you ever wanted to see go someplace far away?"

Had I ever wanted to see some place far away? I told her about my plans to go to Europe and see the works of Michelangelo and to visit the Great Wall of China and to explore the deepest jungles of Africa. Then she said that maybe she would like to go to Africa, too, and see a real jungle and maybe we would get chased by a lion. I said that I would shoot the lion just before it ate her and then she said that I would probably get malaria and die. Then she would be stranded in Africa and have to live with cannibals.

We talked all the way to the Jackson's place.

I handed her books to her. "Bye, Ellie. I'll see you tomorrow."

"See ya," she said.

I watched Ellie turn down the narrow lane that led off into the woods and out of sight. I stood there until I couldn't see her anymore. Then I bounded home, thinking of stars and of Africa. That night I tried to draw a lion, but I fell asleep with my head on my sketch pad.

The next day I asked Ellie to sit at the lunch table with us again. She sat by me and I shared my food with her.

Liddie Grace was unusually quiet. Just before school let out I asked to be excused to go to the outhouse. When I opened the door to come out, there was Liddie Grace, standing in front of the girls' toilet. She ran toward me and stopped when she was about five feet from me.

"Frankie, I never figured you for one to take up with the McThackers."

I shrugged. "What's wrong with the McThackers?"

"Don't play ignorant," Liddie Grace said. "Well, they're dirty and they steal. Ellie stinks. Can't you smell her when you sit by her?"

"I never noticed any smell."

"I'm warning you, Frankie Delano Keilman, if you know what's good for you, you'll quit inviting her over to our table."

It was like Liddie Grace had just stomped my toe and dared me to do anything about it. "Or what?"

"Or what?" she put her hands on her hips and bobbled her head from side to side. "I'll tell you or what, I'm gonna call your mother and tell her that you've been eating with a McThacker."

"What's Ellie ever done to you?" I said.

"It's not what he has or hasn't done. It's what she is," Liddie Grace said.

"I used to like you," I said.

"Used to?"

"Yeah, before I discovered you were such a bigot."

"She's a colored person," Liddie squawked.

"She's got blue eyes and brown hair," I said. "She doesn't look black to me."

"That's even worse," Liddie said. "My mother says the McThackers are part black, part white, part gypsy, part Indian, part everything. For all we know they might even be part dog or goat or something. They take up with anything."

Liddie's words felt like a knife in the gut. "She's human," I said. "Things are changing all over the country or don't you ever watch the news?"

"I watch it all right and I know that all this Civil Rights stuff ain't gonna amount to a hill of beans. Her kind will never be one of us."

"Tell Momma whatever you like," I said. "But if I want to eat with Ellie McThacker, I will and tomorrow I'll ask Sandy Coltrain to join us, too, or is he also beneath you?"

"He's a retard," she said.

I shrugged, "so he is, but he's a got feelings. That's more than I can say for you."

Liddie Grace huffed at me, "I hate you, Frankie Keilman. You hear me? I hate you." She stomped back into the school. I was a little afraid she'd call Momma, but at the same time, I felt good.

For the first time since I could remember I had been able to put Liddie Grace McAllister in her place. She was no longer a lodestone for me.

After school, I approached Miss Mays. She was gathering her things to leave and walk Ellie home.

I cleared my throat. "Miss Mays?"

"Yes, Frankie."

"I'd like to start staying a few minutes late every day."

"Whatever for?" she asked.

"Um…well, it's like you said, I'm going to college next year and I'd like to become better with my math. You know that's my weakness."

She nodded. "True."

So it was decided that I would stay an extra ten minutes each day and work on my Math. That gave Liddie Grace McAllister time to get home. I was counting on being able to walk Ellie to the edge of Briar Ridge again.

At some point Ellie must have picked up on my plan and told the teacher that she didn't need her to walk with her to the Jackson place anymore, because two days later, I came out from the school after helping Miss Mays. I'd gone down into the woods about a hundred yards when a voice behind me said, "Frankie, wait up." I about jumped out of my skin. Ellie came flying out from behind a big tree where she'd been hiding and waiting for me."Want some company?"

"I reckon it'd be all right," I said.

"So, is your math getting any better?"

"Nope, not much," I said. "Looks like I'm going to have to stay late all of the time."

She grinned.

"Well, you know, I don't want to flunk out in college."

"No, of course not," Ellie said. Then she smiled.

"How about you, Ellie? You going to college?"

She looked down, "I hope so."

"Me, too."

"Why so glum?"

"If I go to college," she said, "I will be the first person in my family to ever do so."

"Well, I had an aunt go to college," I said. "She's a teacher in Michigan now, married a guy from Ireland."

"Maybe we could go there on one of our adventures," Ellie said.

"You mean Michigan?"

"No, Ireland. I've heard there are no snakes there. I never did like snakes very much."

We carried on that way, talking silly, until we reached the Jackson place and parted ways.

When I got home, Momma was waiting by the phone. "What are you doing, Momma?" I asked, but I already knew what she was doing. She had a half-full glass of water on the table beside the phone. That water shook whenever somebody on the party line was getting a call.

"Shh," she said. "I'm waiting. I accidentally picked up the phone receiver while ago and heard Irly Garnett tell Edna Mae Jackson that one of them colored Pablo boys from down in Swamp Holler has run off and married an Eastridge girl from town. An Eastridge. Frankie, can you imagine one of them taking up with a colored?"

"Momma, they're not colored. They're Mexican."

"Don't matter," Momma said. "Some folks ought not to mix. It just makes life too hard on their kids in the long run."

"What's wrong with Mexicans?"

"Frankie, ain't you got no sense a'tall, son? It's not right to mix races. If I didn't know better, sometimes I'd say you was touched."

"But, Momma..." Just then the water shook.

"Hush, Frankie." She picked up the receiver and placed her handkerchief over it. There would be no more talking to Momma for a while.

I changed my clothes, helped Daddy feed the cattle, slopped the hogs and split some kindling for the cook stove, then I went up to my room and I read from My Side of the Mountain for a while. I read that poem that Ellie liked, "Annabelle Lee," and I realized that I did like it. I closed the book with a big lump in my throat. I was touched all right, just like Momma said, and so was the man who wrote that poem. Maybe Michelangelo was touched like me, too, and all those other men who wrote poems and painted pictures. I thought right then and there that maybe being touched wasn't so bad, because if nobody was touched like that then where would all of songs and stories and pictures in the world come from?

Then a most amazing thought hit me. It was so amazing that I almost felt like I was sinning for thinking it. Could Jesus himself had been touched, too? I was so scared of the thought that I looked up to make sure nobody was standing in the door, like they could hear me thinking it if they had been there.

Chapter Five

On Saturday morning my dad and I rode up to Goodin's store to pick up some things on a list Momma had given us. Mrs. Goodin, a tall, sturdy woman with gray hair, who always wore skirts and her late husband's shoes, was outside pumping gas into a long black car when my dad cut the engine in our red and white pick-up. I could see a girl's head in the passenger side as we got out and started toward the store.

"Fine day," my dad hollered out to Mrs. Goodin.

She nodded then motioned her head toward the store, like she wanted us to hurry in there. I had been around Mrs. Goodin long enough to know that meant there was someone in her store she didn't trust, meaning the person was either a stranger or what she called "a varmint" from Swamp Holler.

The store was a white concrete block building with a wooden porch, covered by a green tin roof. An old church pew and a couple of straight back chairs sat on the porch beneath various tins advertising cold drinks, cigarettes and gas companies. Mrs. Goodin sold gas, stamps and just about any kind of dry goods, including boiling coffee and can food that you could ask for. She had a shelf dedicated to local molasses makers and one for the honeybee keepers where she sold their produce for them. She would offer credit to upstanding citizens who would and could pay, but if a person was a stranger or from Swamp Holler, she wouldn't give them two cents if they were dying and their pants were already burning with the flames of hell itself.

When Daddy and I entered the store, I noticed right off why she had been so nervous. A tall, thin man in a stylish leather jacket and tight jeans stood with his back to us. He was looking at a bottle of shoe polish.

"Hey," my dad said. He sounded gruff. "Can I help you, son?"

When the man turned around I recognized his face right off, not because I had seen him before but because he looked just like Ellie McThacker. He had the same peanut butter skin, full lips and ice eyes, just like Ellie. There were no other words to describe him except to say that he had a more perfect face and prettier teeth than a movie star. He was better looking than Elvis.

He smiled. "No, sir, I reckon I'll just wait on Mrs. Goodin to come in and check me out. I need to pay for my gas and shoe polish." I looked down and noticed that he had a nice pair of western boots. He looked like he had stepped right out of the pages of one of my momma's fashion catalogs, like he belonged in Chicago or California, but not on Briar Ridge.

Just then Mrs. Goodin came in and rang up his total without so much as a 'thank you for your business' or anything. In fact, I'm sure she grunted at him.

He saluted me with two fingers on his way out the door. "See ya, sport." He grinned and was gone.

"That's what I've been talking about," Meredith Goodin said, before the McThacker car was even out of the parking lot. "I'm telling you, Ancil. That Swamp Holler riff-raff gets more brazen every day. Time was when they wouldn't come flaunting their bootlegger money in this store, but that Mickey, he's the worst yet.

I don't like that boy. Don't trust him. If y'all find me dead and my store robbed, you'll know that it was that McThacker boy."

"McThacker's been bad news round here for years," my dad said.

"I've heard tell that them people down there in that holler are wilder a pack of stray dogs. They's rumors that nobody's seen old Mooney McThacker in years. Came in here once, years ago, asking me to give him credit. Of course I quoted the Bible to him, 'he that will not work, shall not eat.'"

"What did he say to that?" my dad asked.

She shook her head. "I'll never forget it as long as I live. That devil of a man gritted his teeth and called me a hypocrite right to my face. He said if heaven was gonna be full of people like me then he'd rather not go. Only he cussed when he said it.

"Never heard from him again and just as soon that he never came back. Crazy mean man with wild snake eyes, just like that boy of his.

"Still, I'm telling you, something's up. I'll tell you what I think. I think he's run off with a strumpet woman or else his wife's family came after him and he's hiding. Most likely though, that girl didn't have a soul to care about her. She ought to have stayed with her own people."

My dad lowered his eyes. "It was a sad thing, that was."

"As for old McThacker, no lawman in his right mind is going to go poking around down there in that holler to find out why a moonshiner's not been showing himself in public. Thelmer Joseph says that his granddaddy disappeared down there in that holler and was never heard from again. No, only reason we know about McThacker's wife dying was because Rainy Jackson was driving down the road and found her in a ditch. A ditch, I tell ya. I don't care what kind of woman she was; she didn't deserve to die in a ditch like that."

"Why wasn't McThacker arrested for murder?" I asked.

43

"It wasn't murder," Daddy said. "She wasn't dead when he found her, just near death. She died from pneumonia. For all we know old McThacker might have put her in that ditch and was hiding in the bushes to make sure somebody picked her up. They say she was wrapped in a quilt and a man's coat when Jackson found her and took her to the hospital."

"Hmph," Mrs. Goodin said, "I hate to sound harsh, Ancil, but I doubt that's the case. Most likely, Jackson put his own coat on her and took her in."

"Why not ask Jackson?" I said.

"He don't come in here," Mrs. Goodin said. "The Jacksons keep to themselves. Strange people. Always believed they might be a little kin to some of that bunch down in the holler. But I can't say much about a man who won a purple heart in the war and saved my store from destruction."

She was referring the Sunday that Mr. Jackson was driving down the road, saw smoke coming from her chimney, burst into the church, a quarter of a mile up the road, which he did not attend, and hollered that the store was on fire. The preacher said, "It's an ox in the ditch," so all the men jumped up and ran over there. They had the fire out in minutes. Mr. Jackson then helped Mrs. Goodin's late husband rebuild the parts that had been lost. So, that was why Rainy Jackson was the only man on the ridge who escaped lashing from Mrs. Goodin's tongue.

I wouldn't put anything past that McThacker boy. It's just a matter of time before those heathens start robbing and stealing up here on the ridge."

"Has he ever threatened you?" I asked.

"Don't have to," she said. She leaned over the counter. "I can see it in his eyes. That boy's got them steely eyes, shiftless mixed breed eyes. You can't trust a person with eyes like that and the way he grins, all sly like the devil. I'm telling you that boy's got evil in his heart."

"I keep telling you, Meredith," my dad said, "it ain't safe for a lone woman to be running a store on the side of the road like this. Why what if me and Frankie hadn't wondered in here? He might have robbed you blind."

"He didn't look like he was trying to steal anything," I said.

"Frankie, boy, you don't know nothing about people like that," my daddy said. "He probably put it back on the shelf the minute we pulled up."

"Or shoved it in his pocket," Mrs. Goodin said. "I'll have to do an inventory after a while and if anything's missing I'll know where it went."

My dad cleared his throat. "I tell you what, Meredith, you need a man around here. Somebody young and strong that you can trust."

Meredith looked at me. "What I need is a boy like Frankie. Look at him, all clean cut and respectable. He's got manners and knows how to treat his elders. Are you a hard worker, Frankie?"

"Yes, ma'am, I try to be," I said.

She looked at my dad. He looked at her and they both looked at me.

"He can start working for me every Saturday," she said, "because that's when the Swamp Holler riff-raff always seems to show up. I reckon they're out spending their moonshining money on the weekend."

"It's a shame," my dad said.

"Low lifes," Mrs. Goodin spewed. "Ain't got the decency to work like regular folks."

"Well, do you want Frankie to start today? I'll come pick him up at closing time."

"No, no, it's done on up in the day, going on ten o'clock, just wait and bring him up next Saturday about daylight."

On the way home I thought about how I would save my money to buy a car but it only took my mom one and a half minutes to kill that dream.

My dad and I came in and sat the stuff we'd bought on the kitchen table. She was sitting at one end, grinding hog meat, pepper and sage into sausage. My dad took to bagging the sausage for her and told her all that had happened at the store.

"So Frankie's got a job," she said. "That's good. It's about time he started helping pay the bills around here. God knows he eats enough."

"I was hoping to save up for a car," I said.

"You don't need a car," Momma said. "You need to start buying your part of the groceries."

"But we raise our own chickens, our own hogs and our own gardens," I said. "What groceries?"

"Flour, sugar, spices and coffee," she said.

"I don't even drink coffee."

"You eat biscuits don't you?" she said. "Now, Frankie, it's settled. You'll work for Mrs. Goodin and pay for the groceries once a month. If you have a few pennies left, then you can save for a car."

"But, Momma..."

"Mind yourself," she said. "If you don't honor your mother and father, you'll die young, just like Elliot Goodin. He died of that heart attack because Meredith told me that he had a big fight with his mother. Any person who disrespects his mother will die young. That's Bible, son. Can't change Bible."

I just turned and went up to my room. Groceries once a month would take my entire paycheck, seeing how I was only getting paid for one day a week. Momma didn't care though. Shoot, I hadn't gotten a Christmas present since I was eleven because she said it was too expensive, not when she needed a new living room set and a new quilting loom.

46

I looked long and hard at my window. I thought about climbing out, sliding off the roof, heading off into a holler somewhere and living off the land like Sam Greeley had done. There was an old shack in the woods not far from Eugene's. I remembered seeing it a few times when I was a little kid. I could live in that shack and fend for myself. Forget those stupid groceries and living rooms sets and quilting looms.

That night at supper I didn't say a word. I listened as Momma rambled on and on about Aunt Ima Jean's new living room set.

"I don't know how she can afford it," she said. She buttered her cornbread. "Then again, Lester will give her money for things like that. He don't spend every penny he gets on his stupid old hunting dogs."

My dad stood, picked his cap up off his chair post. He looked at Momma and said, "Jesus the Christ Himself couldn't live with you."

He left the table with his food practically untouched. I had seen my dad do that a million times. When Momma got to nagging because some other woman on the ridge had gotten some new gadget for her house that she didn't have, she'd throw up every bad investment my dad had ever made, ever dumb thing he'd ever said. She'd get started on his bad habits, like the way he misplaced things or never seemed to finish what he started. She'd call him lazy and irresponsible and accuse him of not even being able to match his own clothes. There had even been times that my dad would refuse to go to church because Momma would harp on his clothing choices so badly.

"See there, Frankie? See how he does me? Your daddy don't think about nobody but himself. He don't care that I'm stuck here with outdated furniture, while Lester gets Ima Jean anything she wants. It ain't right, I tell you." She took a cigarette out of the package on the table and lit it with a match. Then she puffed and blew out little rings of smoke. "Frankie, if you ever get married and I prefer you don't, but if you do marry somebody, say like Liddie Grace McAllister, then you treat your woman right. Don't you be running off to coon hunt or fox hunt while she sits at home and has to churn butter and make sausage meat.

"A man is supposed to respect and love his wife, putting her above all others. That's Bible, Frankie and you can't change Bible." She took another draw from her cigarette, a really long one.

I looked down. I had been reading a great deal of Bible over the past three years, ever since Momma said I was going to seminary and I wasn't sure that the Bible meant it the way Momma thought it did.

"I guess it's all up to you, Frankie. I can't trust your daddy to take care of me. He ain't got the sense. But you, you're smart. You go on and get that seminary education and become a pastor. You'll have a guaranteed income for the rest of your life and then I know I'll be taken of."

She laid her cigarette in an ashtray. "Are you done eating? I'm done eating. Help me do these dishes." I helped her with the dishes. She talked about Daddy the whole time, about how she nearly died giving birth to me while he was out on a drunk.

I knew that I wouldn't see my daddy again until well after dark or maybe even the next afternoon. He would probably fox hunt with friends from up on the ridge tonight. They'd sit around a fire, listening to their dogs run, drinking whiskey and talking about things that didn't matter. I knew this because Eugene once told me that's what they did.

I went to my room while Momma talked on the phone to Ima Jean. I picked up my Bible and read the story of Jacob who loved Rachel and worked seven years just to be with her then was tricked into marrying Leah. I thought about my dad and my mom. I couldn't imagine that Daddy would do that for Momma. I wondered if they had ever loved each other at all and why they married in the first place. I had never so much as seen my parents hold hands and never did they look at each other with love in their eyes like people did in the movies.

Surely, some people really did love each other like that because here it was in the Bible and then there was that poem, "Annabelle Lee." He had loved her enough to die for her. I pulled out my sketch tablet and drew Rachel from the story and somehow she came out looking like Ellie in Bible clothes.

After I had finished drawing, I sat just feeling of the paper, my precious paper and charcoal, a gift from Miss Mays that I kept hidden in a box under my bed. Momma thought such stuff was nonsense and a waste of time and money and Daddy, he could care less whether I drew or I didn't. The most I would get from him in regards to art would be a grunt. He didn't understand that type of stuff.

Chapter Six

Sunday morning at four thirty my wind-up alarm clock, with an American eagle in the center and gold bells on the top, sounded and woke me. I rolled out of bed and went down to the barn to help Daddy with the milking, provided he had come home last night. If he hadn't I knew I could count on Eugene to be there.

Our milk barn always smelled of cow manure, hay and crushed feed. When I entered the parlor, Eugene was on a stool, milking the first of our ten cows. I yawned, grabbed my stool and then went out and brought in the next cow.

"Frankie," Eugene said.

I braced myself. Here it comes, I thought.

"Your daddy didn't come in last night. You gonna have to talk to that witch of a momma you got and tell her to let up on Ancil. She's a hard woman to live with." He spat out a mouthful of tobacco juice on the ground. "Of course your daddy don't do things right, neither. If he did do something right, he'd take a handful of cow patty and smear on it just to mess it up."

"I'll try, Eugene," I said. "But do you think either one of them ever listens to me?"

He looked at me. "Probably not. You going to church this morning?"

I nodded. Of course I was going to church this morning. If Daddy didn't come home in time, I'd have to listen at Momma go on endlessly about how he was causing her to sin by laying out all night and keeping her from attending service and if he did come home, then she'd pull those curlers out of her head, smear on some lipstick and go sit by Aunt Ima Jean so they could give all the other ladies the 'eye' as they came in. That meant that they'd look at what everybody was wearing and how they conducted themselves then talk about it over the dinner table that afternoon. Because without fail, whether my daddy was home on Sunday morning or not, Momma and I ate with Aunt Ima Jean and Uncle Lester.

"Eugene," I said, "how come you never got married?"

My older cousin laughed and squirted me with hot milk from a teat. "Boy, are you crazy? You couldn't pay me enough to attach myself to a woman, always telling me what to wear and where to hang my hat, always telling me where I can and can't take my boots off. No, I believe that God put women here just torment men."

"Why do you say that?"

"Well, take your momma. Your daddy can't do nothing to suit her, but the truth is, nobody else could either. That woman can't be pleased and she's not the only one, Ima Jean, she's the same damn way. Busybodies, hell cats, that's what they are. I'd rather you take one of them logs yonder," he pointed to a log beam in the center of the barn, "tie me to it and throw me in the deepest part of the Cumberland River than to be married."

"But all women aren't like that," I said.

"The hell they ain't," he huffed. "I'd like to know where you found one that's not. You see here, Frankie Boy, they all start out looking pretty, smelling good and talking sweet, then the minute they get a ring on your finger they turn into the she-devils they are. They all turn into their mothers."

"But your momma wasn't like that..."

"No, no. My momma was a sinless saint what never did no wrong, cept have me out of wedlock. I reckon every once in a while a decent woman comes along but the rest of them will hen peck her to death if you don't watch out. My momma made up for her mistakes. She never married and never knew another man after I was born. She spent her whole life praying for forgiveness."

"That don't seem right," I said.

"What do you mean it don't seem right?"

"Well, I read in the Bible that all of us sin sometimes and that if we do, God promises to forgive us if we just admit and ask."

"That's that once in grace always in grace stuff," Eugene said.

"But without grace, how are we any different than anyone else in the world?"

Eugene spat again. "I wish you'd quit studying to be a preacher, Frankie. Cause you ain't learning old time religion. I don't know what you're learning but it ain't the Bible I learned when I was a boy."

I led my cow out. Why was I even talking to Eugene? He had his own views on everything and none of them made any logical sense to me.

"This is the life for a man, Frankie," I heard him say as he came out to get his next cow.

"Working the land with your own two hands, having everything just the way you want it, having your own little place and nobody to tell you what to do with it."

I sighed. I guessed I shouldn't be too hard on Eugene. After all, he and his mom had been shut up and forced to live in an attic for the first few years of his life. When his mother had him out of wedlock, her parents were so ashamed that they locked them away and then later lied that his mom was his older sister and that he was actually their child, not hers.

He had never been allowed to go to school or interact with people who didn't live on the farm, for fear that the truth would get out and everyone would know there was sin in the family. That was important, because the Keilman name was respected and the Keilman family would do whatever it took to make sure it remained that way, even if that meant sending off any child who happened to be touched or locking a girl in the attic if she messed around and found herself "with child".

"How many y'all got done?" I heard my dad say. I looked up and there he was, leading a cow into the barn. I really was glad he was home. I wanted to tell my dad that I understood why he left so often, but I didn't. Maybe because Eugene was there or maybe because it was just hard to say those things to my dad.

When we got back to the house, there was Momma, looking like she'd just stepped off the set of that Lucy television show. "Take them stinky clothes off and leave them on the porch," she said.

My dad didn't say anything to her as he sat down. He just picked up his fork and looked at her. We ate breakfast. Then my dad put on the clothes she had laid out for him and I put on my only suit, navy blue with a white dress shirt and red tie. It was the same suit I wore every Sunday.

Our church, a red brick building with a pointed steeple, sat in the midst of a well-kept cemetery with enormous oaks scattered about it. Behind the church sat the men's and women's toilets, a barbed wire fence, separating it from the Goodin farm and for as far as my eyes could see there were hills, rolling and covered with timber. For an artist like me, it was breathtaking. Those hills were like waves of the ocean, sprinkled with a million shades of color. This morning a fog rose up and swirled around those trees. That fog looked alive.

"Come on and quite gawking at nothing," Momma said and nudged me toward the church house.

I sat through the choir singing, wondering why so many ladies sang in those high screeching voices. Did they really think that sounded good? Then it was offering plate time and finally we were dismissed for Sunday school. I listened as our former school teacher, Mr. McGinnis, read from a booklet a story about David and Goliath. Then someone knocked on our door and it was time for worship service.

Brother Jullian Van Dyke was a new minister to our church. The deacons had voted out his predecessor because his wife was seen wearing pants at a church picnic. Momma said it was because they were from "off from here" and didn't know that on Briar Ridge we didn't take to those city fashions. That preacher and his wife had been from up around Louisville and even if women were wearing pants there, it wouldn't hold here on Briar Ridge. At any rate, Brother Van Dyke was from Berea by way of Lexington, which Momma said was almost as bad as being from Louisville.

Brother Van Dyke wasn't much taller than my dad and like my dad he was balding prematurely. I suppose he might have been forty or forty-five. He wore black framed glasses and a dark knit suit of clothes. I had never seen him in anything but a dark suit and tie with a white shirt. He had good manners and of course, he had been educated in seminary, just as all our ministers were.

He stood and cleared his throat, and then he began to speak. He read the story of the woman at the well from his Bible. I perked up.

"You see," he said after having read the passage, "Jesus wasn't afraid to be seen with anybody. The disciples could only see a woman with a bad name, but do you know what Jesus saw? Hmm…folks? Well, I'll tell you what he saw, he saw a human being. He saw someone worthy of hearing the gospel. Why do you think that was?"

I couldn't understand why preachers always asked questions. They knew nobody was going to answer them and always ended up answering their own questions. Miss Mays told us that it was to make us think.

"I'll tell you why," he said. "The disciples could only see what was on the outside of that woman. They could only go by the gossip and rumors they had heard regarding her, but Jesus saw her heart. He knew her for who she really was. The Bible says that man looks on the outward appearance but God looks on the heart.

"Do you remember the story of David and Goliath, my friends?"

Of course I remembered it. I just heard it in class.

"David's brothers were against him going out there to face that giant. All they could see was a skinny little teenage boy, about like…" he looked at me and grinned. "About like young Frankie Keilman over there." I heard some people laugh. "See folks if you were to look at our Frankie here, you wouldn't suspect that he might be a giant killer, because he doesn't look much like one. I mean just look at that kind face and those big blue eyes. He doesn't look like a warrior. That's how it was with David's brothers. The Bible says David was a comely lad, a pretty boy. They saw only their kid brother, nothing out of the ordinary, but God, now God saw what was inside David. He saw a great warrior, a man of courage and faith. He saw a giant killer. He saw a king."

He went on with his message, talking about how we are too quick to judge people based on rumors or on appearance. He talked about how Jesus said we should pray for one another, not judge each other, not run other people down with our tongues. Then he announced that there would be a church picnic in two weeks, and he said we should each try to invite someone who didn't already go to church somewhere.

When the service was finally over he and his wife, a short woman with plain features and mouse brown hair, went and stood at the backdoor and shook hands with all of us as we left.

My Aunt Ima Jean, as always, trying to be the first to make good with the new preacher, invited them to Sunday dinner.

"I'll say no more," my momma said when we got in our truck. "That preacher ain't going to last any longer that the other one."

"Why do you say that?" my dad asked. "His wife doesn't look like she'd be the kind to wear britches."

"Oh, his wife is just fine," Momma said. "It's him. There's just something about the way he preaches that I don't like."

"You mean the way he called gossip a sin?" my dad asked.

"Why would that bother me?" Momma said. "I don't gossip. No, no, it's something else."

"You mean the way he said we shouldn't judge people by the way they look or by where they come from?" I asked.

"That's it," Momma said.

"That means that God might see the good in anyone, even say, oh, I don't know, the McThackers or some of the folks from Swamp Holler."

"Oh, good heavens no," Momma said.

"You be careful with that one, son," my dad said. "I don't think that the preacher meant for us to go hanging out with bootleggers and coloreds."

"Then what did he mean?" I asked.

"I think he really meant that we should treat people decent," Daddy said. "Don't mix with them or even spend time with them. Just don't mistreat them."

"Or talk bad about them?" I said.

My dad nodded. "That's right."

Aunt Ima Jean was a great cook. We had her Sunday special, chicken and dumplings, green beans, corn on the cob, biscuits, sweet tea and of course, sweet potato pie topped with meringue. If

I ate at her house every day, I would grow as big as Tiny Elmer. I was sure of that.

We sat at her giant oak table. Uncle Lester asked Brother Van Dyke to say the blessing and he and his wife were told to fix their plates first. Our family always let the ministers be served first. He and his wife both went on and on about how delicious Aunt Ima Jean's food was.

"That was a good sermon today," I said. I normally didn't talk to adults that way, but I meant it.

"Why thank you, Frankie," he said.

Momma beamed, "Frankie wants to be a preacher. We've saved up to send him to seminary this fall."

"That's wonderful," Brother Van Dyke said. "Where do you plan to go?"

"Asbury," Momma blurted. "He's going to Asbury." She bit into her corn.

"That's a great school," the preacher said. "Tell me, Frankie, what did you like best about the sermon today?"

I wiped my hands on my napkin. Now I was nervous. All eyes were on me. "I…I liked that you said God doesn't see the same way we do, that He sees what a person is like on the inside. Like if a person is from a bad family, God doesn't judge the person based on where she comes from."

"Or he," he said. "Remember the second part was about David."

"Yeah, I know. I was getting to that."

He smiled at me. "Tell me, Frankie, do you have a favorite Bible story?"

I nodded. "One of them you preached. The woman at the well and the other one is the Good Samaritan. I like that even though everybody around Jesus said the Samaritans were bad and evil that in His parable of the Good Samaritan, it was a Samaritan, a man nobody liked, that helped the injured man. I keep thinking what if I

58

was a Samaritan and people didn't like me because of who my parents were or the color of my skin then what..."

"Frankie," Daddy said, "you ought not to be...

"No, no," the preacher said. "Frankie's got a point. We live in a segregated world but God does not segregate. The Bible plainly says that in Christ there is neither male nor female, Jew nor Greek. He does not see the color of our skin or the amount in our pocketbooks, but rather he sees whether or not we believe with our hearts."

My momma looked at him so hard that I thought darts would come flying out of her eyes. I knew that down in Memphis and Alabama there were a lot of uneasy people, but those places were hours away. Besides, I knew what was really eating at me. I couldn't understand why the world was against Ellie McThacker when all she had ever done was manage to get born.

It was in that moment, that I thought maybe there was more to being a preacher than getting to live in the parsonage for free and always being invited to Sunday dinners. Maybe being a minister was about saying what was true, whether people liked it or whether they didn't. I took a bite of dumplings and swallowed. I wasn't sure if I was cut out for that.

Chapter Seven

"I can't believe him," I heard Liddie Grace say as I reached the outhouse door. She must have had her little flock gathered down over the hill, just behind the toilet. I imagined it was probably Idy Jo and the handful of girls who followed her around the school yard, walking like her, swishing their skirts and flipping their hair.

I normally couldn't care less who Liddie Grace and her flock were gossiping about but today I stopped and listened, not letting them know I was there, out of sight with my hand on the outhouse door.

"I know," I heard one of the other girls say.

"It's every day," Liddie said, then she emphasized "Every doggone day that he calls her over there to sit with us. I've done warned him, girls. I told him that I was going to call his mother."

"She's not so bad." I recognized Idy Jo's high-pitched voice.

"Idy Jo," Liddie Grace snapped, "you feel sorry for every old stray dog that wanders up the ridge. You don't actually like her, you just feel sorry for her. She's not like us. She might not even be all the way human."

"She is smart," Idy Jo said. "And she is nice."

"Nice?" Liddie snapped. "She won't even talk to anyone but Miss Mays and Frankie and that stupid retard, Sandy Coltrain…"

"But Sandy can't help that his granny dropped him on his head when he's just a baby," Idy Jo said.

"Whose side are you on anyway, Idy Jo?" Liddie Grace snapped. "It better be mine if you know what's good for you."

"Of course I'm on your side," Idy Jo said.

"Good, cause that McThacker acts like she thinks she's better than us. Imagine that."

"Yeah," I heard a bunch of girls chime with agreement.

"I say it's time we told Frankie what's what," Liddie said. "I don't know why he puts that little lice infested piece of Swamp Holler at the dinner table every day, but it's time he stopped.

"My mother would die if I told her I'd been eating dinner at school next to a McThacker."

"Yeah, mine, too," another girl said. "You've done waited too long, Liddie Grace. You better tell his momma."

"But I thought you liked Frankie," Idy Jo said. "You said he was the dreamiest boy you'd ever seen in real life. You know what we talked about? How you would marry Frankie and I would marry Elmer and we'd all stay best friends forever?"

"I still want that," Liddie said. "But if Frankie is to fit into my plans then I'm going to have to lay down the law to him. He ain't gonna be bringing every little floozy that wears a skirt around and he's not going to be hanging out with moonshiners, whores and thieves. And I know for a fact that's all the McThacker's are. I've heard my own momma say it."

"Then let's go tell him," one of the other girls said.

"Yeah, let's tell him," the others said, almost in unison. Then I heard them come walking up the hill like a pack of she lions on the prowl. I jumped in the outhouse and closed the door. So Liddie Grace McAllister was going to set me straight? Going to tell me who I could and could not sit with at lunch?

I almost threw open that outhouse door and gave that girl a piece of my mind, but I didn't. I just bided my time. I would set Liddie Grace straight in my own time and my own way.

When the teacher rang the bell for dinner break I took my lunch pail and walked over to Ellie, leaving the others on the school bench. Sure enough Liddie Grace up and said, "Frankie, ain't you going to eat with the rest of us?"

That's when I stood up, took her by the elbow and led her away from the table. I had never even so much as touched her before but I didn't get all nervous around her anymore. I didn't care how good she smelled, how shiny her shoes were or how white her teeth were. I whispered in her ear. "Liddie Grace McAllister, if Ellie McThacker is not welcome at the table with you, then neither am I."

Her mouth dropped open and her eyes got big, then they looked mad. "You mean you would rather sit with her than with your own friends?"

"If my friends were really my friends," I said, "then they'd realize that Ellie is my friend, too and treat her that way."

"Hey," I heard Tiny Elmer holler from the table. "You two need a preacher to come and read your vows to you?" Then I heard him laugh.

I let go of Liddie's arm. "Like I said, where Ellie's not welcome, I'm not welcome."

"You're gonna be sorry," she said.

"What are you going to do, Liddie Grace? Tell my momma. I'm seventeen. Do you really think that scares me?"

Of course it did. It terrified me but I wasn't about to let on to her that it did. "I'll be moving out on my own in a few months. Go on back to your little girl gang and gossip about how somebody's too fat or their clothes are ugly. Ain't that what y'all do best?"

"I hate you," she hissed. For a moment I thought she was going to cry, but then she gritted her teeth. "You're gonna regret the day you traded me for a piece of Swamp Holler garbage." She went back to the table, grabbed her lunch bucket and stood, "Come on, Idy Jo. We ain't eating where we're not respected."

"But I was going to eat with Elmer," Idy Jo protested.

"I said come on," Liddie snapped. Idy Jo looked at Elmer and shrugged, "Sorry." Then she followed her boss over to the where the seventh and eighth grade girls were eating.

I walked back to where Ellie sat on the schoolhouse steps. "Let's go eat at the table."

"Looks like you lost your woman," Harlan said to Elmer.

"Yeah, but Frankie got his'n," Elmer said.

Ellie's face turned red. "I ain't his woman," she said in her low voice.

That afternoon I waited again until the others were gone then I walked Ellie past the Jackson place. She didn't have an armload of books.

"Tomorrow Mickey's taking me to the library. I don't need to borrow any from Miss Mays tonight," she said.

"About Mickey, does he have a car? A big black car?"

"Yeah, but it's not what you think."

"How do you know what I think?"

She shrugged. "Same as everybody else; that my brother runs whiskey and sells it all over the south, that he's the biggest shiner in this whole state. I've heard all of the stories. I have the power of being invisible and people talk about my family like I'm not even standing there. That Mrs. Goodin, up at the store. She doesn't even see me when I come in. She only sees Mickey in his leather jacket and shiny boots. The minute he walks out, she says horrible things about him. But he's not horrible, Frankie."

"If you say he's not a shiner then I believe you," I said.

"I didn't say he wasn't a shiner," she said. "I said he's not the way people think he is."

"Is he a bootlegger then?"

She stopped and looked down. She didn't have to answer. I already knew.

"Ellie, it's okay," I said. "I don't judge you by what your brother does."

She snickered, "By what my brother does." Then she shook her head. "You don't get it, Frankie. What my brother does is he keeps us alive, me and him. That's what he's always done..."

"But your dad must..."

"You don't know nothin' about my dad."

"Ellie, I'm trying to understand you and your family, but you're not making it easy."

"Ain't nothing for you to understand," she said. "We're poor. We do what we can to survive. You don't need to know nothin' else. Don't you be feeling sorry for me, for that poor little McThacker girl. I won't be stuck here forever, not in Swamp Holler where good people do without, while folks on Briar Ridge point their fingers and snub their noses."

In that moment I believed Ellie really was a hawk, flying way up high with her talons out, flying high so she couldn't hear the flocks of crows who laughed at anyone who tried to rise above them. And she flew high, so she could see the far horizons, beyond Briar Ridge and Swamp Holler and one day, she would land there.

"I ain't feeling sorry for you," I said. "I'm just hoping that one of these days when you fly away from this place, you'll think about me once in a while. It's just that you're not like any other girl I ever came across, and sometimes I wonder what makes you tick."

I didn't go on to say that I really wanted to know why her brother had such nice things and she dressed in rags, but I figured now wasn't the time to ask. Ellie deserved nice things, too. I said goodbye to her just past the Jackson place then turned for home when a notion hit me.

The next day was Saturday. I worked for Mrs. Goodin. Along about noon Mickey's car pulled up for gas. I peered out the window to see if Ellie was with him but she wasn't. Some other guy was with him.

Mrs. Goodin said, "You keep an eye on that McThacker boy for me, Frankie."

"I will, Mrs. Goodin," I said. Then I went out to pump his gas for him.

"Hey, Mickey," I said as if I knew him.

He laughed. "Hey, Sport. How'd you know me?"

"I go to school with Ellie," I said.

"Oh, yeah, the Keilman kid. What's your name? Oh, don't tell me. I know it, Franklin, Frank..."

"Everybody calls me Frankie," I said.

"Well, Sport, y'all got any smokes in there?"

"Just got a delivery yesterday," I said. "How much gas you want?"

"Fill'er up," he said. Then he started into the store but turned back and hollered at the guy in the car with him. "Hey, Joe, you want a cold drink?"

The fellow called back. "Yeah, that'd be all right."

So Mickey went in to buy a pack of cigarettes while I finished pumping his gas.

The other guy, a thin dark complexioned fellow about Mickey's age, got out of the car and said, "Here, Sport. Ain't no use you doing all the work." He proceeded to clean the windshield of Mickey's car.

"Thanks," I said.

"Name's Joe," he said, "Joe Pablo. Mickey and Ellie are my first cousins. Say, Kid, I bet you've heard of me."

I had. So this was the man, the Mexican, who had the audacity to marry a White girl from town and flaunt it in the face of all the snobs on Briar Ridge. This was the fellow that caused my momma to keep a glass of water by the phone so she wouldn't miss out on the latest gossip concerning him.

I must have been staring at him because he cut loose a laughing and said, "What's the matter, Kiddo, you never seen a Mexican hillbilly before?"

I smiled. "No, I really haven't."

"Well, what do you think?"

"I think you're all right," I said, "especially if your Ellie's cousin."

He smiled at me, the same charming and beguiling smile that Mickey had smiled the first time I'd seen him.

"I tell you who's all right, kid. You are. It's a one in a million man what won't stick his nose up in the air at a man who don't have as much as he does, or have hatred hiding behind his words when he sees the color of a man's skin. I can tell you're a fine feller."

About that time another car pulled up and something came over Joe. He went all stiff and his dark eyes became like flint. "Hey, Kid, get Mickey out here now," he said.

I stuck my head in the door, "Um, Mickey, Joe says for you to come out here fast."

Mickey paid Mrs. Goodin for the things he had bought and hurried out the door just as those other fellows were getting out of their car, a black and white one with wings on the back. I recognized them, the Dawson boys. There were five of them. Every one of them had reddish blonde hair and freckles. Two of them were as big as Tiny Elmer and the other three were about the size of an average man. I guessed them to range in age all the way from about my age up to almost Eugene's age. There was one, ruddier than the rest. I figured him to be about my age.

Everybody on Briar Ridge feared the Dawson boys. They were said to be as mean as the devil himself and nobody crossed them or even had anything to do with them, not even the law.

They eyed Joe and he eyed them. If looks could have killed, Mrs. Goodin's parking lot would have been full of dead bodies that day.

One of the biggest ones walked over to Mickey and took him by the chin, "You be a good boy now, McThacker, you hear. Wouldn't want to cause any harm to come to that sweet little piece of meat now would you."

When he said that my blood ran cold. I had no idea what he was talking about but I knew in my gut that Ellie McThacker was in a lot of danger, the kind of danger that made all of my life seem childish.

Chapter Eight

I stood in the parking lot and watched them leave then I went back inside the store.

"Lord a mercy, Frankie Keilman, you're as white as a sheet," Mrs. Goodin said. "What was all that about?"

"I don't know, ma'am," I said, "I was afraid they were going to fight right here in front of the store. The Dawson boys just got out and looked at Joe Pablo like they could kill him and he looked at them the same way. Then they threatened Mickey."

"Mickey, now who's that? Oh, you mean the McThacker boy?"

"Yeah, they threatened him."

"Threatened him? How?"

"I don't know what they were talking about, but I would be scared to be him."

"Well, it's just as well," Mrs. Goodin said. "McThackers are white trash. Pablos are coloreds who think they can go around marrying white people and that it's okay, but it's not. It's a sin. And the Dawsons, oh, good heavens. Briar Ridge would be better off iffen the whole lot of em up and decided to move. Better yet, suit me just fine if every one of em was to get drafted and have to go overseas." She shrugged. "T'ain't gonna happen though."

About an hour after Mickey and Joe and the Dawsons had gone, Mrs. Goodin told me to take the rest of the day off. She said that business had slowed down and she was going to close early because her gout was acting up. As soon as she told me to take the rest of the day off, I caught a ride home with Tiny Elmer and his dad who happened to stop in for some colas and moon pies. When I reached the house my parents were not home. I knew they had gone to town for the day. I wrote a note, saying I had gone to visit the preacher and stuck it on the door. I had a plan. It took me about half an hour to walk to the pastor's house.

His wife answered the door, "Well, Frankie, what a surprise."

"Mrs. Van Dyke," I said, "I really need to talk to Brother Van Dyke. It's concerning a spiritual matter."

Just then Brother Van Dyke came through the door from an adjoining room. He was wearing a sweater and trousers. He carried a newspaper in his hand and at first I was shocked. It was the first time I had seen him without a suit.

"Well, Frankie Keilman," he said, "don't just stand there, son. Come on in."

I stepped inside their cozy home that smelled like apple pie.

"Martha is baking a pie," he said then sat down in a big brown chair by the window. "Why don't you stay and have a piece with us?"

I sat on their vinyl black couch. The coffee table was covered in photographs, beautiful black and white images of birds, old cars, trees, barns and many other common things, but the way this photographer had singled in on these objects turned them into works of art. I picked up a photo of a wagon wheel, tangled in honeysuckle vines. It was the finest piece of art I'd ever seen in real life.

"You like my work?" Brother Van Dyke asked.

"Your work?" I couldn't believe it.

"I sell to one of those country lifestyle magazines. Got my own dark room and all, but still it's mostly, it's just a hobby, I guess."

"A hobby?" I said. "It's the finest thing I've ever seen." I didn't mean to sound so excited.

"Thank you, Frankie. There aren't many hobbies a preacher can engage in without inviting ridicule into his life, but I reckon photographing God's creation is as pure and clean as you can get."

"Yes, sir, but don't folks call you touched?"

He stared at me like a cow stares at a new gate. "What?"

"I know. We're not supposed to talk about it, but my grandpa used to tell me about people being touched." He was still looking at me so funny then I told him the story about the boy who lived with the gypsies for a summer and about Mr. Poe who wrote all those poems and about how I thought he might have been touched.

Brother Van Dyke smiled at me and looked through his photographs, touching them like they were his little babies. "Well, I suppose I'd like to be touched, too," he said. "But I've never heard it called that before. You see, Frankie, what some people see as weird and out of place, others see as gifted, even genius sometimes."

I thought about that for a minute then I blurted something I wouldn't have asked another soul on the planet except maybe Ellie. "Well, do you think God is touched, too?"

He laughed a little. "Look around you. All the things that inspire people to paint and to write and to sing, to create, where do they come from? God made them all, Frankie. I'd say that God is as touched as you can get."

I looked at him for a minute, thinking about how I was glad Momma wasn't there or Aunt Ima Jean or any of the deacons from church. "Maybe you ought not to say that at church," I said.

Well, Brother Van Dyke just about doubled over laughing. I was only trying to help him keep his church. I guess he knew that though, because he wiped his eyes from where he laughed so hard that they watered then he said, "I suppose you're right. Thank you for looking out for me like that. I know you didn't come here to talk about my photographs, so what can I do for you, Frankie?"

"Remember that sermon you preached here while back? About the woman at the well?"

He nodded.

"Well, I know this girl, and she's just like that woman, except she's not been married five times and the only wrong thing she ever did was get born down in Swamp Holler. She doesn't have any nice clothes to wear to school and the girls are mean. They laugh at her and well, it just ain't right."

"I agree. It's not right. But people, even those who call themselves Christian people, can be cold-hearted sometimes."

"Yeah, you might not ought to tell my parents I talk to her. Although, I suspect Liddie Grace McAllister will tell sooner or later, depending on when she gets mad enough."

He took a pipe from a box on the table and lit it. He took a puff from it. "Oh, I see." Then he leaned forward, "Frankie, it's not good to keep secrets from your parents."

"Then you're going to tell them that I was here?"

He smiled. "No, son. I'm not going to say a word."

"You mean you ain't gonna tell me right from wrong?"

"That is the Spirit's job. Not mine. You have to hear the voice of God inside you and obey your conscience. My job is simply to make you aware of His presence, not interpret His will for your life. Now, what about this girl?"

"I just want her to have something nice," I said. "Like a couple of good dresses and some ribbons for her hair. I hate how the other girls treat her, even if she says she can take it. She acts all tough, but well, I can tell that it…you know."

"Bothers her?"

"Yea, but see, I don't know how to get things for a girl and I can't say anything to Momma about helping me because she thinks the McThackers are about like Samaritans."

"Samaritans?" he said. "I see."

Mrs. Van Dkye said, "About how big is she?"

I shrugged. "I don't know. Skinny. Little. Not too tall. Maybe this tall and this wide," I used my hands to indicate her height and weight.

She looked at her husband. "You think maybe she could wear some of Corey's clothes?"

He nodded. "I have no problem with it."

"Corey is our daughter," she explained. "She's always been painfully thin. At any rate, she's off and married now, but she left a lot of her things she outgrew with us. I don't think she would mind at all if her clothes went to help another."

"Thank you," I said. Already I was wondering how I was going to sneak a dress home then to school and conceal if from my mother and the likes of the nosy crows at school. Also what would Ellie say if I gave her a borrowed dress?

"I can't borrow it," I blurted.

"Why?" they both responded.

"I have to pay for it. Or Ellie's feelings will be hurt. She's not a borrowing kind of girl. I made fifty cents working today. I'll give you a quarter for it."

I left the pastor's house that day with a blue checkered cotton dress with a lace collar that Mrs. Van Dyke had made several years ago for her own daughter, but the dress was just like new and as pretty as a store-bought one.

On Thursday afternoon Liddie hung around after school. I thought she was never going to leave, so I kept on washing the board for Miss Mays, then I packed out the trash to burn it for her. All the while Ellie sat at her desk, doing extra work. Liddie followed me out to burn the trash.

"Frankie," she said. "I wish you weren't mad at me."

"I'm not mad at you," I said. And I wasn't. I just wished she go away so I could walk Ellie home.

"Well, good, then," she said. "Your momma called my momma and said you all are having a church picnic this Sunday. Your momma said that you wanted me to come with you."

My stomach did a flip-flop. I may have taken a step backwards, because Liddie said, "Frankie, you okay? You look like you're gonna fall over."

"I...I don't even have a car," I said. "How can I take you to the picnic?"

"Your momma told my momma that you were going to drive your daddy's truck. It's so cool that you can drive, Frankie."

Of course I could drive. Every boy on the ridge could drive. We were farmers. I'd been driving since I was ten years old.

"Frankie, if you don't take me to that picnic I'll tell your mother all about how you've been getting so friendly with a McThacker and not only that, I'll get that leper kicked out of this school. My daddy knows everybody on the school board and they all do what he tells em, so you best be doing what I tell you, lessen you want little Miss Dirt Wad in there to get kicked out."

"You can't do that," I said.

She grinned. "I'm a McAllister, Frankie. Haven't you learned yet? I can do anything I want to. Pick me up at ten o'clock," she said, then bounded off across the school yard. I didn't know what to do. I didn't want to take her to that picnic, but I knew that she was really would stir up a whole nest of trouble. She had me over a barrel and she knew it.

The next day I stuffed that dress I'd gotten for Ellie into a pillow case then crammed a few books in on top of it and tied it shut. I was nervous all day that someone might try to get into my stuff and find the dress, but no one did. I thought the day would never end and I would never get to walk Ellie home, but it did end.

Liddie Grace dropped a note on my desk as she left the building. She turned and looked at me from the door, smiled a most wicked little smile then walked out. I unfolded the note and read, "I can't wait, Frankie Delano Keilman." I waded it up and threw it in the waste basket.

I stayed and practiced my math, giving her and all the others plenty of time to get out of sight. Then I told Miss Mays that I'd see her tomorrow.

As I walked past Ellie's desk where she was working on a report about Madame Curie, I whispered, "See ya in a minute. But don't bring any books today, okay?"

I had just made it into the cover of the woods when Ellie caught up to me. "What's up? You've been jumpy all day."

I took a deep breath. I was sweating, too. I untied my pillow case and pulled out the blue dress.

"It's a little wrinkled, but they will fall out if you hang it up and spray it lightly with some water, then let it dry. I've seen Momma do that."

"It's beautiful," Ellie said. She reached out and touched the lace collar and the tiny belted waist. "Where'd you get it?"

"It's for you," I said. "I bought it."

"You bought it? You bought me a dress? Why on earth would you buy me a dress?"

She looked down at her own homemade flour sack dress then back at me. A look washed over her face, a look I didn't understand at all and was sure right off that I didn't like. She pursed her lips together and started walking off.

"Ellie, what's the matter?" I called. "You don't like it? I could've gotten you a green one."

She whirled on me. "I don't need you feeling sorry for me, Frankie."

"Ellie, wait," I shouted, but she kept walking. "Ellie, please."

She did not turn around. I don't know what got a hold of me but I hollered as loud as I could. "I think I love you, Ellie McThacker."

She froze. Then I realized what I had said. And that I had said it out loud. It was true. I had not known that what it was until that moment, but I loved Ellie, sure as the world and I knew that I had loved her from the moment she helped me wipe the blood off of my leg. And now I was terrified.

She just stood there for the longest time, not looking around at me, not moving. She must have been terrified, too.

Then I said, "Oh, my God, Ellie, I'm touched."

I had scared her so much that she couldn't move.

"You can't tell anybody," I said. "They'll send me off and I'll never get to go to college or see The Great Wall...Ellie, I'm sorry, it's just that you're the most beautiful girl that I've ever seen and when I close my eyes at night, I see your face. I wake up every day excited about talking to you. I see Liddie Grace and all those other girls in pretty things that they don't deserve cause they're mean and selfish and...You're the one that deserves beautiful things."

I saw her shoulders move and I realized that she was crying. I went over to her, "I'm sorry, Ellie. I didn't mean to hurt you. I'm sorry."

She turned and fell into me. I put my arms around her and just let her cry. I could smell her and Liddie Grace had been wrong. She didn't stink. She smelled like the woods, like wildflowers and leaves, like autumn wind. I stroked her light brown hair. It was soft and silky.

"Are you mad at me?" I asked.

"No," she whispered.

"Then why are you crying?"

"Nobody ever said those things to me before and I'm so afraid that you might not really mean them."

76

"I do mean them," I said. She looked up at me and when she did, something happened inside of me that I could not explain. Her eyes cut right through my soul and all I wanted was to be with Ellie. I kissed her and I just kept kissing her. I couldn't seem to stop myself. I was kissing those lips I had drawn so many times. My heart felt like it was swelling up inside of my chest and the spirit that was housed inside my chunk of marble was about to pop right out and take off flying. I didn't care if tomorrow or Sunday or any other day ever came. I could have spent the rest of my life just standing right there, kissing Ellie McThacker, but we heard voices coming through the woods. I grabbed her hand and we took off running. We slid down the embankment and hid behind a giant boulder.

It was men's voices we heard. They stopped right about where Ellie and I had stood kissing. Then I heard one of the men say plainly, "I'm paying you so you better come through for me. If you don't rein him in, you're gonna have to start worrying about yourself, you hear?" He sounded like his throat had a frog in it that he couldn't get to clear.

"Yeah, yeah, I hear you," the second man said. "You'll get what you pay for. You can bet on it. Come on, let's go."

I heard the sound of their steps getting farther and farther away. I had no idea who they were or where they were going. Ellie and I sat there, afraid to breathe until they were long gone. Then we headed back out onto the main road, near the Jackson place. "Who were they?" I asked.

She looked down and shrugged. "No telling."

I kissed her on the cheek and we parted ways.

Ellie wore the blue dress the next day and she was by far the prettiest girl in school. She had combed her hair differently, kind of parted on the side and placed an old silver barrette in it and she still wore her boy shoes, but to me, she looked like a fashion model from my momma's catalog. When I looked at her, I wanted to sneak her off somewhere and kiss her again. I wanted to touch her hair and feel smell of her. She was so gorgeous that even Tiny Elmer up and said, "Ellie McThacker, I didn't know you were so pretty. Where have you been hiding?"

Then Idy Jo hit him as hard as she could with her tiny fist, right in the stomach and she didn't speak to Ellie all day.

Liddie Grace stared at her all morning and I begin to feel bad that I had given her the dress, because maybe it was backfiring.

At lunch Liddie Grace had the audacity to 'accidentally' spill her water on Ellie, then feigned how sorry she was. Afterwards, she and her little gang would look at Ellie and giggle. But Ellie turned away from them and continued reading as if they were of no matter at all. I did not want to go to that picnic with Liddie Grace and because I now knew for sure that I loved Ellie, I was going to tell Liddie Grace that no matter what happened to me, I had decided not to take her to the picnic, but on the other hand, she was a she devil as Eugene would say and I feared she might make life miserable for Ellie.

At recess Harlan and Elmer got a baseball game up. All the boys from about twelve on up headed out to the field to play, including me. Liddie and her little flock of crows gathered at the fence to watch us. I looked up to see if I could see Ellie and sure enough she was watching me from the far end of the fence. I waved at her and smiled.

She waved back. Then I saw Liddie Grace leave her spot at the gate and walk over to Ellie. I knew my day was about to get nasty. I couldn't concentrate on the game for worrying what Liddie was saying to Ellie. Our side was losing and Harlan was madder than a hornet at me. I was thankful when Miss Mays came out and rang the bell, but it was too late. Ellie wouldn't even look at me when I entered the room. Liddie Grace looked up and grinned like the Cheshire cat.

As soon as Miss Mays dismissed us, Ellie was out of her seat and out the door. Liddie Grace started toward me but I brushed past her and a bunch of other kids and ran after Ellie. She did not carry books today. I had no idea that girl could run so fast. I saw her head into the woods. She wasn't even going to stay on the trail today. I took off right after her, not caring who saw me or who said what about it. We were almost to the Jackson place, coming up on the backside of their barn when I finally caught her.

We were both out of breath, especially me since she could run like a deer and had a head start on me to boot.

"Ellie," I said then gasped for some more air, "what's the matter with you?"

"You know what's the matter?" she said. "How could you? After yesterday, after you told me that you meant what you said?" her eyes were filling up with tears.

"How could I what?"

"Take Liddie Grace on a picnic."

"She threatened to have you kicked out of school," I said. "She told me that she'd get her dad to have the school board remove you."

Ellie's brows creased. Her entire face wrinkled in confusion. "Why would she do that?"

"Because she's used to getting her way," I said. "All of her life people have told her how cute she is and have bought things for her and given her whatever she's asked for…and now, apparently…"

"She wants Frankie Keilman."

I nodded.

"You're too good for me," she said. "The people on this ridge, they're never gonna let a boy like you and a girl like me be together. And as long as you live your life to please the people on this ridge, you'll be just another one of them."

"I don't want you getting kicked out of school, even if it means having to take Liddie Grace on a stupid picnic."

"Frankie, you don't get it. If you give into her on this now, she'll be forcing you into spending the rest of your life with her before you know and you can kiss those dreams of yourn' goodbye."

"I can't...I won't let her get you kicked out of school," I said. "You've just got to finish this year and I know you've got to make the top grades. I won't let her destroy your dreams, even if I have to give up a few of my own to do it."

She stared at me. It seemed like forever then a sound in the underbrush broke our intense moment. Then someone gasped, "Help me. Ellie, help me."

A man dragged himself out to where we could see him. He wore a leather jacket. I could tell right off that it was Mickey McThacker and he was bleeding bad.

"Mickey," Ellie screamed and ran to him.

"They shot me, Ellie. Shot me in the back."

Chapter Nine

Ellie fell on her knees beside her brother, trying to lift him. "Get Joe," he moaned.

"I can't leave you," she said.

"Joe," Mickey grunted.

At first I just stood there as numb as frozen lizard, then something came over me and I knew that if Mickey McThacker was going to live to see another day, he had to be helped by somebody who knew what they were doing and he had to be helped now.

"Ellie, run up to the Jackson place and get somebody out here to help us. I'll stay here with Mickey and try to slow down this bleeding."

Ellie took off running. I was shaking all over as I lowered myself on the ground beside him. I remembered that Elmer told me that when his brother about shot his foot off that they had to get the bleeding stopped first, and they had to keep Elmer warm.

"You hang in there, Mickey," I said, "We've got to slow that bleeding down," I could see that the bullet had gone through the lower part of his jacket, hitting him just above the rear end on the right side. I had no idea how deep it was or what it had done once it got inside of him. I raised his jacket up, took out my pocket knife and cut the back of his shirt away. The hole was small, but the blood was about to make me sick. I had to hold it together. I knew that, for Mickey's life, for Ellie's sake, I had to be stronger than my weak stomach.

"Are you shot anywhere else?" I said.

"No," he moaned.

"I'm gonna feel you to see if there's a hole in your belly," I said.

"Ain't no hole in my belly," he gasped.

"Just be still then," I said. "Stay calm."

Then I took off my shirt and used it to seal up that bullet hole. I applied all the pressure I could to the gunshot wound in the lower part of Mickey's back. I don't know if I prayed out loud or just in my head but I was praying, "Oh God, please don't let Mickey die. Please help us, Lord."

"Hang in there," I said again. I think I may have said it a bunch of times, but I was scared to death and couldn't think what to say, and half of what I was doing was just instinct or something like it.

I could hear him breathing so I knew he wasn't dead yet. I kept on applying pressure and praying that he would not die. Then I heard a car coming across the field in back of the Jackson place. I saw Ellie and Joe Pablo running through the woods toward me, and behind them was an elderly man in a light blue shirt and suspenders, Mr. Jackson. I had heard of the little old man, but I had never met him. He and his wife was an elderly couple that kept to themselves. I had no idea how Ellie had gotten a hold of her cousin so fast, but stuff wasn't registering right and I wasn't even sure how long I'd been there.

"Oh, Mickey," Joe said. "What have you gone and done to yourself?"

"The four of us can put him in my car," Mr. Jackson said. "This boy needs a doctor now."

"He'll be dead before we can get him to the hospital, sir," Joe said. "Let's get him to Granny Flor. She's picked a many bullets out of folks. Then somebody can go for the doctor while Granny works on him."

"I've got to keep pressure on the bullet hole," I said.

"All right," Joe said. "Then the rest of us can lift him. He ain't as heavy as he looks. His jacket weighs more than he does."

Mr. Jackson nodded and the three of them lifted Mickey as gently as they could, while I kept his wound covered. They carried him to the old feller's station wagon. We loaded him in the back. I got in with him, never letting go of the shirt I had pressed against his body, and the old man let Joe drive.

I had passed through Swamp Holler on my way to town before but I had never been off the main road that ran right through the middle. I had never been where the people lived. Joe was at the foot of Briar Ridge in seconds and the next thing I knew we were bouncing down a dirt road past chickens and cows and peacocks and goats. We passed a hog lot and a bunch of little shanty houses that didn't look fit to live in. Then we passed a corn patch with nothing left but the stubs from the crop that had already been housed in the barn to cure. In fact, there were corn patches all over the place. Every house had a corn patch behind it or in front of it or beside it. Swamp Holler was full of corn patches and animals. The smell of oil was so strong it almost gagged me. I had heard that the Georges and the Dawsons owned a lot of oil wells in the holler.

The sight of the car and the sound of engine had brought a stream of onlookers racing after us. We stopped in front of one of the little shanty houses. There was a porch, roof held up with knotty logs, running all the way around the little shack. The door stood wide open and the windows were so dirty no one could have seen out of them.

As Joe cut the engine and we unloaded Mickey from the car, a frail brown woman came out of the house, in a tattered gingham dress and dirty pink house slippers.

People crowded in on us. I noticed, even in the excitement, that many of them had dark faces.

"Mickey's been shot," Joe hollered. "He's a dyin'."

People went to hollering and crying and leaning on each other.

The old woman from the porch pushed her way through. "Oh, my Lawd, it's Mickey," she said. "All y'all get outta the way and let em get up to the house."

"He's been shot, Granny," Joe said.

"Jim Elee," Granny hollered over her shoulder, "you jump in your car and get to town. Find a doctor." A young man with sandy hair and a pink, sunburned face, who looked about Joe and Mickey's age, took off running. He didn't say a word, but he was on the move.

"Git'm on the eating table," Granny ordered. "All you other ones, stay out here on the porch, until we know something. I can't operate with a room full of people." I assumed that all those faces, some white, some black, some brown and some all in between, were neighbors, friends and family. I had no idea so many people lived so close together in Swamp Holler.

We carried him in the house and laid him on her homemade eating table in the kitchen, which was really just a section off to the side of the living room. I heard a motor hum and knew that boy, Jim, was on his way to town.

Granny's house looked like it had one other room besides the living room/kitchen. I could see her quilt-covered bed from the living room. Her little shack smelled like a woodshed and was crowded with an old, overstuffed couch and mismatched chairs. The kitchen area consisted of a wood burning cook stove, a table with water buckets and a big dish pan near the far wall, her eating table which was white on the top with brown, unpainted legs and four wooden ladder back chairs with bark bottoms.

There were spider webs on the ceiling rafters which were so low that anybody as tall as Elmer would have had to duck to keep from bumping his head. Coal oil lamps sat on almost every flat surface atop handmade doilies so I figured that Granny Flor did not have electricity.

"Now, Ellie Mahala, you get over yonder and boil some water on that heating stove," Granny ordered, "and while it's a heatin' you run out yonder to the shed and get me some of that strongest liquor. Joe, go get my doctoring herbs out from under my bed. Little blonde boy, you come over here and hold him down. Now, don't you let go for nothing, son, you hear? What I'm about to do to him is gonna hurt worse than a bullet in the butt and he might want to flop all over the place, but don't you let him."

"Yes, ma'am," I said. She spat a wad of chewing tobacco in a can then went to saying something in a foreign language while she checked over Mickey, feeling of the bullet hole, sticking her hands under his belly and all around.

"It's just a flesh wound," she said. "That means our boy might live. Course he might be crippled. I pray the Lawd he won't be."

The little woman's hair was gray and streaked with black. I could tell it had once been dark and her face was the color of thin molasses. Joe brought her the herb bag.

She opened it and took a clean scalpel from it. Ellie brought her the liquor. Granny drunk a big swig then handed the bottle to Ellie. "Hold that, girl," she said. While I held Mickey down, she dug that bullet out of his back. He hollered and tried to move around, but I put all I had into holding him down. Her hands and mine were covered in his blood and I thought I was going to gag my head off but I didn't. He hollered out a couple of more times;, then he passed out. I never had felt so sorry for anybody in my whole life as I did for Mickey McThacker that day.

I have no idea how long it took her. I only know that I could feel my heart beating in my stomach and I was sweating all over the whole time.

With a pair of big tweezers she pulled the bullet out, a small one, and put it in a can that sat nearby. "It's a pistol that he was shot with," she said. "Joe, get over here, youngin, and put your hands on the hole while I mix up a poultice."

Joe applied pressure to the wound while Granny Flor mixed up a pasty looking poultice which she applied to Mickey's back. "That's to help the blood clot up," she said. Then she took a needle and thread from her bag and she sewed Mickey up.

"Well, praise be to the Lawd," she said, "that was a slow moving bullet and it wasn't at close range, otherwise our Mickey would be dead right now, and if somebody hadn't a helped him he'd a bled to death. Well, let's get him in there in the bed."

Joe got a couple of men off the porch who came in and helped us move Mickey to Granny's bed where they laid him on his stomach and covered him with a quilt. Then Granny prayed over him in that foreign language. I knew she was praying because everyone bowed their heads.

"He's gonna live?" Ellie said.

By this time the house was full of people who had come in off the porch once the surgery was over.

The old lady shrugged. "I hope so, but he ain't in the clear yet. We got to wait twenty-four hours before we know for sure. I wish Jimmy Elee would get on back with a doctor, but this is why I went on ahead and did what I did. If we waited for the doctor to get here Mickey'd be dead now. Still, he's got more powerful medicine than I do. I'm telling ya, it's a miracle that Mickey's alive. That bullet could of gone way in, but it didn't. It stayed right there in the muscle. Still, that there bullet hole could set up an infection or anything. He's lost a lot of blood, too, but that Mickey, he's a tough'n."

She turned to Mr. Jackson who had just stood with his mouth open and his cap in his hands, watching the whole ordeal.

"We owe you, sir. Don't never let it be said that a Pablo won't pay her debts. You tell that wife o'yourn that I'll be a cleanin her house ever Saturday and she ain't to pay me nar a penny."

"Oh, Granny Flor," he said. "You'll do no such thing. Your family's helped mine more times than I can count, so there ain't gonna be no debt payin." He put his cap on. "But it's getting mighty late so I best be a getting home. My old lady is probably worried out of her mind about Mickey."

He started out the door then looked at Ellie. "Now don't you worry, little girl. That Mickey, he's gonna pull through."

By this time Granny Flor was in the kitchen sterilizing her instruments and getting them ready for the next emergency while all of Mickey's cousins and other kinfolk gathered in the living room, talking and growing louder by the second. I had never seen so many kinfolks in one house. I just stood and stared. Then I felt someone touch my hand. I looked up and saw Ellie. She just squeezed my hand. "Thank you, Frankie."

I was so stunned. Nothing made sense, the shooting, the strange little grandmother who spoke a foreign language, all these multi-shaded faces, the shanty houses, the smell of oil, the unbelievable amount of corn patches.

"I think I'm going to be sick," I said. "I need some air."

Ellie led me out of the house and onto the porch. It was already dark and the cool autumn breeze felt so good. I could breathe again. "Your granny is a doctor?"

"Sort of. She's a faith healer and a little bit of a medicine woman. She learned it from her pa. He was a…I don't know the word for it…witch doctor maybe?"

"What language…?"

"Granny still speaks the old language sometimes. It's an Indian language."

"So are you part Indian?"

Ellie smiled at me. "Are you part Keilman?"

I wasn't sure I understood the question, but Granny Flor walked out on the porch just then and I thought no more about it.

"Who did this?" she asked.

I thought she meant who shot Mickey, so I shrugged.

"Who was the one that found Mickey and saved him?" she asked.

Ellie said, "Granny, Frankie and I were on our way home from school when we found him. He'd already been shot. I ran to get Mr. Jackson and told him what was the matter. We picked Joe up on the way. He was walking up to the sti..."

"I was coming home from working in the backer," Joe said. I hadn't noticed he was standing in the doorway.

"Frankie here, he stayed with Mickey until we got back with the car," Joe said. "This boy knew how to stop the bleeding and he saved Mickey's life."

For the first time Granny Flor turned and looked at me, really looked at me. Someone had lit all those lamps because light was coming from inside the little house and I could see that Granny's eyes were black, beady and as shiny as glass marbles. She worked her toothless gums around in her mouth and stared me up and down for the longest time. I could feel myself sweating and my heart racing. Then she said, "How'd you know what to do?"

"I don't know," I said, "I just remembered a tale about somebody getting shot one time and that the most important thing was to stop the bleeding. Everything else was instinct."

"Bugs got instinct. You don't look like no bug to me," she said. "You got the giftin'," she said.

"Gifting? I don't understand. What's that mean?"

She grunted. "Just as well. Still, more n likely, you're the reason Mickey lived long enough for y'all to get him to me. Who are you, boy? You one of them Cravens boys from the far end of the holler?"

"His name is Frankie Keilman," Ellie said.

"Keilman?" Granny squawked. "You mean you're from up on Briar Ridge?"

"Yes, ma'am."

Granny fanned herself and meandered over to her threadbare couch, "Well, I swany. I never in all of my life knew of a Keilman that'd come into Swamp Holler for anything."

"A man's life is reason enough," I said.

A pretty black-haired girl with a creamy white face came and stood in the doorway just behind Joe. She didn't look to be any older than Ellie. I took her to be fifteen or sixteen, seventeen at the most.

Granny looked from the pretty black-haired girl to me and grinned a toothless grin. "Well what on earth is the world coming to when and Eastridge and a Keilman got enough heart to come down into Briar Ridge and see about us po'folk?"

She looked at me again, not as long and as hard as the first time, but still, she made me uncomfortable.

"Come in the house, boy, and sit down. Ellie Mahala, you go in yonder and make this here boy some coffee. Use the good stuff. I reckon anybody who'd save the life of my grandchild deserves the best of whatever we got."

Ellie did exactly as Granny told her. And Granny led me to her couch. "I'm an old woman," she said. "I am done worn out. I can't take much more of that standing."

"Who are all of these people?" I asked.

Granny smiled. "Now this here little gal with the coal black hair, this is Jewell Eastridge, only she's a Pablo now because her and Joe done gone and got hitched. You see, she's from up town and her family didn't want her mixing with no Mexicans or Indians on account a they think they're better'n us, but she's a good girl and she knows how to listen to the Lawd inside of her. Most people with money can't do that, Frankie. You know why?"

I shook my head. I didn't know why.

"Well, it's on account'a they are afraid that being po' can rub off on em. They're afraid that it's like the mumps or the measles or the TB of the lung, something they can catch. And I reckon a lot of people go to them fancy churches up there on the ridge but they don't really believe in the afterlife or they wouldn't be so afraid of being without in this one. I reckon they're all just afraid of dyin' when you get right down to it. Maybe they're so afraid of dyin' that they don't know how to live."

"Anyhow, Lawd a mercy, Jewell's daddy bout passed rocks outta his bowels, but I reckon she loves my Joe. And them Dawson boys, they tried to kill Joe. Beat him half to death and left him for dead down yonder in the creek. See, one of them had his eye set on Jewell Eastridge and it didn't do him no good that a Mexican boy from down in Swamp Holler caught the eye of the very uptown girl he wanted for himself.

"Anyhow, Jewell here, she's brave, Frankie. Her family won't have nothing to do with her right now, but they'll come around, you'll see. If they love her, they'll come around."

I looked up at Jewell Pablo. She was beautiful, far more beautiful than Liddie Grace McThacker and I could tell that she was what my momma would call well-bred. I could see it in the way she carried herself. She was a lady, a girl with proper upbringing. She came from a world like mine, yet she had thrown it all away for Joe Pablo, a smooth talking, fun loving half Mexican boy with a big grin and a big heart. In our world, Jewell's and mine, that was about like marrying one of the colored folks that worked for our parents in the tobacco fields.

"Anyways," Granny said, "how come you to be with Ellie if you're from the ridge?"

90

"I was walking her home," I said. "The teacher said she's afraid of dogs and so I had to walk her past the Jackson place."

Granny laughed.

"Why is that funny?" I asked.

"The Jacksons ain't even got no dogs," Granny said.

I felt my face flush. "What?"

"I'll explain later," Ellie said. "Just don't be mad at me on account of it, Frankie."

"I'm beholden to you," Granny said. "You been a friend to Ellie and went out of your way to save Mickey. You see, Ellie and Mickey, they don't have no momma or daddy and they live off to themselves in that little house down there behind the George's sawmill, but I take good care of em."

I shot a look at Ellie and she shot one at me. I did not know both her parents were dead.

"Look around you. See all these people. Over yonder's Joe's mammy and pa and Jim Elee is his brother and all of these girls are his sisters and his cousins. And down the road a piece is more of us, family. We're a big family, boy. And family sticks together. Blood is thicker than money but love is thicker than blood. That's why Jewell is a Pablo and that's why you helped Mickey here. You got a lot of love in that heart of yourn. Lawd knows I don't know how though, ain't nobody else on Briar Ridge got no love in their hearts. Them folk up there care about one thing, money and the sound of their own names."

Ellie brought me a cup of coffee and I took a drink. It was so strong that I almost choked, but Granny was beaming with such pride that I swallowed and said, "That is the most favorable coffee I've ever tasted."

"I knew you'd like it," Granny said. "Everybody loves my coffee better n anything."

Joe came back in and it was apparent that he and Jewell were having a strong discussion about something. He took a cigarette out and lit it. "I know who did this, Jewell, and the kid here," he pointed at me, "he knows it, too. He was there the day they threatened Mickey."

"The law will not listen to you without proof," Jewell said. "It'll just be your word against theirs and they've got the money to pay off any judge they want to."

"Then we'll leave the law out of it," Joe said. He gritted his teeth and clenched his fist then went on. "It's time they pay for all they've done to this family. And how we know they're not the ones what killed Mooney?"

"Joe, that's enough," Granny Flor said. "Frankie and Ellie don't need to be hearin' that kind of talk."

We heard Jim Elee pull up and then he brought a doctor into the house, a small pink, bald man in a gray suit. There was nothing remarkable about him, except he had sleepy eyes.

"I'm Doctor Finis McGrain," he said. He held his hand out to Granny. She wiped her hand on her dress then shook.

"Y'all all git on outta here now," she said. "This here doctor's a gonna look at Mickey."

On the porch, Jim Elee, pushed his dark hair back and rubbed his forehead with the back of his sleeve. "I'm sorry it took me so long, Joe. I was scared Mickey Wayne would be dead before I got back. This doctor was on the only one on duty and he was working a bad wreck that happened out on fifty-five, and they wouldn't let me back there. I went off on em though, started cussing and climbing the walls. That's when them nurses told me that if I didn't settle down they's gonna call the sheriff and have me locked up then my cousin would die for sure. There ain't enough doctors in this town, Joe."

"You know Granny," Joe said, "if there's any way this side of heaven to save a man's life, she can do it. She put Mickey back together just like she put me back together. You did good, little brother."

Jewell touched Ellie on the shoulder, "Honey, why don't you bring Frankie over to the house and we'll feed the boy while Granny talks to the doctor. He's got to be hungry and so do you. I've got a pot of black-eyed peas and a pone of cornbread made."

"Oh, no, that's all right," I said. "Momma will have supper..." Then I stopped. How late was I? It was way past dark. My parents had to be worried out of their minds.

"I better get going. Will I see you at school tomorrow, Ellie?"

She shrugged. "I don't know. That depends on how Mickey is doing."

I started for home then I realized something and turned around. "Where's Mickey's car?"

"He loaned it to his girlfriend," Joe said.

I nodded. So Mickey had a girlfriend? Made sense. He did look like a movie star. I started to leave again then another thought hit me. "Ellie, will you walk with me a little ways?"

Ellie came down off the porch and walked beside me. "Why didn't you tell me your father was dead?" I asked.

She shrugged. "He's been dead a long time, Frankie. I was just about nine or ten years old. One day Mickey was picking up corn and Daddy was up the holler a ways. When Mickey came in we waited and waited but Daddy never came, then we went looking for him. We took off up through the woods and...and...we came upon..." She put her hands over her face.

"Oh, Ellie," I said. I wrapped my arms around her and she laid her head on my shoulder. "He was shot. Shot in the back, just like Mickey, only there was no one there to stop the bleeding or to go for help. My daddy," she sniffled. "He was mean to us, Frankie. He hit us and everything all of the time, but at least he fed us. Me and Mickey, we were just kids and we didn't know what to do so we got Granny and Uncle Willie Jose and Aunt Sadie Rose and they said that we should bury him in the woods behind the house and keep it quiet, because with me and Mickey being orphans somebody might come and take us away from Granny and away from each other. So we still live in the house and we took over daddy's business."

"Ellie," I said, "are you telling me that you are a moonshiner, too?"

She bit her lip. "We gotta eat, Frankie. Don't hate me. I can take all those other people hating us, but I can't take it if you hate me."

I didn't hate her. My heart broke for her but I didn't hate her. I couldn't even imagine a father who beat me. I couldn't imagine finding my father dead in the woods, shot through the back, not knowing who killed him or why. And I couldn't imagine a ten year old and a thirteen-year-old wandering up on a moonshine still and taking over the operation.

"Oh, Ellie, I could never hate you…but…"

"Don't feel sorry for me, either, Frankie," she said. "Just tell me that you still believe in me and that one day I'm gonna leave this place and never look back."

I traced her face with my hand, a face that I had been drawing over and over ever since that first day I walked her past the Jackson place.

"And your still? It's hidden down below the Jackson place isn't it?"

"Don't tell nobody, Frankie. That's the only way me and Mickey have got of making a living and now Mickey's laid up and…oh, no…oh no…" she took off running in that direction.

"Ellie, wait," I called then took off after her.

As we passed the Jackson place she turned a sharp left and went deep into the woods. I caught up to her and took her by the hand.

We heard voices and ducked into the thick underbrush. By the light of the full moon, I could see that three of the Dawson boys were destroying the McThacker still.

Chapter Ten

There was a full moon that night and I could see the faces of those guys as they hacked away at Mickey's moonshine still. They were for sure the Dawson boys. Ellie clapped her hand over my mouth like she thought I might holler out or something. We eased back the way we had come.

Once we made back to the main road that ran by Mr. Jackson's place she whispered. "We got to put some distance between us and them." Then she sighed. "I don't know what's gonna happen next."

"What exactly is going on?" I asked. My head was swimming. In one afternoon, I had seen a boy almost get murdered and discovered the girl I loved was not only an orphan but was making and selling whiskey. No wonder there was so much corn growing in Swamp Holler. "Start from the beginning and tell me everything. My head feels like it's spinning backwards."

"Mommy died of tuberculosis. Daddy couldn't take her into town to the doctor on account of the law was looking for him, so he wrapped her in a quilt and took out to the edge of the road where he knew Rainy Jackson would be passing on his way home from work, because back then he worked over at the cheese factory. Sure enough, Mr. Jackson saw her and he knew that it was Daddy that put her there and he tried to save her. After she died, Granny Flor and Aunt Sadie Rose say that Daddy wasn't the same. He took the business to heart, thinking that if he didn't do better he'd lose me and Mickey, too. He would take Mickey out in the woods and keep him for days at a time, and him just a little kid. He was teaching him how to make the liquor, you see.

"Anyhow, our daddy ran liquor and was making a good living at it. He bought himself a fine car and started selling his liquor in Lexington and Danville and Frankfort and all over the place. He even made several runs across the border down into Knoxville and all up around Celina. He had a lot of customers. He had all kinds of nice clothes. He had a lot of girlfriends, too, but he never brought any of them home with him. Sometimes he would leave and stay gone for weeks at a time. Then one day he sent Mickey to the house to fetch him some supper and when Mickey got back to the still he found our Daddy dead, shot. That's why Mickey's got the car and the jacket. It was all Daddy's stuff and he never let us touch it, but when he died, Mickey grew into it.

"Me and Mickey took to running the still but neither one of us could drive legally yet, so the Dawsons came down and offered to run our liquor until Mickey came of age and could drive. Only trouble was they took most all of the money and barely even left us enough to live on. Me and Mickey did all of the work and they got the money. When Mickey came of age, he started making some runs on his own and told the Dawsons we didn't need them anymore. Only trouble was the Dawsons said we still had to give them a cut of the money because they were only collecting it for their boss. Mickey told them to tell their boss he wanted out of the deal and wanted to run his own business. The boss, whose name we have never been allowed to know, sent word by the Dawsons that if we didn't continue to turn over the profits then we would see what happened to our daddy happen to Granny Flor and the

Pablos and all of Swamp Holler. So, about three years ago, Mickey made a run into Lexington and delivered shine to this guy who turned out to be a lawyer. Can you believe that? Anyway when Mickey realized it was a law person he was scared to death, but the guy liked Mickey and they became friends. He told Mickey that if he'd make a plan to go straight, he'd help him get out of the business. So, that's when me and Mickey put together a plan to get ourselves out of Swamp Holler and out of the moonshine business.

"We were at Joe's house; he's got a television that he found at a barn sale over in Liberty. Anyway, a man was talking about the future on the news and he said that the key to the future was education. If a person could learn to read and write and make it to college then that person would have a secure future.

"Mickey said he was already too old to go for it and that one of us would have to stay home and run the business while the other went to school and got an education. Only trouble was, I'm a girl. Mickey said that meant I'd have to work ten times harder and make better grades than any boy, lessen I wanted to end up be some bootlegger's wife for the rest of my life." She gripped my hand. "And I don't want to be, Frankie. I just want to do something good with my life. I don't know what yet, but I know I can't be nothing iffen I don't get out of Swamp Holler. So, anyway, I started coming to school.

"Mickey said I had to be quiet about my life so that nobody came nosing around. He said I had to learn twice as fast as a normal kid and he took to taking me to the big library in the city on weekends whenever he had a run to make, and once I learned how to read well, I started reading every book I could get my hands on. I study all of the time. I study way into the night and I read everything. Mickey buys me the paper every time he goes into town and we keep up with all that's going on in the world. I read to him. I tell him about the war over in Vietnam and about how things are changing everywhere."

Then she took a deep breath, "If Mickey dies I don't know what I'll do. I never really knew my momma, can't even remember her hardly and my daddy, he was a hard man to know, but Mickey, he's never been nothing but good to me and I love him more than anything in this whole world. I don't think I'll have the gumption to go on living out our dreams without Mickey."

I was thankful that is was night. Ellie couldn't see how my eyes were threatening to get all teary. So she kept right on talking. "Mickey wants out, Frankie, and I want out, too. Only it's taking us a while to work out our plan and now Mickey's done been shot and what if he doesn't pull through and what if he never can walk again like Granny said?"

I put my arm around Ellie and drew her close to me as we walked. "He's going to pull through," I said in a voice so firm that I scared myself. "He's going to pull through and the both of you are going to leave Swamp Holler." I swallowed.

Ellie was like that Samaritan woman at the well. She just needed a fair chance in life and I determined right then and there in my heart that I wasn't giving up on Ellie and no matter what it cost me; I was going to see that she got a chance, and Mickey, too, for that matter. Maybe he was a moonshiner, and according to my parents, a low life, but he was willing to do whatever it took to give his little sister a better life, and that made me believe that he had a lot of good in him.

The familiar sound of a my dad's truck caused me to let go of Ellie and look up just as he pulled up beside us and rolled down his window, "Frankie D. Keilman, where the hell have you been?"

"D…Daddy," I said. "I, um I…"

"Get in the truck," he said. "Both of you." I opened the door and we got in.

"Who's this girl and where does she live?"

"Ellie McThacker," I said.

"McThacker?" My dad almost gagged on the name. "You got some explaining to do, boy." He put the truck in gear and we were headed back toward Swamp Holler.

"Your momma and Eugene are out walking the path from the school house to home, carrying a lantern, looking for you," Daddy said. "And here you are, out runnin' round with a girl after dark. I never thought I'd live the day that I was ashamed of you, Frankie."

If my dad had beat me with a whip it wouldn't have done much more damage. He hadn't even let me begin to explain. He just figured that if I was out after dark with a girl from Swamp Holler then I had surely done other bad things, too.

"Daddy," I said. "A man almost died today. If you came upon a man who had been shot and was dying what would you do?"

All of this time Ellie sat quiet as a mouse.

"Oh, Frankie, don't you turn this around and go trying to mess my head up with your questions. You laid out late. I suppose this is the first time and I'd let bygones be bygones, but you're with a...well, you done gone and disgraced us..."

"I'm not trying to mess with anybody's head," I blurted. "Mickey McThacker was shot in the back today. I came upon him on my way home from school today. He was bleeding to death and I took off my shirt and stopped the bleeding. Then Ellie here went and got some help. What was I supposed to do, Daddy, let a man die?"

"What have you got yourself into, boy?" my dad said. I wasn't sure about his voice if he was more angry or scared. We came to the end of Ellie's gravel road.

"Turn here," I said. My dad followed the road. Lamp light filtered through the shack windows and open doors, telling me that most everyone in Swamp Holler was still awake. We followed the narrow road until we came to Granny's house. "This is it," I said. My dad pulled into the driveway and as Ellie got out, I could make out Joe's silhouette, standing in the doorway with a lit cigarette in his hand. "Good night, Ellie," I said. "Will I see you tomorrow at school?"

"Probably not," she said. "I'm staying close until I know how Mickey's gonna be. See ya later, Frankie Keilman." She closed the door and ran toward the house. I scooted over to the passenger side of the pick-up.

"Frankie, don't you be messing' with these people," Daddy said. "I ain't saying you did wrong in helping that boy, but leave it alone now and stay away from em. That there girl ain't nothing but trouble and she won't cause you nothing but trouble. Your momma's gonna die when she hears that you were with a McThacker."

I wanted to tell him everything, the whole truth. I wanted to tell him that I had been walking Ellie home every day since the first week of school and that I had bought her a dress and that we dreamed about running away from Swamp Holler and going to see the Great Wall of China, and I wanted to tell him that Momma was trying to force me to take Liddie Grace McAllister to the picnic and force me into one day marrying her or somebody else just like her, but I couldn't. The words wouldn't come. Maybe I knew that he wouldn't understand or that he would flick my feelings off like he flicked the fleas off of his coon hounds. So I sat back in the truck seat, trying to imagine how I was going to bear all of Momma's nagging and then Eugene would have to retell the horror story of the man who had gotten eaten by a catty mau in those woods. I dreaded going home that night worse than a kid dreads a shot in the butt. It seemed like the ride was way too short and before I could even straighten out all that had happened in my head that day, we were pulling into the driveway.

The porch light was on and our house looked like a patriotic post card. Momma had the yard all done up in little white fences and flowers. There were flower boxes and potted ferns on the front porch. An American flag hung from the porch post on one side of the entry and a small mock of the Liberty Bell hung on the other. Above the porch roof, the window to my bedroom was dark. Many times I had thought about how easy it would be just to climb out that window, slide down that slanted metal roof, scurry down the antenna pole and set out on a great adventure. But I had never tried it.

I heard voices coming from the backyard then looked in that direction and saw two lights moving through the woods and toward our house.

"He's here!" Daddy shouted.

Eugene and Momma shouted back and in about two minutes we were all standing on the front porch.

"Where the dickens have you been?" Eugene started. "We thought you were dead, Frankie. I was scared to death that I was going find just your head or your foot or some other body part or maybe we never would find you at all. It'd be just like Old Mallory McGreggins what got eat by a catty mau back in '43…

"Hush, Eugene," Momma snapped

We all went inside. Momma and Eugene started yelling at me at the same time, asking me where I'd been and hollering a bunch of other stuff, but my head was swimming and my ears went numb. I reckon I tuned them out until they got through hollering at me. Daddy didn't do any hollering. He just stood over behind the wood stove, which wasn't being used on account of the weather was still plenty warm, with his shoulder up against the wall.

Momma lowered her voice. "Frankie, aren't you even gonna try to tell us where you've been?"

I started to, but then my dad said, "Frankie saved a man's life today. He came upon one of Billy George's work hands. The boy had piece of metal sticking in his back and was bleeding plum to death. Frankie here, he stopped the bleeding and saved the feller's life. Of course he had to go get help and that took him a long time. Y'all let up on Frankie. He couldn't get to no phone. George's work hands don't have phones. They're just renters passing through til winter sets in."

I knew my mouth was hanging open but I didn't have the strength to close it. My dad was lying. He was flat out lying to protect me.

The house was dead quiet, except for the hum of the refrigerator in the kitchen and the ticking of a wind-up clock in the adjoining room, my parent's bedroom.

"Well," Momma went in the kitchen and put her apron. "Put some coffee on, Ancil. Frankie, let's warm you up some supper. I reckon it was a good thing you did today, saving that man's life, but I was worried. If anything ever happened to you, I don't know what I'd do. Lord knows your daddy ain't got the sense to move up in this world. I'm counting on you to take care of me when my arthritis and slow bowels gets the best of me."

Eugene grunted and shook his head.

"Don't you shake that head at me, Eugene," Momma said, "You know good and well that I'm not well." She looked at Daddy with hard eyes. "I have to work like a man. You don't see Ima Jean out in the fields setting tobacco or in the barn stripping it. You don't see Alice McAlister in no tobacco barn neither." She was referring to Liddie Grace's mom. I was pretty sure that Liddie Grace's mom didn't even change her own underwear but I wasn't going to say that to Momma.

"No sir," she went on, "I tell you, Frankie, if something happened to you, I'd be all alone in this world and I'd be without a hope of ever having a better life."

My dad didn't say a word, he just poured himself a cup of coffee and went in the living room. I noticed how he walked, eyes down, feet shuffling.

"Ancil," Momma scolded, "don't you dare leave that cup sitting in the floor behind the heating stove." I knew that he would leave the cup in the floor behind the stove and he'd probably lie right

102

down in the living room floor and go to sleep. Sometimes he slept in the floor all night. He and Momma didn't share a bedroom anyway. They hadn't shared a bedroom since I was a small boy, which Eugene said was the reason that I was never going to get any brothers or sisters. He said that one day Momma woke up too fragile for Daddy to touch. I was about eight when he told me that and I didn't ask what it meant. Now I knew and wished that I didn't.

Momma fixed her eyes on Eugene. "Well, you might as well stay and have a bite, too, seeing how you've been out looking for Frankie with us."

Eugene lifted his straw hat and scratched his head, "I think I'd rather eat with the catty mau." He turned and walked through the living room and out the front door.

Momma went on the whole time I ate about how I had worried her and about how her bowels were acting up on account of it and she probably wouldn't be able to sleep without some nerve pills which she was out of and the doctor wouldn't give her anymore because she had already taken two whole bottles this month.

"Nerve pills can eat the lining outta your stomach," she said. "Course that's why I'm so skinny. I stay nervous all of the time. Your daddy keeps me tore up. He won't do nothing to help out around here, always leaving his clothes on the floor and shoes just wherever he takes em off and spitting and leaving dishes all over the place. And now, well tonight, I just about had a nervous breakdown, Frankie, when you were three or four hours late from school. I came an ace of calling Alice McAllister to ask her if Liddie Grace knew anything about your whereabouts, but I didn't. I didn't want to run the chance of them thinking harsh of us on account of if something else had come up. Course if you hadn't shown up when you did, I was ready to call the sheriff to come find you..."

"Momma," I said. "You know that I don't want to disappoint you…but…"

"But what?"

"I can't take Liddie Grace to that picnic."

"Oh, Frankie, don't gone on with such foolishness. I mean sure I was worried but I ain't aiming to keep you from seeing Liddie Grace. I know how sweet you are on her and I wouldn't want…"

I braced myself. "I'm not sweet on her," I said. "I don't even like to be in the same room with her."

My mother's face was terror stricken but I went on. "Momma, she makes fun of people. She makes fun of their clothes and their hair. She makes Sandy Coltrain feel stupid"

"Sandy Coltrain is stupid," she said. "So what?"

"He's slow, Momma. He can't help it. Liddie Grace makes Idy Joe feel like she's ugly and she makes El…she tries to boss me around all of the time. I don't want to be bossed around." I almost said, like Daddy, but I didn't.

"You're just tired," she said. She spilled a little of her coffee. "You go on up and get some sleep, Frankie. You'll feel better in the morning. You can stay home from school if you want to."

"No, I'm going to try to go to school," I said. I had hopes that Ellie might be there. I hoped that she would be there and tell me that Mickey was doing okay.

Momma smiled. "Suit yourself, son, but I wouldn't go saying anything about not going to the picnic yet. Liddie Grace is a real sweet girl."

Hadn't she heard anything I had said? Liddie Grace was a nightmare, an attractive, stylish nightmare of a girl who was destined to make some man as unhappy as my daddy had been for the past twenty-five years.

I rose from the table and meandered through the living room. Daddy was sitting behind the stove with his hand on his head. "Daddy, you all right?" I asked.

He nodded then got up, stumbling a little as he did. "Maybe need some air," he said.

I decided to walk out on the porch with him. He sat down in one of the ladder back chairs that we kept on the porch and I leaned against a post. I was exhausted but I was also puzzled. I didn't know why my dad had lied, but he had. I couldn't rat him out. He had put himself on the line to keep Momma from jumping me about being with the McThackers.

"Daddy, why..."

"Some questions are better not asked, son," he said. "Just keep your notions in your head for once."

I sat in silence a few minutes, scratching a horse head into the post with my thumbnail which had gotten a little longer than I liked. "Did you ever have any girlfriends other than Momma?"

He grinned and let out a low grunt. "Oh, Frankie, you ought not to ask such things."

"I just need to know," I said.

"It don't matter," he said. "I ended up with your momma." I wanted to ask if he had ever loved her, but that was one of those questions that I couldn't get to come out of my mouth. I could not imagine my dad ever being in love.

"Your momma was the pick of the litter," he said. "A purebred pup. Now go to bed, boy, before you doze off and fall off the porch. If you was to break your neck your momma wouldn't have nobody to take care of her slow bowels." He grinned again and I laughed.

"Lucky me," I said. I got up and went up to my room. I was so tired that I didn't fix myself any bath water. I set my clock and lay across my bed. I intended to just rest my eyes for a minute or two then take off my clothes and get under the cover. Next time I opened my eyes it was because my alarm sounded. I got up, groggy, washed my face in the basin and went down to the kitchen. Just like every other morning I ate a bite, downed some coffee and went out to help Daddy and Eugene milk. I was in a daze and almost got kicked by a cow. I stepped in a cow pile and walked right into a barn post. Eugene laughed and laughed at me. My dad just shook his head and sent me back to the house.

I combed my hair, changed my clothes and headed out to school. I looked for Ellie when I got there but she wasn't there. I watched everyone file in and still, no Ellie.

Miss Mays wasn't there and Sally Wittle, an elderly retired teacher from farther up the ridge was filling in for her.

Mrs. Wittle was so heavy set that she waddled as she walked up to the board and scrawled her name in chalk. Maybe it was a lack of sleep, but I couldn't stop thinking of the phrase, "Mrs. Wittle waddles." I slid down in my seat, biting my lip to keep from laughing out loud. It was wicked, but it was true.

She wore a blue flowered dress, which matched her blue hair. She turned around and took off her cat eye glasses that hung from a chain around her neck. "My name is Mrs. Wittle," she said in her sweet little old lady voice as if we hadn't seen her before and we didn't know who she was. "I will be filling in for Miss Mays today as she has gone on an important trip today."

At recess I handed Liddie Grace a note. I know it was a coward's way out but I was too worn out from staying up most all night to care. I had scrawled on a note:

Dear Liddie Grace,

I think you are a pretty girl and you are also smart, but I do not wish to go steady with you as my future plans do not include marriage or babies or beauty shops. I hope to travel the world one day. I think you are a fine person, the pick of the litter and a purebred pup, but I do not wish to go to the picnic with you.

Your friend,

Frankie Delano Keilman.

When I got home that afternoon, I headed into the house to change my clothes and go help with the farm work, but when I walked into the living room, I froze. There stood Momma, arms folded, staring at pieces of paper that she had laid on every flat surface in the room, staring at my drawings, drawings of hawks and horses and the Great Wall of China and the Leaning Tower of Pisa, but mostly they were the drawings I had done of Ellie, all of the drawings I had done of Ellie.

"Who is she, Frankie?" Momma said. Her voice shook. She turned and looked at me as she sniffled. "I've about cried my eyes out this afternoon. Who is this little tramp that you keep drawing over and over? And don't you lie to me. I have been on the phone with Alice McAlister and Liddie Grace is inconsolable. Who is this little piece of Swamp Holler riff-raff that you're trying to destroy my life for?"

Chapter Eleven

"A Garney? A Pablo? A McThacker? Is she Black, Mexican or just plain old White trash? Never mind, I know who she is, Mrs. McAllister told me everything that Liddie Grace told her, how you sit with her and share our food that I work hard to cook and how you hold her hand when you think nobody's looking." Momma put her hand on her head like she was about to faint.

"She's a friend," I said. "And it's not right to let another person be hungry. Remember the story of the rich man and Lazarus the begger?"

"Don't you talk to me about right and wrong," she screeched.

"Don't you try to turn this around on me, young man."

My stomach felt like it did the time I got sick off eating a whole jar of sorghum molasses by myself.

"A friend, you say." She shook her head and laughed a sarcastic little laugh, the kind she used on Daddy when she lit in on him and made him leave the house. "Elmer Page is a friend. Idy Jo Darling can be your friend or your Cousin Harlan. Why Sandy Coltrain as mentally afflicted as he is, can be your friend, but a girl from Swamp Holler?"

I backed up against the door, "She's a good person, Momma."

"A good person?" Momma picked up one of my drawings, the first one I had ever done of Ellie, the one I stayed up all night drawing. "Good girls don't look all...all... like that." She ripped the drawing in half and I felt like she had just kicked me in the stomach. No spanking, no nagging, nothing had ever hurt me like seeing my momma rip up my art like it was nothing more than a letter from a bill collector. She ripped it again then threw it in the wood box behind the stove. "You're not going with a girl from Swamp Holler," she said. "What did you think was going to come of all of this, Frankie? Were you planning to marry her?"

"I'm not planning to marry anybody," I said. "I just want the freedom to find out what I'm supposed to do with my life. Maybe I don't want to be a farmer like Daddy and I don't know for sure that I'm meant to be a preacher. What if I'm not? Maybe that's not the reason I was born into this world. I have to find out for myself."

"You're seventeen!" Momma hollered at me. "What on Earth makes you think you've got enough sense to decide what you're future should be. I'll tell you what you're gonna do with your life, starting with right now. You're going to forget all about this little tramp and march yourself up to the McAllister house and beg Liddie Grace to go to that picnic with you. And this art business," she grabbed another drawing, one of Ellie laughing, looked at it then ripped it, too.

"Stop it, Momma," I might have screamed. I don't know. I might have even cried a little. When a man's that torn up, he doesn't know what he's doing, but watching her rip my work was like she had pulled my soul right out of me and was telling me how ugly it was and how disgusted she was with the real me, the person I had been hiding under my bed for the past ten years. Momma had discovered just how touched I really was and she was using it against me.

I braced my insides. I couldn't let her tear up all of my drawings. It was true that they were just paper, but to me they were little pieces of my soul. I started grabbing them right out from under her. It was a war of the wills; Momma would try to grab a picture before I could.

"You had no right getting in my things," I said.

"I'm your mother. I've got the right to get into anything I want to get into. I'm not gonna let you throw a promising future away on some…some..."

"Don't call her trash again!" I yelled. I didn't mean to yell at my mother. I knew to respect her, but my guts were rumbling and I felt like I was falling to pieces. "Future? What future? A life like with Liddie Grace McAlister and her family's money? She makes me feel the way you make Daddy feel." My precious drawings were crammed under the crook of my left arm by then.

"And how is that, Frankie?" Momma said. "How do you think I make your daddy feel?"

I looked at her, standing there with her carrot colored hair up in curlers, at her tiny waist dress and her brown shoes with little black heels. I looked at her apron, stained from years of wear and use. "Like that apron," I said. "You wear it around here and it serves your purpose, just an old everyday thing, but when you go out and you want to be fancy, you just take it off and throw it down." I took hold of the door knob and said, without looking at her, "I can't be no apron, Momma." I pulled that door open and ran out. I could hear Momma screaming behind me, "You get back here, Frankie. Obey your parents or something awful will befall you. That's Bible."

I kept running, my heart pounding so hard that I could feel it in my ears, sweat running down my back and neck, not because it was hot, but because I had never flat out disobeyed either of my parents before. I had no idea where I was going or how long I would stay. All I could think of was a scripture somewhere in the

Old Testament where Solomon said that it was better to live on a roof top with nothing but bread to eat than to live in the house with a brawling woman. I ran, I didn't look back, not on the house or the barn or Momma.

She would probably send Daddy out looking for me, but I wasn't going to be in any of my usual hangouts. I wouldn't be at Tiny Elmer's or Harlan's. I started to go toward Ellie's and check on Mickey, but then I changed my mind. Daddy would come there looking for me and I wasn't going home until I was ready. I needed time to think and I needed a friend, someone with experience and courage. I thought about Brother Van Dyke. I wanted to go there but I knew that his duty to his congregation would cause him to want to call my parents and tell them where I was. I needed someone who wasn't quite so duty bound. It was almost dark when I reached Swamp Holler and a skinny old yellow dog with no hair on its ears ran out and growled at me as I neared Joe Pablo's house.

"Hey!" I hollered. "Anybody home?"

I could see a flickering black and white light and could hear the television through the open door and could smell meat frying.

The house was little more than a shack. It had a lean for a front porch, just a roof held up by some skinny posts and a screened area in the back. The whole thing couldn't have had more than three or four rooms. Flat creek rocks formed a walkway from the gravel road up to the front door and I could see the remnants of zinnias and marigolds from an exceptionally long summer. I hollered again, scared that the yellow dog was going to eat me.

Joe Pablo stuck his head out the door. "Hey, sport," he said and smiled. Then his smile turned upside down and he hollered, "Get outta here, mutt." He picked up a rock and threw it at the dog, which went whimpering and running back out into the road before it turned and growled at Joe.

"Stupid stray," he said. "I'm gonna shoot that dog if airy one of Mammy's chickens turn up dead or chewed on. I tell ya, Kid, I'm gonna shoot that dog."

"It's probably just hungry," I said.

Joe laughed. "Well, we're all hungry but we don't run around growling at people and sniffing their butts. What're you doing walking down here this time of day anyway, son?"

I shrugged. "I'm in a lot of trouble."

"A respectable boy like you, in trouble? Tell ya what, Jewell and Mammy, they've about got supper ready and Ded'll be home any second now. Why don't you come on in and have a cup of coffee and stay for supper and tell us about it."

Inside I realized that though the house was small, it was clean, much cleaner than Granny Flor's had been. A maroon couch sat facing away from the door with a small television about six feet in front of it. Between the two items was a home-made rough cut coffee table with a giant black Bible on the table. It was worn and had colorful little ribbons sticking out of several places.

To the right of the couch and up against the wall beside the kitchen doorway sat a rocking chair with a quilt thrown across it. Family pictures and religious icons covered the walls.

"Hey, Mammy," Joe shouted. "Bring my friend Frankie here a cup of coffee."

A few seconds later a small woman in a checkered dress came from the kitchen.

She carried a cup of coffee on a saucer, the brown liquid spilling over the sides.

"Hey, Mammy," Joe said, "this here's Frankie Keilman from up on the ridge. He's the one that saved Mickey's life."

The woman couldn't have been more than five feet, if that, and I doubt she would have weighed over ninety pounds if she was soaking wet and full of pinto beans. She stretched her bony hand out to me. "Hidy, I'm Sadie Rose Pablo," she said. "Ellie and

Mickey are my sister's babies and we all thank you for what you did for Mickey and the way you been helping Ellie out at school and the dress that you bought for her."

So they knew? Had Ellie told her entire family everything?

"Does Ellie talk about me?" I asked.

Mrs. Pablo grinned. "Does a bird dog have spots? We know everything there is to know about Frankie Keilman." Her dark eyes sparkled and I could tell she had a kind spirit. I also knew that the Bible belonged to her so I up and said, "That's a nice Bible. Is that yours?"

"Lawd have mercy," she said. "That was my daddy's Bible. My great granddaddy was living down in Georgia back in the days of old President Jackson, as mean a man that ever lived that president was. Anyway, neither here nor there, that there president up and decided that my people had to leave the land they'd been borned on and he comesd to just sending his soldier out and rounding up my great-granddaddy's family and my great granddaddy was just a boy. Now there was this Irshmen family what lived down the holler from em and they was good people, so his daddy, when he heared that the soldiers was a comin', he took my great-granddaddy down there and hid him in their root cellar and told him not to come out for seven days. There was a little knothole in that cellar door and he told my great-granddaddy not to come out until he had seen the light and the dark trade places through that peep hole seven times.

"He gave the boy a sack full of corn bread, a jug of water and this Bible. My daddy told me that as far as he knows great-granddaddy's ma and pa died on the way out west but in seven days the boy came up out of that root cellar and went to the Irsh woman's house and she took him in an raised him as her own youngin and when come to the age of marrying, her and him traveled by a horse and wagon over into North Carolina and met up with some of his kinfolk and he married a girl from there. Her name was Wakni Falling Leaf and I reckon she was my great-granny. Anyhow, that's how come me to have that Bible. I didn't mean to talk so long about it."

I smiled. "It's okay. I wish I had a family story like that to be proud of." I looked up and noticed Jewell Pablo standing in the doorway. She smiled. "Supper's ready fellas."

"Well, Willie Jose's not in yet," Mrs. Pablo said. Just then a short man in a straw cowboy hat stepped into the house.

"Looks like I'm just in time," he said.

Then he looked at me. I couldn't help but notice that although the man's skin was as dark as Granny Flor's his eyes were as blues as Ellie's and Mickey's. He pulled off the straw hat, leaving salt and pepper hair plastered flat against his head. He held the hat against his chest and extended his hand, "Howdy, I'm Willie Jose Pablo. You must be the boy what saved Mickey."

"Yes, sir, I'm Ellie's friend from school." I heard Sadie Rose Pablo snicker as she took tiny steps into the kitchen. She reminded me of those women I'd read about in China who had their feet bound and couldn't walk fast on account of it. We all followed her into the kitchen where we gathered around a hand-made table with mis-matched chairs. The food was simple, pinto beans, corn bread, fried chicken, fried apples and black boiling coffee. I drank three cups of that, even though it was as stronger than the smell of fresh cow poop.

All during supper Joe cut up, laughing, telling jokes, poking fun at his boss, Mr. George, whom he kept referring to as the Fat White Man. Then Willie Jose would scold him and Mrs. Pablo would giggle. I thought Joe had forgotten that I needed to talk to somcone, so I up and said, "How's Mickey getting along?"

Joe nodded, chewing his meat. He waved his fork at me. "He's sore as a castrated bull, but Granny says he is going pull through. Now, what was it you needed to tell me about, Frankie?"

I looked around the table. Did I dare pour my story out in front of this whole family? Would they laugh at me? I wondered if my troubles would even seem like troubles to them at all. But then Willie Jose Pablo took a drink of coffee and set his cup down. "Go on, son, it's all right. You saved Mickey's life. You're family now."

"T'ain't nobody here gonna judge you," Sadie Rose said.

I didn't mean to sound like a girl or a baby, but I started with the day I ripped my pants on the fence and they all roared when I got to the part where I looked down and saw my underwear. I thought Jewell was going to spit coffee through her nose she laughed so hard.

Joe waved that fork at me again, "I wish that'd been me that done that!"

Then I told them about how Ellie helped me and Miss Mays said I had to walk her past the Jackson place on account of she was afraid of their dog. Again they all cackled and took on about how the Jacksons didn't even own a dog. Then I told them about Liddie Grace and Momma and the picnic. I told them about how I bought Ellie a dress from the preacher's wife and how she got mad at me and said I was trying to give her a hand out, but I didn't tell them the part where I hollered out that I loved her. I just couldn't tell anybody that part.

I told them about my drawings, which were lying in their living room on the couch while we ate, about how Momma didn't want me associating with Ellie or Mickey and how she planned my whole future out and had her heart set on me being a preacher but I wasn't sure that was what I was meant to be and if I wasn't meant to be that, then it wouldn't be God that was calling me to preach, it'd be Momma and I didn't think that she always had the mind of God as her real motive. While I spoke their faces became solemn and when I had finished, Sadie Rose Pablo rose from the table and

116

came over to me. She patted my hand. "Come in here, Son," she said.

I followed her into the living room and she handed me the Bible from the coffee table. "Open it to where the yellow ribbon is," she said. So, I did.

"Now read that to me. Read the one that has a star beside it."

I cleared my throat and read, "Children, obey your parents in the Lord for this is the firsts commandment with promise."

"Yer momma's right about one thing," she said. "It does say to obey your parents, but catch the next part, in the Lord. Now turn to that pink ribbon and read that page."

I turned and came to the book of Proverbs.

"I believe it's chapter three," Sadie said. "You see, I can't read a lick. Ellie reads it to me, her and Jewell, and just anybody else that'll come along and do it for me, but I reckon I got a good memory and when I hear a verse I know I'm gonna need to remember I have the person reading to put a star by it and I put a ribbon on that page so I can find it. Now you read down there around verse five or six or somewhere down in there where it talks about not leaning on your own ways."

I scanned the chapter then read, "Lean not to your own understanding, but trust in the Lord and He will direct your paths."

"A-ha," she said. "There's your answer, Frankie. You got to obey your parents as much as you can, so long as they're not asking you to do anything against God, but you got to put your life in the Lawd's hands and trust Him to work everything out for you. Here's what I'd do iffen I was you. I'd go on back home to my mammy and tell her that I was taking that biscuit tooth girl to the picnic. I'd say something like, 'I been thinking, Mammy. That I should do what you ask me to and I reckon I will take, um what's her name?"

"Liddie Grace."

"Yeah, Liddie Grace to the picnic, providin' she'll still have me. Then your momma will be happy."

"I won't be happy," I said. "And I don't think Ellie will be happy either."

Sadie smiled. "You just leave Ellie to me. That girl's got an understanding beyond her years. Smartest kid that was ever born, I reckon. I didn't say you had to marry Liddie Grace. Just take her to the picnic to get your momma off your back. In the meantime, you talk to you your pa, just a little bit."

"I can't talk to him," I said. "He doesn't talk, about anything."

"Then let him listen," she said. "You got to tell him. Your mammy and your pa, they didn't come from the same mold. Just talk to him."

I sighed. I didn't want to take Liddie to that picnic and I didn't want Momma thinking she was right and I sure didn't want to talk to my daddy, but there was something about this eighty pound woman that seemed older and wiser than anyone I knew except for Granny Flor, even though the lack of gray hair and wrinkles told me that she was probably not more than forty years old.

"Okay," I said, "but can I leave my drawings here? In case Momma has another hissy fit?"

"Of course you can," she said. "I might hang some of them up iffen you don't care and I'm sure Granny Flor would like to have some of these of Ellie to hang in her house."

I smiled. No one had ever wanted to hang up my drawings before. It wasn't a museum in Rome or Paris, but at least my work would have an audience that appreciated it.

"Why don't you run over and see Ellie?" Joe said from the kitchen doorway. "I'll walk over there with you."

"I will," I said, "and thanks for supper and everything."

"Anytime," Joe said. We headed over to Granny Flor's. As before, the front door stood open, and I could hear Mickey hollering all the way out in the yard.

"What's got him so upset?" I asked.

Joe snickered. "Granny won't let him smoke in bed, unless somebody's standing in there watching him, on account of he can't turn over on that sore butt of hiss'n, and she's afraid he's gonna catch the bed on fire. That feather tick that she's got Mickey on is older than she is and she don't want nothing happening to it. So, he's about to have one of them fits like your momma had when you told her you didn't want to take that little snob to the picnic."

I laughed. Then I said, "I thought he was in pain."

"Oh, he is, but it's the not being able to smoke that might kill him. Course, the bed bugs could be a bitin' him."

We walked up the flat creek rock walk that someone had made to keep Granny out of the mud and neared the porch with its dilapidated home-made chairs and loose floor boards when Ellie rounded the corner of the house a bucket of water in each hand.

"Frankie," she said. "You came back."

Chapter Twelve

"Of course I came back. But I can't stay long. My dad will be out hunting for me." I reached and took one of Ellie's water buckets. Joe took the other one. "I sort of stormed out of the house and my momma's so mad at me that when she blew her stack the roof of our house nearly exploded."

"That's pretty mad," Ellie said. "What'd you do to get her so worked up?" She wiped her hands on her brown dress and opened the screen door for me.

"Three words," I said. "Liddie Grace McAllister."

"Oh?"

"It's a long story. Your Aunt Sadie Rose said she'd tell you all about it. I have to hurry out of here, but first I wanted to say hi to you and Mickey." I stepped in and saw Granny Flor sitting at the kitchen table, working on a quilt. "And of course, Granny Flor, too. How you doing?" I nodded.

Her eyes twinkled with mischief, "Too old to marry. Too young to die." She snickered at her own wisecrack and I couldn't help but chuckle a little bit.

"Frankie," I could hear Mickey yell from the bedroom. "Frankie Keilman, you get in here, boy, and bring me a cigarette. I gotta talk to you."

Joe pulled a cigarette from his shirt pocket and lit it with a match. He handed it to me then gave me a gentle shove toward the bedroom.

Ellie followed me in there and stood in the doorway. Joe went into the kitchen with Granny. I could hear them talking in there but tuned them out as soon as I handed Mickey the cigarette.

He was lying on his stomach with his head turned toward Ellie and me. "Well, you've gone and done it now, Keilman," he said.

"What do you mean?"

"I mean you've crossed the people that did this to me and if they know that you were involved they're liable to come after you. I just want to warn you, sport. Keep your eyes open and don't turn your back, not on anybody, especially not on anybody up on the ridge." He took a draw off the cigarette. "Everybody on the ridge ain't the upstanding folks you might think they are. Me and Ellie, our lives been endangered more than once and Joe, well, some of them fine ridge folks about beat his brains out just before him and Jewell got married. If it hadn't been for Granny and my cousin, Sam Lee, Joe wouldn't be here now. So, you watch your back, Frankie."

He took another draw. "And watch Ellie's too. She's got to go to school. Our plans have got to be carried out and she needs somebody..."

"I can look out for myself," Ellie said. She sounded sullen.

"Now, Ellie, we been over this before. You are going to school and you will complete the plan. I'm gonna be better before you know it."

"I just hate leaving you. That's all," she said.

"What's got to be done has got to be done. Soon as my rear end heals up me and Joe are gonna get with Jim Elee, Sam Lee, Finus and a bunch more of our kin and we are gonna get even with them what did this to me and what tried to kill Joe. Just you watch your back, Frankie. They're like timber rattlers. They just hang around, waiting and watching for a chance to strike. And you never know what part of your life they're gonna strike at neither.

"Could be your momma or your daddy or your girl. Could be that old buzzard you work for on Saturdays or that preacher up at your church and they'll do it in such a way that you can't pin nothing on em, lessen you catch em red handed with the sheriff standing right beside you. Even then, they're liable to pay him off and get off scott free while you end up burying somebody..." he stopped there and just stared out in space for a moment, puffing at that cigarette.

I stood there glaring at him. Fear had a hold of my feet and was holding them fast to the floor and there was a lump in my throat about the size of a hornet's nest.

Mickey flicked ashes into a can on the floor beside the bed. "You can't talk to nobody, Frankie. You don't tell nobody on the ridge about me getting shot or about me and Ellie not having a daddy and you don't tell nobody about our still. You understand?

I nodded.

"They'd send me off and take Ellie to a home somewhere. We can't be split up. You got that, don't you? Can't nobody know what you know about me and Ellie."

I looked up at Ellie. Her eyes pleaded for me to heed her brother's advice then I looked back at Mickey. "I won't tell a soul. I swear it with my own life."

Mickey put his cigarette in the can then reached out and clasped my hand in a firm grasp. "You're all right, Keilman. You're all right. Now get out of here before somebody shows up looking for ya."

I stood.

"Oh, and one more thing," Mickey said. "If you up and make Ellie cry or if you get my sister pregnant, I'll kill you and bury your little body so fast the buzzards won't even have time to eat you."

"Mickey," Ellie gasped. "Oh, God, Mickey. I can't believe you said that!"

I know I turned eight shades of red. Although I had kissed Ellie and held her hand, I had not even imagined going where Mickey's mind was already sending us.

"Look," Mickey said, "Ellie, she's gonna be something someday and I won't let anybody keep her from that dream. You understand?"

I cleared my throat. "I want your and Ellie's plan to succeed more than you know. So, you don't have anything to worry about."

Mickey smiled. "Good. Now get out of here."

I stepped into the living room to say good-bye to Joe and Granny when I heard a vehicle.

"Hide," Ellie shouted and shoved me into the kitchen.

Joe pulled back the curtain covering the bottom of the water table. "Under here," he said.

I didn't know who I was hiding from but I obeyed and crawled under the table.

I crouched there, feeling my heartbeat against my knee. At first I thought it might be my dad, but then I recognized the sound of the car. It was Mickey's car. Why were they hiding me from the person in Mickey's car?

The car stopped in front of the house and the driver cut the engine. I heard Joe holler "howdy" from the porch and could make out the muffled sound of a woman's voice. Then there were footsteps on the porch.

"Hey, girl," Granny said as the mysterious visitor entered the house. "You finally get back?"

124

"I'm exhausted," the woman said. Her voice sounded familiar. "How's my guy?"

"In the bedroom. Been shot," Ellie said.

"What?" I heard her run into the bedroom. It sounded like she was crying over Mickey's being shot or maybe she was crying over him still being alive, but there was a lot of whispering going on. Then Ellie stuck her head through the curtain and whispered. "Come on."

She and Granny Flor ushered me to the door, urging me not to say a word or make a sound while Joe stood in the bedroom doorway blocking both the woman's view of me and my view of her.

Outside, Granny said, "Now, Frankie, don't you be too rattled up by all that's happened here tonight. But you need to realize that life is hard for us folk down here sometimes. We don't want you getting yourself hurt. That's all."

I wanted to say something back to her. I wanted to sound like I had some sense in my head, but the truth was, I felt like a gun-shy dog on the Fourth of July.

She and Ellie walked with me a ways out toward the road. It was starting to get dark and even though it was October, it was still warm enough that the frogs were hollering and the crickets chirping. Dogs barked at us and the mutt Joe had thrown rocks at raced along behind us.

I took a deep breath. The outside air felt cool and fresh compared to the stale air in Granny Flor's house. We passed a twisted tree stump, sticking up out of a patch of golden rods. Ellie plucked up a golden rod and picked at it as we walked.

"I think I'll put this in water," she said.

"Isn't it a weed?" I asked.

"A weed?" Granny Flor said. "A weed is just a flower with a free will, Frankie. Weeds are useful, too."

"And sometimes beautiful," Ellie said.

I thought about the wild flowers that grew in the McGinnis field near my house. I loved that field. "Yeah, I guess you're right. Funny how we're all taught to see things differently while we're kids and when we grow up somebody else comes along and causes us to see things in a way we never thought about before."

"I'm gonna tell you a little story," Granny Flor said, "Used to be a beautiful woman lived down here in Swamp Holler and a man from Briar Ridge was sweet on her, but when it all came down, she wasn't good enough for him. So, he left her and went his way. She married and he married, but the hole in her heart never healed and I reckon it up and kilt her and him, well, he spent the rest o' his life in prison. Your daddy, he knows the story, Frankie."

Then Granny Flor stopped. "This is as far as I go. Ellie, you take him out to the road then turn back."

"Okay, Granny." Ellie held my hand and we walked toward the highway.

"Ellie, what's going on here?" I said. "Who's in there?"

"We can't tell you, Frankie. I swear if I could I would, but I can't. A lot of things could go very bad if anybody knew who was seeing Mickey right now."

"It's his girl, right?"

"She's more than that, Frankie, so much more. And if the people who shot Mickey know about her, then we're all in more trouble than we can say. Nothing can happen to her, nothing. We need her to complete our plan. Please understand. We only want to protect you."

I rubbed my head. "Oh, Ellie, what have I gotten myself into. What are you involved in? Why didn't you tell me about this before we..."

"You were never supposed to find out. I only meant to have somebody to walk with and talk to about little stuff. I just wanted a friend, Frankie, but the truth is that now your life is in danger. All of our lives are in danger. You got to trust us and do what Mickey said." She tiptoed and kissed me on the cheek. "I do love you, Frankie. Please stay safe and I'll see you at school in a few days, after Mickey's able to sit up and stuff."

Ellie turned and ran back toward the house and I set out for home. My head was spinning. Momma was mad. Liddie Grace was mad and Swamp Holler was more of a mystery now than before. And me, I was terrified.

Chapter Thirteen

I hadn't walked a hundred feet up the roadside when I heard the unmistakable sound of my dad's truck and saw those little round headlights coming straight at me. He pulled over to the curb and got out, the truck still running. "This is getting to be a habit with you, Frankie," he said. He had his belt in his hand.

"Yep, I know. You aim to hit me with that?"

He drew the belt back like he was going to lay into me right there on the spot.

I braced myself then blurted, "I only do what you've done a million times. I couldn't stand it, Daddy. I couldn't stand how she was talking. So, go ahead and hit me but I was only..."

"Get in the truck," he snapped then lowered the belt.

I got in the passenger side of the truck as he threw the belt in the seat and slid his legs under the steering wheel. "Why, son? Why couldn't you just do what she wanted?"

I looked down, picking at a loose thread in the truck seat. "Because she wants me to be somebody that I can't be."

"I was headed to Swamp Holler. I figured you'd run off to see the McThacker girl. Don't you ever go down there again, you hear?"

I didn't answer.

"I mean it, son. You stay away from that McThacker girl. Her daddy's the devil himself and you been raised better than to mingle with the likes of Swamp Holler."

"Have I?"

"Watch your mouth, Frankie."

We sat in silence on the side of the road with the truck engine running, then Daddy mumbled something about the price of gasoline and how I was costing him a fortune because this was twice he'd had to come looking for me as he pulled out onto the highway and headed home.

"Daddy," I said, then paused, trying to figure out how to tell him how I wasn't going to give up my art for Momma, that it meant more to me than fox hunting meant to him or getting in with the big shots meant to her. I wanted to tell him that I wasn't giving it up for anybody because it would be easier to give up food or air.

"What?" His voice was angry, yet somehow still sounded tired and defeated.

I took a deep breath. "Aw, nothing. I just dread going home. That's all."

"Umph, you and me both. I can't take the fall for you this time, Frankie."

"I know. I can handle Momma from now on."

"Well, Lord I hope so. It'd be the first time anybody could handle her."

We turned into the end of our lane.

"How'd you and Momma get together?" I asked.

A person would've thought I'd ask him to tell me where babies come from all over again like when I was six, because it sounded like he stopped breathing and then he cleared his throat. "It's a long story," he said, "and not anything you really need to hear."

We pulled into the driveway. "No matter what," he said, "you don't mention Swamp Holler to her and if you were there, you don't even tell me."

"You want me to lie? You taught me to always tell the truth."

"Keeping your mouth shut ain't lyin, boy."

Momma was on the couch crying when we went in. She looked up and saw me, then Daddy right behind me. She laid her head back like she was an actress in a soap opera. "I am your mother. I gave birth to you, laid in that labor room for thirteen hours and me so skinny and poorly that the doctors thought I would die. You know that's why I've never had another child. I'm too frail to go through it again, too frail and too tender-hearted. I laid on the couch and cried for a solid month after you were born.

"I can't believe how you've treated me today, Frankie Delano Keilman. I never in my life thought that my child would be so thoughtless of his own momma who has loved him and sacrificed for him. Ain't nobody else ever gonna love you like I do and this is how you repay me? By running out, going God only knows where? Were you with her? That little strumpet that has caused you to fall from the grace of God and everybody who matters up on the ridge? Don't you go fooling around with her. No good can come of it."

I looked at Daddy. He threw his hat on his rocking chair behind the door and went into the kitchen. He really wasn't going to put into our discussion at all.

"I'm sorry that I hurt you." That much was true. I didn't really want to hurt my mother, but I wasn't sorry at all about liking Ellie and I wasn't sorry that I felt like God had somehow put me on Earth to draw. "And I'll try to straighten things out with Liddie Grace tomorrow."

Momma sat up like a puppet master had just pulled her string. "You will? You'll apologize?"

I nodded.

"You go to her house right after school. I'll go bake a lemon cake. You take it to her mother and apologize to her, too, for causing Liddie Grace to cry and Lord-a-mercy, I hope it's not too late."

"I'll do my best."

My dad came and stood in the doorway, eating a cornbread muffin as if all was right with the world.

"Now about this drawing," she said. "You've got to stop it."

I felt my heartbeat getting faster again. I stuck my hand in my pants pocket and made a fist, reminding myself to stay calm. "What harm does it do?"

"Because, them kind of people get big ideas in their heads and they just drift, Frankie, never amount to nothing and always dreaming. We don't need no dreamers in this family, none of them weirdos like out in Californy, not when you got a good mind to do something sensible, like being a pastor of a respectable denomination or becoming a doctor or something that'll get you a good woman and that'll make you some good money."

I stared at her. I would be gone in a year. College was looking better all of the time. "Okay," I said. "You won't find anymore art in my room or anywhere else." I crossed my fingers inside my pocket. I didn't say that I wouldn't draw, only that she wouldn't find them. I would find another place to hide my masterpieces, even if I had to send them home with Ellie to give to her Aunt Sadie Rose.

Momma got up, went into the kitchen and started making a cake for the McAllisters. Daddy went outside to whittle on the porch and I went up to my room where I would usually draw, but instead I picked up my Bible and read a passage in Ephesians, "Children, obey your parents in the Lord for this is the first commandment with promise." It went on to say that wives should reverence their husbands and husbands should love their wives and that parents should not provoke their children to wrath. I though on that for a few minutes. What did the word provoke mean anyway. I kept thinking of how one of our dogs once had a squirrel and I was going to try to get the squirrel away from him and my dad said, "Don't provoke him, son. He'll bite you." So, I figured that to provoke was to nag at a child and to pull at him until he up and bit somebody. Seemed to me like my momma did a lot of provoking. I must have fallen asleep while I was reading because the next thing I knew my alarm was sounding and it was time to help with the milking. It was still plenty dark outside, but the rooster was crowing and I could smell bacon.

Momma was at the table, flipping through her recipe book when I bounded down the stairs and into the kitchen.

"Your daddy's already in the barn," she said. "Remember, after school today you come straight home and take the pie that I'm going to make over to Liddie Grace's house."

I stuffed a piece of bacon in my mouth. "Pie? I thought you made a cake last night." I picked up a hot biscuit and started in on it.

"I changed my mind. The cake can be for the picnic. I'm thinking that a lemon meringue pie will do just fine."

I knew that it was more than Liddie Grace's feelings my momma cared about. She wanted to impress Liddie's mother.

I dreaded going to Liddie's house and knew that this day was going to be another long one.

"I don't know whatever possessed you to write Liddie Grace that note anyway and just about ruin everything. But never the less it may not be too late to fix it all. And if that Swamp Holler girl is at school, you do not go near her. Don't you dare share the food I cook with her. Just being seen with the likes of a body like that could ruin your reputation as a minister before you even get to college."

I laid my half-eaten biscuit on the table and stood, "Yeah, imagine that a man who is supposed to be like Jesus being seen with sinners and lost people. Why I don't know, Momma, that's like a doctor being seen with sick people. You're right. It makes no sense at all."

"You watch your mouth," she said. "Don't go trying to twist my words around with your fancy talking. You know good and well what I mean."

I took my jacket from the coat rack near the backdoor. "Unfortunately, I do." I put my jacket on and scampered out the door. Outside I breathed as deeply as I could. "Frankie," Momma's shrill voice drifted out the window, drawing my name out until it had about twenty syllables. I turned and there she was, her face filling the window screen while she held the window up with her left hand. "I just wanted to remind you that the Bible says to honor your mother and your father, because if you don't something terrible is liable to happen to you. That's Bible, son and you can't change Bible."

She slammed the window shut and her face was gone.

I stuck my hands in my pockets and headed for the barn. "Why not?" I mumbled to myself. "You do it all of the time."

Milking should have been a quiet time but instead Eugene was on about something the minute I walked into the parlor. Daddy had left his stool in the wrong place again and had forgotten to hang up the extra buckets.

They were arguing and cussing. I got my stool, sat down and milked three cows without a word to either of them. Then I left the barn went back to the house and changed my shoes on the porch. Momma never even heard me out there and I was glad.

The walk to school was a welcome quietness. I would do what Sadie Rose Pablo had said. I'd take Liddie Grace on the picnic and I'd somehow get through the rest of this year, but when next August came, I was leaving home. If that meant going to seminary, then I'd go to seminary. I wasn't sure that God had called me to preach, but I was sure that I couldn't stay on Briar Ridge.

When I was little Momma had seemed different, but I suppose that all little children love their mothers because they're the most important person in their world, and they don't know to do anything else. Even now I did love my momma, because she was my momma but I didn't want to be around her.

When I arrived at school I was so relieved to see that Miss Mays was back. She looked so young compared to the substitute who had been there. As I took my seat I realized that Miss Mays couldn't have been more than a couple of years older than Mickey, if that. And she was pretty, even if she was a teacher. I looked around the room at the little kids studying their spelling words for their Friday test, at the middle graders all working on math problems and at the bigger kids. Everyone of them would probably do just what Ellie said, grow up, marry somebody on the ridge and take over their parents' farms or stores or businesses.

Well, except for poor old Sandy Coltrain and he would probably live with his parents until they died of old age then I had no idea what would happen to him. He sat back in the corner. He couldn't read any better than an eight-year-old and he stuttered something awful, but everyone of us, even Liddie Grace and her little girl gang, understood that Sandy was special and we all felt sorry for him.

I looked over at Tiny Elmer. I knew that my friend would never leave Briar Ridge that he would never want to leave. Life was perfect for him here and there was my cousin, Harlan, who was so much like my own daddy that it was scary. Harlan would marry somebody just like Momma, maybe one of Liddie Grace's gang or Liddie Grace herself, because come hell or high water, I wasn't marrying her. I might end up alone like Eugene, but in that moment while sitting in my little wooden desk, I made two decisions that would carry me for the rest of my life. Number one,

I wasn't going to marry any girl from Briar Ridge and number two, I wasn't going to stay on Briar Ridge. As soon as I had said that to myself, like a New Year's resolution, I felt different on the inside.

I sat up straight and smiled. I decided right then and there that I was going to college, but I wasn't going to let Momma pick the school for me. I waited, watching the door, wishing to see Ellie but knowing that she wasn't coming. Then Liddie Grace came in and went straight to Miss Mays's desk. They whispered for a minute then Liddie came and took her seat directly in front of me. I started to write her a note, but then I decided that I would not. I was going to talk to her face to face. I had seen a man shot. My life was possibly in danger and I had just seen my mother rip up the things that mattered most in my life to me, so there was nothing that anybody on this ridge held over me or could use to intimidate me ever again, least of all, Liddie Grace McAllister.

That morning I volunteered to give the spelling test to the little ones. I thought Miss Mays was going to pass out and Liddie would wet her pants. Elmer, Harlan and a bunch of other boys giggled. I didn't care. I was leaving this place in less than a year and these little kids needed to see a boy who wasn't afraid of becoming a man. They needed to know that some people could see beyond the hills surrounding Briar Ridge. At least that's the way I felt about it that morning.

After that, I sat down at my desk and finished a history report I was writing on Homer Winslow, a great American artist. I wrote about his life and about how he captured not only the effects of light in his works but snippets of American life.

When I went up to hand my report in to Miss Mays she looked up at me and said. "I don't know what happened to you while I was gone, Frankie, but I like the results. This is the guy I always knew you were." Then she smiled at me, not a teacher kind of smile like she used on the little kids to make them feel better, but a real person kind of smile, like I was her equal.

"Thanks," I said. "What now?"

"Your math?"

"Finished it already," I said. "Finished assignment from this morning."

She nodded toward Liddie Grace. "How about being my assistant again. She is really struggling with areas and circumferences."

Liddie was staring out the window, not concentrating at all. She had her pencil in her mouth, pushing on her teeth. "Okay, Miss Mays."

"Thank you," my teacher whispered.

I pulled a chair up beside Liddie Grace. She looked up, puzzled and then that annoyed, spoiled look took over her face. "What do you want?" she huffed.

"I'm going to help you with your math," I said.

"I don't need any help."

"Sure you don't. Listen, Liddie Grace, you can either let me help you or fail and have to do it over. The choice is yours."

"Ugh," she rolled her eyes and shoved the math book over to me.

"Also," I said, "forget that note I sent you. You are going to the picnic with me."

"Oh, am I? What if I don't want to?"

"Then don't go," I said. "Again, the choice is yours."

"Well, I suppose I could take you back," she said.

"We're not going steady, Liddie Grace. We were never going steady. I only sent you that note because I was mad at my mother. She's always trying to boss me around and I hate to be bossed around." I looked at her, trying to copy Miss Mays look the day she caught me jumping that fence.

I could tell Liddie Grace was taken aback. She just stared at me.

"I'm coming to your house today," I said. "I'm bringing a pie. Will you be home?"

She just nodded.

I picked up a pencil and looked at her paper. "Now, here's what you're doing wrong on this," I said, and I sat right there beside the queen snob of Briar Ridge and I taught her how to find the circumference of a circle then I taught her how to find the area of a rectangle and a square.

"Where's Ellie McThacker?" she asked me after a while, clear out of the blue.

"Her brother's sick," I said. She'll be back in a few days."

"Why do you mess with them, Frankie. My mother was appalled and so am I."

"Don't worry, Liddie Grace, I'm not going to wipe McThacker cooties on you."

At that moment the back door opened and we all looked up. Old man Dawson walked into our room and in behind him came the youngest of the Dawson boys. I had seen him before, that day at Goodin's Store when his brother had threatened Mickey and Joe.

"Teacher," he bellowed, sticking his chest out like he was a hairy red peacock. "My boy here wants to come to school."

Liddie Grace's face went white, like she might just pass out.

Miss Mays stood. "Please, let's go outside so we can talk without disturbing the children's studies."

Then she followed the big man with rust-colored hair and skin, along with his younger duplicate of a son, out the back door.

I don't know what happened out there that day, but when Miss Mays came back in she was in a bit of a huff and the rusty teenager came back in with her.

"Class this is James Russell Dawson and he likes to be called Rusty."

Well that made sense. He was the color of rust and so was his hair. I mean that was like calling me Blondie.

Before long it was noon, dinner time or lunch, as Miss Mays called it, and Rusty Dawson came over to our table. He looked at

Idy Jo Darling and picked her out as the weakest link. "Scoot over, midget," he said.

Tiny Elmer stood up, several inches taller than Rusty. "I'm Elmer," he said, "and this is Idy Jo. She's my girl."

Idy Jo scooted over and Rusty sat down. I was thankful that Elmer was just big and not prone to fighting just for the fun of it, but I didn't doubt that if push came to shove, Elmer would defend Idy Jo's honor.

Liddie Grace was so quiet during lunch that it was creepy. Even her little girl gang, which followed her around, was quiet. So what was it about Rusty Dawson that struck terror into the core of Liddie Grace McAllister? How did she know him?

When Miss Mays rang the bell for us to go back in, I motioned for Liddie Grace to come over to me. She trotted over to me while the others packed up their lunch buckets and I whispered, "How do you know the Dawson boy?"

"That big ugly toad? I don't know him." She crossed her arms and pursed her lips but the fear in her eyes told me that she did know him and if anybody could strike fear into Liddie Grace then he had to be in cahoots with the devil or something.

"I just don't like the looks of him," she said.

As we walked toward the building Rusty popped up behind Liddie Grace. He touched her cheek, "Hey, McAllister," was all he said, then he ran his finger down her cheek and let it rest under her chin. I really thought Liddie Grace was going to pass out. Then he grinned, showing his tobacco-stained teeth. "Be seeing ya."

Liddie Grace grabbed my hand, not to show off like in the past, but because that girl really was afraid. She pulled me into the school house. "Sit by me," she whispered. "Please, Frankie, sit by me." So I did and Miss Mays didn't tell me to go back to my seat or anything, as if she was just as afraid as Liddie Grace. I was so glad Ellie wasn't there, because I knew that this boy showing up had something to do with Mickey's being shot, but what I didn't understand was what he had to do with Liddie Grace or Miss Mays.

Chapter Fourteen

When recess came Harlan, Elmer and some other boys got a baseball game up, like they always did unless it was raining and we had to stay in.

"Hey, Frankie, wanna play?" Elmer yelled.

"Yeah, I'm in," I said and headed toward our homemade baseball field just on the other side of the fence I had jumped. Of course, I hadn't jumped it anymore. No, nowadays I just went through the gate, like everybody else.

Sandy Coltrain came running out onto the field. He couldn't read or write or do a math problem to save his life, but the boy could knock a homerun like he was Babe Ruth himself. Everybody wanted Sandy on their team which made our mentally afflicted classmate smile and cackle.

Then Rusty Dawson walked onto the field. "I'm playing," he said, "and I'm on the blonde boy's team."

I wondered what I had done to deserve that honor, but I didn't say anything. My team was first in the field today so I positioned myself as pitcher. And Rusty went up to Tommy Gist, a seventh grader who always played hind catcher and shoved him out of the way. "This is my position," Rusty said.

I felt for Tommy Gist. What was the boy to do? He walked away, head down.

"Hey, Tommy," I yelled. "You play short stop today. Ernie's not here." Ernie was an eight-grade boy who always played short stop for my team.

So, the game took off. Tiny Elmer hit a home run. Then Harlan made a hit and got to second base. Jesse Smallwood struck out and gave them their first out, then it was Sandy Coltrain's turn to bat. The outfielders backed up and everyone got ready for a ball to be knocked clear to Kingdom Come.

Sure enough, Sandy hit the ball and it went far over our heads and past our outfielders.

"Homerun!" his team mates yelled and Sandy ran, wind whipping through his unkempt hair, him laughing and yelling and none of us usual players really caring that he was going to make it. This was Sandy's thing, his only thing.

As he reached home plate, Rusty Dawson caught the ball, stuck out his elbow and hit Sandy right in the face. Sandy went down just short of base, blood shooting out everywhere.

"Out retard!" Rusty yelled. He swept his hands though the air in front of him. "Out!"

Scooter Jones, first baseman and I reached Sandy first.

Sandy was wailing and bleeding like a hog at slaughtering time.

I rested his head against my leg and started trying to stop the bleeding with my own handkerchief and when it was soaked I used Scooter's. Someone must have gone for Miss Mays because next thing I knew she was there beside me, helping me and she had the clean white bandages she kept in her desk in case of an emergency.

I don't know how long it took us to get Sandy's bleeding under control, but when we did, it was clear that his front teeth were knocked loose and his nose was possibly broken.

Miss Mays kept saying, "Don't cry, Sandy. It's going to be okay." She looked up, scanning our faces while she held Sandy's head back. "What happened here?"

Liddie Grace blurted. "Rusty Dawson elbowed him right in the face."

"McAllister," Rusty said with a snarl, "it was an accident." He looked at Liddie Grace like he was going to eat her for super or something.

"It was not," Elmer said. "I saw the whole thing. Sandy was about to touch base and this new guy didn't want him to so he elbowed him as hard as he could."

"I did not. The retard ran into me," Rusty snapped.

"We'll get to the bottom of it later," Miss Mays said. "I had better get him home. School is dismissed for the rest of the day. Elmer, will you help us?"

"Sure, Miss Mays," Elmer said. He reached down and lifted Sandy up like he was a sack of feed corn.

"Liddie Grace," Miss Mays said. "You live closest to the school. You run home and call his mother. Somebody may want to meet us on the road with a car."

Liddie Grace took off across the field. Her house was less than a mile from the school which made it weird that she was late sometimes.

"Frankie, lock up the school. The keys are in the top drawer of my desk. You can bring them with you on Monday morning."

I nodded and did what she said. All of the children took off toward their homes, except Rusty Dawson, who hung around, watching me lock up the building. Then he walked across the baseball field and into the woods.

I felt uneasy, not just because Sandy was hurt but there was something more, something I couldn't name. It was the same feeling I would get when the sky would turn yellowish in the spring and everything would go dead still, the anticipation that a

143

storm was coming and the not knowing whose house might get blown away before it was over.

When I opened the living room door to our house Momma was on the couch watching her stories.

"Frankie, what're you doing home so early? It's not even two o'clock yet."

I told her about the Dawson boy showing up and all that had happened. Then she looked up at me and said, "But you made up with Liddie Grace?"

I couldn't believe her. Poor Sandy's nose was broken and all she could worry about was whether or not I was in good graces with the McAllisters. For a second, I wanted to scream, then I said, "Yes, Momma. Liddie Grace and I are in good standing and she is terrified of the Dawson boy."

"Well, why don't you take that lemon meringue pie on over there and see about her?"

So Momma gave me the pie in a nice little covered carrying pan and I set out back up Briar Ridge, toward Liddie Grace's house.

About halfway there I heard someone scream. At first I didn't know whether to run toward the scream or away from it, but Mickey's words about the people who shot him striking out against people in my life came loudly in my head. So, I ran toward the sound and about a quarter of a mile from Liddie's house I came upon voices. Rusty Dawson's and Liddie Grace's. I hid under the cover of undergrowth for a moment to figure out what was going on.

"You get away from me, or I'll scream again," Liddie Grace said. "My daddy will hear you and he'll be right down here. He'll shoot you."

"Your daddy owes us," Rusty said. "I aim to send him a message. We want what's coming to us. I ain't afraid of him." Then he shoved her against a tree and started kissing on her. I froze. I forgot that Liddie Grace had been a brat her whole life, that

144

she somehow always managed to intrude upon all of my plans and had been the whole cause of my momma's conniption fit. No, in that moment, all I could see was a big mean boy, forcing himself on a frightened girl. I sat the pie down and tried to think what to do to save Liddie Grace.

All at once Rusty Dawson yelped like a dog caught in a rabbit trap and he hauled off and hit Liddie Grace so hard that he knocked clean down to the ground. She landed on a rock and was crying, clutching her arm, which was bleeding. He grabbed hold of his belt and started unfastening it. "You little bitch," he said. "You're gonna pay for that." He grabbed her legs and pulled them apart.

There was no more time for thinking, I took off running and as I got close enough I leapt into the air and plowed right into Rusty Dawson from the side, knocking him off her. "Run, Liddie Grace, run!" I said. "Get your dad."

He rolled over faster than a tom cat out for a killing and came at me. He hit me so hard that I felt like my whole head was coming off. I had never been hit by another person in my life. It hurt so bad and I know I hollered like a whipped dog, but I swung at him.

He ducked and came up with a big piece of wood in his hands and whacked me in the side so hard that I flew off the ground and landed almost on top of Liddie Grace who hadn't run at all, but was still there, too scared to do anything but holler and scream. Then he hit me again, so hard that he broke the stick this time. I'm not sure if the cracking noise came from me or from the stick, but I knew I was hurt pretty bad, mostly because everything was spinning. I looked up and saw him with part of that stick still in his hand. He was standing over me, laughing. Then he said, "I'll kill you, you little twerp." I tried to get a handful of dirt and sling it in his face, but then I saw something, the top of a blonde head popped up behind him and I heard a clicking sound. Rusty heard it, too, because he froze.

"You step away from my students," a woman said. "Or I'll blow your eyeballs out the backside of your skull."

I knew that voice, but I'd never heard those kinds of words spoken by it.

Rusty backed up and laughed a nervous laugh. "Now teacher, you just put that gun down. You don't know how to use that thing."

"You going to bet your life on that?" she said.

"I don't want no trouble with you," he said.

"Too late for that. You don't pretend to be a minor, break a kid's nose, try to rape another one and beat a boy half your size. These students are under my protection and if you mess with them you're messing with me. You got that? I'm going to count to three and you had better be out of my sight."

"Umph," Rusty said. "Come on, teach. You don't understand. You don't want to make enemies with my family."

"No, I don't think you understand. You don't want to make enemies of mine," she said. "One."

"You ain't gonna shoot me."

"Two."

He backed up toward the woods. Then he turned and ran. "You'll pay for this!" he hollered as he went.

Liddie Grace must have come to her senses, because there she was taking on over me. "Oh, Frankie, you look bad. Are you going to live?"

Miss Mays was at my side in a flash. She didn't even ask if was okay to look at my bare belly, she just yanked up my shirt and grimaced. "Oh, Frankie, you're really hurt."

"What gave you that idea?" I tried to joke, but I hurt like everything and every breath felt like somebody was stabbing me in the side.

146

"Let's get you to Liddie Grace's house and her parents can take you to the hospital from there and I can give Frankie's folks a call to meet us there. How's your arm?" she looked at Liddie Grace.

"It's not broken. I can move it but it's really sore."

"I'm going to make you a sling for it anyway, just to be on the safe side." She grabbed her long skirt tail and tore it all the way around. "Exactly what happened here?" she asked.

Liddie Grace straightened up and dried her eyes. "I had just come home from school and told my parents about what happened with Sandy and then I told them that I needed to study with Maggie for tomorrow's test and they said that I could walk over to Maggie's house." Maggie was one of Liddie's little gang that lived about a mile to the west of the McAllisters. "I was walking along, minding my own business, when all of a sudden I looked up and there he stood and he…he…" she started to cry, really thinking about what Rusty meant to do to her.

"Just take it easy," Miss Mays said. "He's gone now."

Liddie hiccupped. "He said my daddy owed his daddy money and that my daddy was a crook and a gambler and that if he didn't pay up, that they were gonna take it out of me and Momma. Then he grabbed me and started touching me…" She looked at me. "So I screamed and he kissed me so I bit him. Then he hit me and knocked me down. That's when Frankie saved me."

She just kept staring at me. "You saved my life, Frankie. He's way bigger than you, but you tackled him and you got him off of me."

"Can you get up?" Miss Mays asked me. I tried to but it hurt so much that I howled like a fox hound.

"That's okay. Just take it casy," she said, "we'll figure out something."

"Just help me to stand and don't listen if I holler. I have never been hurt before and I'm not good at it."

She smiled at me and instructed Liddie Grace to get on the other side of me and together they helped me to me feet. It was everything I could do not to bawl like a baby.

I know I said, "Ouch," a million times or more, but I was really hurting, maybe not as bad as Mickey had been, but bad enough.

"My momma sent Liddie's momma a pie," I said. "In the bushes. Will you get it?"

Liddie Grace went and got the pie.

"Thank you," I said.

"Where'd you get that gun?" I asked as we poked along the trail, them supporting me like I was a doggone invalid or something and me such a soft boy that I was letting them, because I knew if they let go of me, I'd fall over faster than a two-legged chair.

"Christmas present from my daddy. I keep it in my teacher bag."

"Well, that explains why you're not afraid to go walking this ridge day or night," I said.

She laughed. "Yes, it does, doesn't it? Nobody is ever what they seem, Frankie. No matter how much you think you know a person, there's always more to them than what meets the eye, either for good or for bad.

"And those who try to cover their bad spend their whole lives to trying to protect their lies.

"The Dawsons use other people's fear of the truth getting out as a means of extortion. They know a lot of secrets on a lot of people and they use that to blackmail and control. And when the blackmail and control fails to work, then they resort to violence."

"Well, he was lying about my daddy," Liddie Grace said. "My daddy don't owe them money for anything. He would never have any dealings with the likes of the Dawsons."

Miss Mays didn't say anything to that and for just a second I wondered what more there was to our teacher. She had just saved our lives and I never in a million years, would have imagined proper Miss Mays as always having a sawed-off shot gun hidden in her bag of papers to be graded.

"Why were you walking this way, anyhow?" I asked.

"I took Sandy home then I just had a gut feeling that I should come back by and check on Liddie Grace. Call it a teacher's intuition, I guess. But there was something about the way he looked at her today that unnerved me."

I wondered was it Liddie Grace that had brought the Dawsons to school or was it Ellie McThacker?

It was no secret that the McAllister's had a beautiful home. It sat on a hill, surrounded by serene woodlands. The trees were starting to turn now and that house looked like something out of an early American painting. It was a wide white two-story structure with a red tile roof. A porch, supported by numerous columns went all the way from the front left corner of the house to the back right corner. The Pablo's entire house could fit on the McAllister's porch twice. An American flag flew from one of the columns on the front of the porch and mums bloomed all along the flowerbed between the sets of porch steps.

"Momma!" Liddie Grace hollered as we neared. "Momma!"

Mrs. McAllister opened the door and stepped out onto the porch. She looked just like Liddie Grace, only older with shorter hair. She stared blankly at us for a moment then ran to her daughter.

She examined Liddie's bandaged arm. "What on earth?"

"Oh, Momma," Liddie Grace handed her momma the pie. "Me and Frankie were almost killed today." She started crying. Her momma sat that pie on the ground and folded her into her arms. She stroked her hair and kissed her head. Then she looked up at Miss Mays who still carried the shot-gun with angry, confused eyes.

"Would somebody care to explain?"

"Rusty Dawson attacked Liddie Grace on her way to Maggie Russell's house," Miss Mays said. "Frankie was on his way to bring you a pie that his mother when he came upon them."

Liddie Grace's looked up. "Frankie saved my life, Momma. He tackled Rusty Dawson and knocked him off of me." For the first time Mrs. McAllister took note of me and I could tell that she felt sorry for me, because of her eyes.

"But Rusty broke Frankie's ribs," Liddie Grace continued, "then Miss Mays came up and said she was going to blow Rusty's eyeballs out the back of his head if he didn't leave us alone. He was scared of her shot-gun so he ran off into the woods."

"Are you saying that one of Udell Dawson's boys attacked my daughter a half mile from our own front door?"

"Yes, ma'am," Miss Mays said," that's exactly what we're telling you."

By this time I was hurting more than when Rusty had first hit me. It was all I could do to breathe and it felt just like what I imagined it would feel like if somebody had run me through with a tobacco spear. I don't know if I made sounds or not. I was gasping and was pretty sure that I was dying. For all I know I might have even cried. I heard Mrs. McAllister yell, something about a car.

Chapter Fifteen

I was aware of the pain in my body and of that fact that I was lying down. I felt like I was made out of wet clay and knew that if I tried to get up some of me would stick to the surface I was lying on and I'd surely fall to pieces. Even my eyes wouldn't open, so I just laid there, wherever there was. Then I realized there was someone with me. I could hear a man's voice. "He's gonna be all right," the man was saying. Whoever he was he needed to clear his throat. It was all full of gravel.

"Oh, I can't believe this has happened," a woman said. She was high-pitched, nasal and frantic sounding. That had to be my mother. "If anything happens to Frankie I don't know what I'll do."

"Your son's a hero," the man with the gravel in his throat said. "Now, it's agreed upon then. You folks say won't anything about who it was that attacked our daughter, seeing how that we don't want word of it getting around and we'll make sure that Frankie never wants for a thing during his college career."

I know I was in pain, but was I hearing what I thought I was hearing. Was that Liddie Grace's dad going to pay my way through college to protect Rusty Dawson that had tried to rape and kill his only child?

"Frankie saved your daughter's life," that was my dad talking, "I think it should be up to him to de…"

"Frankie's life depends upon your co-operation," McAllister said.

"Seems to me like the Dawsons have been running the ridge too long? Somebody ought to do something," my dad said.

"And who's going to do it, Ancil? You?" my mom jeered. "You gonna stand up to the Dawsons like you stood up to Mooney McThacker?"

What was she talking about?

"The past is the past," my dad said.

"We'll do it," Momma said. "You take care of Frankie's schooling and we'll see to it that no one ever knows about what nearly happened to Liddie Grace."

"You're a fine woman, Sarah Jean," he said. "Now mind you don't say anything in front of Liddie Grace or my wife. They don't know and I can trust you to make sure Frankie keeps quiet, too?"

Just then I heard a door open.

"Is Frankie going to live?" that was Liddie Grace's voice.

"Yes," her father said. "He has a couple of broken ribs and the doctor says that he has passed out from the pain, but they can't detect any internal injuries."

"Let's go in the hall and talk," her dad said. Then I heard their footsteps leave the room, and for a second I thought I was alone, wherever I was, but then my dad said.

"You should let bygones be bygones, Sarah Jean.

"You still think about her, don't you?" Momma said. "No, you're not even a man to me and if I'd have known that you had been with her I never would have married you."

Who was she talking about? Did I dare open my eyes and let them know I was awake? Did I really want to know what deep dark secret my mother was holding over my father's head?

"I made a mistake," my dad said. "It ain't like you've been the perfect woman either."

"I have made a name for myself," she said. "A name you've tried to tear down with all your drinking and carrying on. What is it that sends you to drinking? The memory of a piece of white trash up in your bed?"

"Shut up," Daddy said. "She may have been poor, but she was never trashy."

"She married a McThacker didn't she?" Momma snapped.

No. No, I didn't want to know this. I couldn't hear anymore, didn't want to know anymore. I moaned as loudly as I could. I had to make them think I was waking up.

"Frankie," Momma said. I opened my eyes and there she was, her face leaning right over me, orange hair, orange lipstick and a yellow dress. "Frankie, son, you saved Liddie Grace."

"Hey, son," Daddy said. "You did a real brave thing."

"Where am I?"

"Hospital," Momma said. "Alice McAllister called me. I thought she was calling to thank me for the pie, but then she went to crying and saying somebody had attacked Liddie Grace and that you were hurt. When she told me you were unconscious, well Lord a mercy, I about died myself, me being so poorly and all.

"Why you just about put me in an early grave. And your daddy here, he was down in the little barn and I had to yell and yell for him. He couldn't hear me so I had to go down there and get him. By the time I got down there I was so winded I thought I was going to die."

"You're not gonna be fit for much over the next few weeks," she said. "The doctor said that wouldn't nothing for you to do but lay around until your ribs heal up. I just don't know what I'm gonna do without you helping me around the house on account of I just ain't able to work hard."

"I'm sure you'll manage," Daddy said.

"Oh, you wouldn't care if I fell over dead," Momma said.

Daddy just stood there with his hands in his pockets and his hat down low over his forehead.

"Oh, here's the good news," Momma said. "Elbert McAllister is so pleased with what you did for Liddie Grace that he has offered to pay your way through seminary."

"Huh," I moaned because I really was still in a lot of pain. "Well, what do you know? Guess that means I'm going be a preacher whether God wants me to or not then."

"Of course He wants you to," Momma said. "What kind of fool talk is that? This is His way of providing the money for you."

"Tell him the other thing McAllister said," Daddy added.

Momma looked at him like she could bite his ears off and throw them out to the hound dogs. "He has asked that you don't say anything about it being Rusty Dawson that attacked Liddie Grace and that you don't repeat anything the boy might have said about him in your presence."

I stared at Momma, unable to believe the words coming out of her mouth. Was Elbert McAllister really that afraid of the Dawsons? Or did he have something else to hide?

"Where's Miss Mays?" I asked.

"Miss Mays," both my parents said at once. "We haven't seen her."

"She's the one that scared Rusty off," I said.

"She was gone by the time we got here," Momma said. "Ethel said something about her not wanting to be mixed up in anything that had to do with the Dawsons and she has agreed not to say a word about what has happened today."

"So are we all going to just lie to protect a rapist?" I asked.

154

"No, no, we're not going to lie," Momma said. "We'll just tell people that you hurt yourself helping out at the McAllister place, which is true."

It wasn't true. It was a half-truth, a twisted piece of what really happened.

I looked at my dad, standing beside a window that looked out into the street. How many half-truths had my parents told me in my life? Which part of who Frankie Keilman was were true and which parts were just smoothed over things which were meant to be hidden in order to protect our family name? For example, there was Eugene. His mother had been my dad's sister. She had become pregnant by a passing woodsman. Rather than let the community discover that she had been with a man, they locked her in the attic until the baby was born then pretended the child was their own, so that Eugene had lived his entire life calling his momma his sister. The only reason I knew the truth now was that I had overheard my parents arguing when I was ten. They thought I was outside but I wasn't, I was in the pantry while they argued in the kitchen.

A tall man in a white lab coat came into the room. He was almost bald, wore thick black framed glasses and wore a stethoscope around his neck. I didn't need anyone to tell me who he was, but he told me anyway.

"Hello, son," he said. "Glad to see you're back with us. I'm Doctor Gregory. You've got yourself a couple of cracked ribs. The little girl who was with you when they brought you in tells me that you got into a fight with another boy from school and that he hit you with a pole."

"Something like that," I said.

"That child must be made of steel or something."

"Or something," I said. "He's as big as a horse."

"You need bed rest and lots of it. I've wrapped your ribs, but there's not much I can do for you other than that. I'll write you a prescription for pain medication. I want to see you back in my office in about three weeks. Remember, no activities. Any sudden moves, heavy lifting or exertion could cause your ribs to puncture your lungs and that's serious business. So, it's complete rest for you for the next three weeks."

"I can't do anything? Not even pump gas on Saturday?"

"Today's Saturday," he said. "And I don't want you pumping gas for at least two weeks."

I think the news of being laid up for nearly a month hurt just about as much as being half beat to death by Rusty Dawson. "Oh, shucks. I'm never gonna get enough money to buy a car at this rate."

The doctor took a pen out of his pocket. "That's about it. Any questions?"

"No sir," I said.

He turned to my parents. "If you folks will follow me, I'll give you the prescription for Frankie's medicine."

My parents followed the doctor out of the room, leaving me alone for the length of time that it took the door to close behind them. Then it opened again and Liddie Grace's dad came in. I had seen him a few times before out in the community. He always reminded me of a bowling ball with limbs and the thin black belt he wore on his high-waist pants made him seem even rounder. He had on a white shirt with the sleeves rolled up and gray pants. He was one of those people who was always red. His face looked sunburned all year long or maybe like he was hot and no amount of rolling up his sleeves or wearing white could cool him.

"Frankie," he said. "I don't believe we've actually ever talked." He took a slender box from his shirt pocket. "Cigar?"

I shook my head.

"Just as well. They get upset when I smoke in here. Doctors and nurses think they've got the say over everybody. It's people like you and me that keep them in business."

He chuckled, "Seems we got ourselves a dilemma here. You see, on the one hand I owe you a great debt of gratitude. You have spared my daughter and my family from great heartache and humiliation. On the other I need your word that you won't say a word as to who it was that wanted to hurt my little girl."

"I don't understand," I said. "Don't you want him brought to justice?"

"In due time, my son, in due time." He pulled a cigar out and stuck it in his mouth. I wondered if he were actually going to light it or just hold it there between hi lips. He took the slender brown stick between his fingers and smelled of it.

"Some things, like fine tobacco, come at a great price. Take for instance, coal. It's a wonderful thing, provides fuel and electricity but you let somebody light up one of these near a pocket of methane and the whole mountainside is liable to explode. I used to work the coal mines, Frankie. Bet you didn't know that."

"No, sir. I didn't."

"Thing about a mine, things can be done down there in the dark that the wife and kids back at the house never need know about. Well, life up on the ridge, it's not so different than the mines. Things are done in the dark, deals are made and there's no need for the wife or the children to be involved. Sometimes a man makes risky deals to provide his family with the things they need."

He sat in the chair my mother had previously occupied and then bent so close to my face that I could smell the tobacco on his breath. "I will pay for your education, send you to that seminary your momma's got her heart set on and in exchange you will not say a word about the Dawsons, because if you was to, things could happen. Things I might not be able to fix as easily."

"What if he comes after Liddie Grace again?" I asked. "What if I'm not there or Miss Mays isn't there?"

He stood. "Don't you worry about Liddie Grace, son. I'll take care of her. Your momma promised me you wouldn't say anything about who it was that attacked her and I need you to make me the same promise."

"What if I don't? What if I got to the sheriff and tell him everything?"

"Mooney McThacker talked that way, son, and no one has seen him in quite some time, of course with him, nobody's looking. There would have to be convenient explanations for someone like you, you being just a kid and all. It'd be a terrible thing if something were to happen. Then there's your sweet little momma and your daddy and oh, yeah, your cousin... or should I say, uncle? Eugene. There's a lot riding on you keeping quiet, son. Remember that."

The door opened and my parents came back into the room. Mr. McAllister smiled at me and said, "Now, you get better, boy, you hear?" He nodded at my parents and left.

Had Liddie Grace's father just threatened to kill me if I talked? Or was he warning me that the Dawsons would kill me if I talked? Either way, I didn't think I would be able to sleep. I looked at my dad and my mom and thought about the practical little world we had lived in my whole life, a world of milking cows and tobacco crops, of molasses grinders and corn crops, of hog killings and feeding the chickens. Momma had been wanting to get in big with the McAllisters for years. I think that the real McAllisters and the fantasy my momma had concocted about them were as far removed as honey and sheep dip. If it took my being quiet to protect them, then I would be quiet, but sooner or later I was going to get to the bottom of it all.

Chapter Sixteen

The truck ride home from the hospital was the most uncomfortable ride of my life. First, because my side felt like it had a knife sticking in it and second, because my momma went on and on about how Mr. McAllister was going to pay my way through school. That may have been the biggest reason I begged to stay at Eugene's while I healed up. I told my parents it was because it hurt so much to climb the stairs to my room. I could sleep in his extra room. I could just lay around and read. Eugene spent a lot of time outside. Even in the fall he found things to do that kept him outdoors. I would have time alone. No television. No telephone. No parents always arguing.

I wouldn't have to listen to Momma declare the glories of the McAllisters or go on endlessly about my dad's many faults. However, Momma decided that she would cook for me and send it up with Daddy every night at supper time on account of she was too poorly to walk up there.

Eugene's extra room was adjacent to the living room and it was his guest room, not that he ever had any guest, except me, but he kept his best furniture in that room. A four-poster oak bed sat against the right wall of the room, across from the only window which was covered with green checkered curtains. Next to the window was an oak dresser, then there was a door and in the corner near the foot of the bed was a dark oak table. These precious pieces of furniture sat on a hardwood floor covered by a hand-braided rug. He kept a quilt that my Granny Keilman had made on the bed and at some point in the distant past, he had painted the walls a muted green. It was a manly room and I had always liked it.

To make me more comfortable, he had gone out to the shed and gotten an extra milking stool. He sat this beside the bed so I could have a night stand to set a glass of water and my pain medicine the doctor had given me.

Sunday came and went. The church picnic that had caused me so much trouble, that I was supposed to take Liddie Grace to also came and went. I slept most of the day, even when my parents stopped by in the pickup truck, I pretended to be asleep.

On Sundays Eugene would put on good overalls, his good straw hat and smoke his good tobacco. He would eat cornbread and coffee for breakfast then listen to preachers on the radio all morning. In the afternoon, he would go and sit under a shade tree in the front yard and wait to see if he was going to have any visitors. My being there did not change his routine at all, except for the fact that he asked me if I felt like sitting in the front yard with him for a while. So I did. I got up and sat with him on the front porch, but no one came to visit and we both went to bed early.

The next day Eugene meandered around the house until mid morning then he went outside to work. I found a Bible that had belonged to his mom on the dresser, picked it up and thumbed through it. I read for a little while from the Book of Psalms. Then I turned on the radio and listened to some music. It was Bluegrass, of course. Eugene would be outside a long time so I turned it over and listened to some more modern music.

I must have drifted off because the next thing I knew somebody was beating on the door and waking me. The door was locked so I would have to get out of bed to answer it. I struggled past the pain and stood to my feet.

As I came into the living room, I peeked out the front window to see who I was about to let in, because if it wasn't someone I wanted to see, I wasn't going to open that door. It was Miss Mays and she had her teacher bag with her.

I unlatched the door and let her in.

"Miss Mays, what are you doing here? How'd you know I was at Eugene's?"

"I'm here to check on my top student," she said. "And your mother told me you were here."

I hobbled to the couch and eased myself onto it.

"Have a seat," I said.

She sat in a green chair next to the couch. "I've brought you some things." She pulled a leather-bound notebook from her bag and handed it to me. I flipped through it. Every page was blank, a sketch tablet, a really nice one.

"I ordered it a few months back," she said. "Got it from a special art catalog that I found when I was in Nashville."

"Gee, Miss Mays, this is great."

She pulled a box of charcoal out of that bag and set it on the seat beside me. I touched it as if it were the finest China on the planet. Real charcoal. Then I remembered Momma.

"My mother has forbidden me to draw," I said.

She gasped. "What?"

I couldn't stop touching the box of charcoal, couldn't take my hand off it. I looked up at Miss Mays. She was biting her lip and shaking her head. Sitting there on Eugene's chair with pink cheeks from being outside in the cool air and disheveled hair from having walked so far through the woods to get to where I was, she seemed so down to earth and I remembered something Ellie had once told me that sometimes she wasn't a teacher. Sometimes she was just a regular person.

"Frankie." She interrupted my thinking. "Why does your mother forbid you to draw?"

I thought about how to answer that question for a few seconds then I said, "Miss Mays, do you think it is dishonoring your parents if you don't always agree with them?"

"I don't always agree with mine," she said. "I still love them. I still respect them, but there are many areas on which we don't see eye to eye."

"You are a Christian aren't' you?" I said.

"Of course, why?"

"Well, Momma says that if a person doesn't follow the plan his parents have for his life then he is disobeying God and dishonoring them. She says that terrible things will happen to the person who disagrees with what his parents want for his life."

"Oh, Frankie," she said and when she said it, her face looked sad. "I don't mean to contradict your mother, but you're a young man now. You're not a little boy. Your momma is not going to have to live the life you make for yourself. You are. If you choose your course in life based on some unfulfilled dream that your mother is trying to recapture through you then you will never discover the person you were meant to be. Each of us are given a life, Frankie. That's God's gift to us. Let me ask you this? What do you want to do with your life?"

I shrugged. "I don't know." Then I looked down at that box of charcoal and that leather sketchbook. I started just rattling off what came up inside me. "I want to see Paris and Rome. I want to see the tower that leans and the Great Wall of China. I want to paint the pyramids of Egypt and the Grand Canyon I want to see the sun come up over the ocean just one time. I want to go to the jungles of

Africa and I want…I guess I want to help people the way I helped Sandy when Rusty mashed his face and the way I helped Liddie Grace learn her math or the way I want to help Ellie."

"What do you mean? How do you want to help Ellie?"

"She wants to go to college and study outer space. I wish I could make her dream come true. Or maybe I just want the freedom to know when the time is right for me to do a thing. I just don't understand. That's all."

"What do you not understand?"

"Why God would make me the way he made me then want me to be something else."

"Oh, Frankie," she said again.

"I mean if He didn't want me to paint then why did he make it where colors look like living things to me and why did he make me where I would notice the changing leaves and the sunset to the point that I could stand and stare at them forever, drink them in like they're the air I'm breathing."

"There once was a boy," she said. "He was born with extraordinary fingers. They weren't like yours and mine. No, they were long, thin and webbed. He could stretch his fingers further than anyone else. When he was a child his father asked him what he wanted to be when he grew up. He looked on the wall and saw a painting of Beethoven and do you know what the boy said?"

I shook my head.

"He said, 'I want to be him.' And do you know what his father did? He went and hired the boy the best piano teacher he could afford and in time the boy grew to a man. He was the most skilled pianist in his country. He became so well-loved that women would faint when he played publicly."

I would have laughed at that if it didn't hurt so much. "Imagine that," I said. "Girls fainting just because some guy is good on an instrument."

Miss Mays grinned. "Yeah, imagine that. Well, people respected this fellow then he started hanging out with gypsies. The people in his society felt the same way about gypsies as your parents feel about Swamp Holler folks. He even took gypsy children into his homes and taught them to play piano. He had the dream of helping others make their dreams come true. He was born with a gift, Frankie, and he learned to use that gift to change the lives of others. His music was so ahead of its time, so complicated that even today, some of his pieces are impossible for the best musicians to play."

"What was his name?" I asked. "Was he a really person?"

"Franz Lizts," she said. "And yes, he was very real. When he became an old man, he turned his heart completely toward spiritual things and composed some of his most profound and beautiful pieces. His goals in life were to help others, to do the thing he was created for and to honor God. To do those things he had to sometimes go against the norms of his society. But how he blessed the world because he did."

"He was kind of like the Michelangelo of music."

"Yes. He was."

"Momma wouldn't like him," I said. "He didn't play a banjo or a mandolin or a guitar."

"Oh, but he sometimes played the fiddle," Miss Mays said.

I smiled.

"My point it, Frankie, you and you alone must decide your path in life. Your mother, no matter how good her intentions may be, cannot determine your future."

I nodded and she took a deep breath. Then she folded her hands in front of her and said, "I learned today that Liddie Grace will not be back to school for the rest of this year."

"What?" I said. "Why?"

"Her father has pulled her out of school and is sending her mother and her to Atlanta to spend the remainder of the year with an aunt there."

I couldn't believe it. No more Liddie Grace on Briar Ridge. "Just like that?" I said. "Does she get any say in the matter?"

"No, neither does her mother. Mr. McAllister can be very overbearing at times."

I wanted to tell her how he had threatened me when no one was around, but I was afraid. What if whoever he was talking about found out I had told Miss Mays?

"It'll be okay," she said. "Things will work out."

How could they with so many lies floating about and no one really telling me anything that made any sense?

"Why did you leave at the hospital?" I asked. "Why didn't you report what happened to the sheriff?"

She looked at me long and hard with her steely eyes then she said. "There are things going on in this community that neither you nor I are supposed to know and the less the people involved believe we know, the safer we are."

"What kinds of things?" I asked. "I'm not a little kid anymore. Tell me."

"I can't." She looked up at the clock and said, "I've got another wounded soldier to check on before it gets dark and it's a good little walk down there. I don't want to meet up with the Jackson's dog after dark. I'll be back in a few days. Hope you decide what to do with the paper and charcoal."

I started to get up. "No, stay, I'll let myself out." She opened the door and was gone.

I managed to raise myself up off the couch and locked the door behind her. I watched the top of her blonde head bopping down the road and remembered the blonde hair that I had seen barely beyond Joe Pablo the night Ellie made me hid under the water table. Then it hit me. The Jacksons didn't have a dog. That was a code word for the still site. Miss Mays knew about the still? The thought that came into my head next just about caused my head to spin around backwards. Miss Mays had just spoken to me in the same muted tones as the Mickey's mysterious visitor. Joe had said Mickey's girl had his car. Miss Mays was gone to Nashville the next day.

I walked back to the bedroom and eased myself onto the bed. My hands were shaking as I got back under the covers. My teacher was Mickey McThacker's secret girlfriend? No, surely not. That just couldn't be, could it? They were near the same age. She spent an uncanny amount of time making sure that Ellie learned. But mostly it was the way she handled that sawed-off shot-gun and threatened to blow Rusty's eyeballs out the back of his skull. Somehow I imagined that only a woman capable of doing something like that could be Mickey's girl. Still, she was educated, refined, from a well-to-do family and he was, well, he was a McThacker, a bootlegger's son. How on earth did they hook up and why?

Miss Mays had been the one to encourage me to draw. She taught us about all the far away places I wanted to visit and caused me to read My Side of the Mountain and Edgar Allen Poe and now. She was a symbol of freedom to me, of life beyond Briar Ridge and she was dating Mickey McThacker. The relationship just didn't add up? I don't know why but I felt sick inside. I felt like something precious had been stolen from me, some idea had been destroyed. Was there nobody who was what they seemed to be? What was it she had said that day Rusty beat me up? "Nobody's who they seem to be, Frankie."

I wanted to bring her back and make her answer my questions straight. I wanted to know some truth and all of a sudden, I wanted to see Ellie. I wanted to see her so much that I hurt inside, not my cracked ribs but a yearning in my chest similar to the one I felt when my grandpa died and I knew that I couldn't go fishing with him again or just sit on the porch and whittle with him when Momma was on a tangent and Daddy was gone hunting.

I knew that if I could just talk to Ellie, then everything would be all right.

Chapter Seventeen

I didn't expect to have any more visitors but Miss Mays came every other day. She brought me books to read and homework. I just couldn't look at her the same, knowing that she was Mickey's girl, but I couldn't ask her about it either. What if I was wrong? And what right did I, a student, have to pry into my teacher's personal life? A couple of times Eugene was there when she came and commented on what a fine teacher she must be to walk all the way down the ridge just to check up on my learning.

Once she came when Momma was there and I felt sorry for Miss Mays because Momma got to asking her if she knew anything about bunions, seeing how she was a teacher and teachers were supposed to know about all sorts of things. Of course she didn't know anything about bunions and I'm sure she didn't want to see Momma's but Momma showed it to her anyway.

No one said a word about the Dawsons, but a week after I got home from the hospital Eugene and I were in the kitchen, eating the supper that Momma brought up to us. For all of her complaining and whining and nagging, Momma was a good cook. I was thankful for the meals. Mostly because Eugene ate cornbread, beans and coffee all of the time. Momma had brought us fried chicken, mashed potatoes, roastin' ears, which was corn still on the cob, all hot with butter and salt running off of them. She brought Johnny cakes and we were planning on eating them with molasses for desert when we heard a vehicle outside.

Eugene shuffled into the living room and peered out the window. "Don't know that car," he called toward the kitchen door. "Reckon it must be somebody here to see you." He took his rifle from the rack above the couch. "Man can't be too careful with all the heathenism in the world now-days. You sit right in yonder, Frankie, lessen I tell ye to get up."

Eugene was a fearful man. He slept with a pistol under his pillow and kept that rifle in easy reach at all times. He was always concerned that someone would steal from him. Momma, Daddy and I were the only ones who knew that he kept his life savings in the attic, sealed in canning jars. He had lived through the Great Depression as a child and had known deep hunger. He had seen men shoot each other over a hog. He would often say, "Ye never know when hard times are a comin' back. Ain't no way to see em comin' til they're done here."

He opened the door a peep and hollered out, "Who are ye?"

A girl shouted back. "Liddie Grace McAllister. Elbert McAllister's girl. I'm here to see Frankie. We go to school together."

Eugene closed the door and put his rifle back. "Lord have mercy, Frankie. It's a woman here to see you. You know I don't like no women folk in my house lessen it's the teacher or your momma and I don't like having your momma none much. Get rid of her as fast as you can."

He opened the door and hollered, "Well, come in."

I heard her bound up onto the porch and I knew she was in when Eugene said, "Frankie's yonder in the kitchen. How'd you get here?"

"Oh, Daddy's out in the car waiting on me," she said.

"Well, he might as well come in," Eugene said.

"Oh, no. He just ran me by so I could say good-bye to Frankie." She came into the kitchen and stood just inside the doorway, staring at me. "Well, Frankie Keilman, you're just not gonna believe what's happening."

"What's happening?"

She flipped her black hair, which was hanging loose tonight and not in the usual high ponytail. "Daddy is sending Momma and me to Atlanta for the winter. I'm going to be going to a city school down there. No more walking through the woods for me, getting attacked by big old ugly boys. Daddy says it's because we're the richest ones up on the ridge and there are people who just hate us on account of that."

"Yeah, that's probably it," I said. She stood there, thrilling her hair, staring up at the light fixture and smacking gum. "Only thing, Frankie, there is a chance that I might come upon a boy down there and I just wanted you to know that he might fall for me."

"Well, I reckon that's a part of life," I said. "You'll probably be an old married woman by the next time I see you."

She stopped twirling her hair and stomped her foot. "I will not be old and I won't be married. I just said that to see if you had any feelings for me. But it looks like you don't. So, why did you save me if you don't have feelings for me?"

"No sense in you getting mad," I said. "I would've done it for Sandy Coltrain or Idy Jo. I'd have done it for anybody in your situation."

"Ugh," she huffed. "I hope I do find somebody down there in Atlanta that I like." She wheeled, her flighty self around and marched right out of Eugene's house. That was the Liddie Grace I was used to. I guess the scare of nearly being killed by Rusty had already left her and she was back to her snobby self. I heard the door slam then poured some molasses on my johnny cakes.

171

"Eugene," I hollered. "Your food's getting cold."

He came poking back into the kitchen. "Smart thing you did. That girl wouldn't bring a man nothing but trouble. She's one of them I been warning you about, a hellcat, a she devil. I feel sorry for the man that ends up with her."

"Yeah, me too, Eugene. I know one thing for sure. It ain't gonna be me."

"Her daddy's got money," he said.

"You always told me that money's not worth your freedom."

"You see how I'm livin' don't ye? No fancy frilly stuff in my house. I go to bed when I want to and get up when I want to. I eat what I want to and wear what I want to. If I miss the spit cup and get yam berry in the floor, ain't no woman fussin' at me to clean it up. I got peace. A man can have money without having a woman from a rich family. Work hard and save it instead of spending it on fool things like Lester and his woman and like your momma's always naggin your daddy to do."

I smiled. Eugene probably had thousands of dollars upstairs in those jars, but no one would ever spend it. He didn't even have indoor plumbing or a telephone.

The day after Liddie Grace had come to visit me I discovered I was feeling better. I decided that I would go for a walk. I promised Eugene that I was feeling fine and that I wouldn't go far. I meandered around the yard for a little while then decided to walk across the field adjacent to Eugene's garden spot. On the far side of the field, where it met the woods, I came upon a little path. I knew where it led. I had been down that path many times as a child, but in recent years I had forgotten all about it. The path led to an old smokehouse that Eugene no longer used. He had abandoned it in favor of using the shed behind his barn to cure meat, on account of the shed behind the barn was closer.

I ventured down the path. By now my side was hurting a little, but I kept walking until I came to the old plank building, sitting there, gray against the colorful late October leaves of the trees surrounding it. The structure had been built as a house for slaves that once worked for my great-great-grandfather. I thought how ironic that the old plantation style home he had lived in had long ago burned to the ground, but the slave shack still stood, almost as sturdy as the day it was built.

The door stood partially open, so I stuck my head in, observing the shack's one room. There were leaves on the floor and lots of spider webs on the walls, but that was it. A fireplace occupied the wall opposite of the door and there was an old cabinet on the other wall. Ropes still hung from the ceiling rafters where Eugene had once hung his meat to cure and there was a huge salt box near the door that no longer contained anything but leaves.

I stayed there a few minutes, listening to the silence of the woods. I walked inside and leaned against the old salt box. The shack could be cleaned up. It could be made useable again. Somebody should use it for something, but for what? It was a hide-a-way, a haven. I could ask Eugene for it, but then he would want to know what I needed it for and what I planned to do with it. The truth was I didn't know. It just seemed like somebody ought to use it for something. It was right then and there that I decided how I could use that shack. I had promised my mother that she wouldn't find any more of my drawings in our house, but I never promised her that I wouldn't draw.

The next morning when Eugene went to do the milking, I waited until he was out of the house then I took the charcoal and art paper Miss Mays had given me out from under the bed and carried them to the old shack. I hid them in the cabinet and secured the door with a rope that had fallen from the ceiling. In the days that followed I often took a walk in the woods and I drew without fear of discovery. I was careful not to be gone too long as to alarm Eugene which meant that I had to work on my drawings in small sessions rather than hours at a time as I had done in the past, but still I drew.

My three weeks were up the first of November and it had already begun to chilly in the mornings. On my first day back at school I wore a denim jacket and what we called a togie, which was a type of knit cap that a person could pull down over his ears. Elmer was absent. Idy Jo said he was stripping tobacco, which meant he was helping his parents peel the leaves off the dried stalks, put them into grades and get it ready to haul to the tobacco warehouses where it would be sold.

Harlan wasn't there either and I knew he was doing the same. I probably would have been stripping tobacco, too, but my mom was more adamant than ever about my attending seminary now that Elbert McAllister was putting up the money.

School seemed quiet without Liddie Grace there. I waited outside the door for Ellie. Miss Mays rang the bell and still no Ellie. I thought she wasn't coming, then I heard a car engine and Mickey McThacker's car came around the bend in the road and pulled right up to the school house door. Joe Pablo was driving it. Ellie got out, school books in hand and hurried toward the building. She smiled when she saw me.

Once we got inside I noticed that half the kids were absent, especially the older ones. It was tobacco stripping season. School would be a barren place for the next few weeks.

At lunch Ellie and I ate together on the back steps instead of eating at the picnic table where Liddie Grace's former gang of girls gathered and hackled. I imagined that now that Liddie Grace was gone, they'd have to peck each other until one of them emerged as the top hen. It didn't matter to me and I don't think it mattered to Ellie either. She was beyond them. She had always been beyond them, even the few times they managed to hurt her feelings. She was beyond them because her life was serious and she had dreams. They just wanted to be stars in their own eyes.

I shared my cornbread and bacon strips with Elllie. The way I figured it what Momma didn't know wouldn't hurt her and Liddie Grace wasn't around to tattle.

"How's Mickey?" I asked.

"He's up walking now. Meaner than a striped snake. Granny says he'll be driving again soon. I'm glad you're back, Frankie. It's been so lonesome here since you've been gone."

"Since I've been gone? It was lonely when you weren't here, too, you know."

"Everybody said you got hurt working for Liddie's Daddy on his farm. Is that true?"

I looked around to make sure no busybodies were close, then I motioned Ellie closer and made her swear to never tell anyone what I was about to tell. Then I told her. I told her about Rusty Dawson attacking Liddie Grace and about Miss Mays with a gun. I told her about Liddie's dad saying I couldn'ttell anybody. Then I told her that if she told even a soul that somebody could end up dead, because that's what Elbert McAllister said to me. I was afraid as soon as I told her. What if someone found out I told her?

"I won't say a word. Won't anybody find out," she said. "I can keep a secret."

I knew that was true. Ellie had kept it a secret for years that she had no parents. So, she really could keep a secret.

I heard Miss Mays moving around inside the school. "Ellie," I said. "I have to know something. Who is Mickey's girlfriend?"

'Oh, you don't need to know that."

"Yes, yes I do. I have to know."

She looked down.

"Is it..." I felt stupid for asking because it seemed absurd, but still all the pieces fit. "Is it Miss Mays?"

She didn't answer. She continued looking down.

"Well," I said.

She nodded.

"But how? When? Why?"

"You mean why would an educated girl from the city go with my brother, a McThacker? Because he's a wonderful person despite the fact that he smokes too much and tells nasty jokes and says cuss words. Miss Mays doesn't see people like everyone else around here. She sees them for who they are, kind of like you."

"Does anyone else know?"

"No. It's a secret."

"Why? Is she...you know."

"Ashamed? No. It's just not what you think. That's all. When the time is right then they will tell people." She dug at the grass with her shoe. "She's more than she seems, Frankie. She's better than anybody around here. At least I think she's better. She pays attention to stuff that nobody else sees and she, well, she found out right off that Mickey and me were living by ourselves. She came right down to Swamp Holler to meet my family. No teacher, nobody, ever did that before."

"Has she been walking you home since I've been out?"

"Ever since I came back. I guess you know that the reason she walked me home all along was because she knew about the Dawson boys and she had a gun in her bag."

"But why did she send me? I don't have a gun. Wasn't she afraid the Dawsons would attack both of us?"

"They wouldn't attack somebody from the ridge, somebody like you that everybody knows. There would be too many questions asked, but a kid like me, if I came up missing nobody on this ridge would notice and there'd just be my family down in the holler. Nobody would listen to them or care. Frankie, the sheriff, half the people on the ridge, rich folks in town, a lot of people are in co-hoots with the Dawsons. Miss Mays is about the only person up here you can trust, on account of she's an outsider."

"Brother Van Dyke is an outsider."

"Yeah, but he's never even been to Swamp Holler and he wouldn't know if any of us were dead or alive. No, Miss Mays, she's the one we all trust."

I took two apples out of my lunch bucket and handed one to Ellie. "I don't get it."

"What do you not get?"

I took a bite from my apple, "The connections."

"What are you talking about, connections?"

"Come clean with me, Ellie. Everybody beats around the bush hiding the truth from me like I can't handle it, but I am knee deep in the middle of something and don't even know what it is, something that involves the McThackers and the McAllisters and the Dawsons and maybe even my own father. I have to know, Ellie. Tell me."

"I don't know anything about the McAllisters," she said, "only that they wouldn't spit on me or my kin to put us out if we were on fire. But the Dawsons…" She looked around then whispered to me. "My daddy used to run liquor for the Dawsons. He gave them a cut of everything he made and in return they supplied him with equipment, names of buyers, addresses and gave him protection from the law. Then my daddy turned up dead."

She looked to her left and then to her right to make sure no one was approaching then continued. "He kept a map of his local customers and Mickey used the map to continue making his runs even after he died, that's when we cooked up our plan that we would only do it long enough to get me through school. Only thing is Old Man Dawson sent his oldest two boys to the house one day and they said to Mickey, 'you better give us a bigger cut than your old man did and you better not think of getting out and crossing over to the competition.' We didn't know what competition he was talking about. Heck, up until then we didn't know that Daddy was running for them. We thought Daddy was doing his own business, but those two explained how that their daddy was expecting up to

177

sixty percent of all Mickey made in every run. Sixty percent or they might not protect us for other bootleggers who wouldn't take kindly to a couple of kids cutting in on their territory."

"So let me get this straight," I said. "You and Mickey have been giving the Dawsons sixty percent of all you made from the liquor you sell? In exchange they are supposed to offer you protection from some other big time bootlegger?"

"That's right, only we don't think there is another big time bootlegger. We think the Dawsons are the ones that hurt people when they don't give them what they want. Must be that Liddie Grace's daddy is not as all fired rich as he lets on."

"Unless," I said, then I realized that the notion that had just hit me was so far-fetched that I was afraid to say it out loud, even to Ellie.

"Unless what?"

"Oh nothing," I said. "I don't even know exactly what I was going to say. It just doesn't make sense about Elbert McAllister. That's all."

It was right at that moment that a fine-looking powder blue car pulled up with chrome trim and fins coming off the back fenders. Everybody in the school yard stopped what they were doing and gawked at that car. Two men got out, one in a gray suit with a black tie, the other in casual tan linen britches and a blue button shirt. The man in the suit was maybe thirty-five. He was thin and lanky with sandy hair and fair skin. The other fellow was younger and although he was also lean, he looked more like a tennis player or a runner. He had golden skin that contrasted with his almost white hair, as if he had spent many days in the sun. It was hard to pinpoint his age, but I guessed him in his late twenties to early thirties. Both men had a foreign air about them and it was just easy to tell that they were from somewhere else. Everything about them screamed that they were foreign to Briar Ridge.

Miss Mays came to the door, a surprised look on her face that collapsed into a big smile. "Martin! Jerry!" she shouted then ran down the steps and hugged first the older man then the younger. She turned to all of us who had gathered around and said, "Students, I'd like you all to meet my brothers, Martin and Jerry Mays. They've come all the way from Memphis."

Chapter Eighteen

I walked Ellie home that afternoon after Miss Mays's brothers came to school. She let us out about an hour early. Of course we all knew it was so she could spend time with her kinfolk.

I knew Momma would spit three ways from Sunday if she had any idea I was walking Ellie home, but I didn't promise her I wouldn't. All I promised her was that she wouldn't find anymore of my art around the house.

Sandy Coltrain, whose nose was all better, followed us down the lane. I turned around, "What is it, Sandy?"

He ran toward me. He reminded me of a half-grown hound dog when he ran. His feet and hands were the biggest part of him and they just flopped when he ran while his head wobbled from side to side and his tongue tended to stick out a little bit.

"Fr…fr…fr…ankie, th…thank you for help…helping me."

"You're welcome, Sandy. What are friends for?"

"You… my f…friend, F…frankie? You my friend?"

"Of course, I'm your friend."

"I'm your f…friend, too, Fr…Frankie." He stood there, just staring at me and smiling a mindless kind of smile with his eyes all big and his tongue half sticking out then he turned and ran back toward the school.

"Looks like you've made a friend for life," Ellie said. Then she took my hand, "Actually, you've made two of them."

I squeezed her hand. "Yeah, but I don't plan on kissing Sandy Coltrain."

"You don't, do you? Well, just who do you plan on kissing?"

"I don't know. I was thinking that maybe I might kiss that McThacker girl, the one from Swamp Holler."

"Is that so? What if that McThacker girl doesn't want to kiss you back seeing how you got all busted up trying to save Liddie Grace McAllister instead of her?"

I pulled her toward the cover of the trees, "Well, in that case I'd tell her that I was a hero for sure, having to save a girl I can't even stand to be around on account of her big biscuit white teeth and her loud mouth."

Ellie laughed. "Some hero. Talking bad about the person you rescued."

"Speaking the truth ain't talking bad, now is it?"

"No, I reckon it's not and Lord knows that every thing you said about her is as true as it can be. But you're my hero, too, helping Sandy Coltrain, standing up to Rusty Dawson and mostly, saving my brother's life that night. So, you might as well go ahead and kiss me."

We leaned up against a tree and I did. I kissed Ellie and it was just as wonderful as it had been the other time, back before the world went crazy and people started getting shot and beat up.

I walked Ellie all the way home that day, not to Joe's house or to Granny's but to her house, the one she and Mickey had lived in before Mickey got shot. Swamp Holler was all flat and no matter where you stood you could look up and see the hills, Briar Ridge was the biggest and closest but all around for miles and miles, there were hills. In some ways, it was the most beautiful place in the world and in other ways, it was a sad place, hemmed in on every side by those hills. They reminded me of ghosts, always present, never speaking. I discovered why it was called Swamp Holler that afternoon. Ellie led the way after we passed the Jackson place. The trail was the same as if we were going to Joe's house except when we came to the dirt lane we had always gone down, we didn't turn, instead we went about a quarter of a mile down the main road and turned down a gravel lane.

"My house is at the end of this road," she said. We hadn't gone far when we passed a swamp, a true blue swamp on the right side of the road. It stretched out as far as I could see, green and brackish water with scrawny trees standing in it.

"It's a real swamp," I said.

"Of course it's a swamp," Ellie said. "But it isn't very big."

We followed the road beside the swamp until it slanted upward and we were on higher ground, not much higher, but higher than the swamp. The swamp gave way to thick woods and the dirt path led to a small house, covered in black tar paper and overshadowed by large beech trees and oak trees. The yard was grown up and water stood. Strange mud mounds littered the yard like giant wet ant hills.

"What are these?"

"Crawdad holes," Ellie said. "Sometimes you can see the crawdads just crawling around the yard, unless it rains, then they swim."

"Do you and Mickey own this land?"

"Well, sort of. Our daddy owned it and then he died, so now I guess it's ours until somebody decides to take it away from us."

"Now who would do a thing like that?"

She shrugged. "I don't know. Dawsons maybe. Old man McAllister. Whatever rich man decides it's worth taking."

The house wasn't much to look at. It was a rectangular box with a roofed porch made of planks and tin. There were two front doors. One of them was a mustard yellow color and the other was painted black with a tiny peep hole that someone had bored into it. Ellie lifted a loose board from the porch and retrieved a key. "Now, if you tell anybody where we keep our house key, I'll have to kill you, Frankie, so you better not tell on account of I love you and I don't want to kill you. Well, it'd probably be Mickey that killed you but I'd still be sad."

"I reckon if I gotta be killed it might as well be you and Mickey that does it to me. Except I won't tell and you know it."

"I was just kidding," she said. "I wanted to see your face turn all white and your eyes get all big like they do when you get spooked."

"My eyes don't get big," I said.

She just looked at me as if to say that I was touched in the head. Then she unlocked the door and invited me into her home. I stood there for a moment, letting my eyes adjust to the darkness. The windows were partially covered with cardboard, allowing light to come in through slits in the top, which were too high up for a person to peer through from the outside without the aid of a stool or ladder. As my vision came back to me I saw that the walls were covered in newspapers. Somebody had collected old papers and used them as wall paper. A heat stove made from an old oil drum sat in the middle of the floor and a discarded church pew covered in homemade cushions served as a couch. Beside the stove was a real chair, made from wood. It, too, was homemade.

On either side of the living room was a doorway, neither of which contained a door. The one on the right was easy to see into. It was the kitchen which contained a cook stove, the kind that you had to build a fire in to use, a water bucket table with a bucket on it, and an old metal cabinet. There was no refrigerator. That's

184

when I realized that Ellie and Mickey had no electricity in their house.

"This is home," Ellie said. "Of course, most of the time we stay over at Granny Flor's or Aunt Sadie's or at some of our other cousin's houses. Still, this is ours and when I want to be alone, I come here. Wanna see my room?"

"Okay."

She took me by the hand and pulled me toward the other doorway which was covered by a ragged blanket. She pushed the blanket back and we entered another dark room which contained nothing but a bed and a dresser. A jacket hung on each of the foot bed posts and a cowboy hat lay on the dresser. Again, the walls were covered in newspapers.

"This was Daddy's room," she said. "Mickey gets it and all of the clothes in the dresser. My room is right through here." We passed through another blanket covered doorway into a room that contained a smaller bed, a roll away bed. On the wall above the bed hung two dresses, one of the flour sack ones Ellie always wore and the one I had bought her. Today she was wearing her brown one. I felt like my heart was in my throat. Ellie only had three dresses. How many dresses did my mother own? Ten? Twenty? More? That was all that was in Ellie's room. She owned nothing except a bed, a pair of boy tennis shoes and three dresses.

She dropped to her knees beside the bed. "Look here, Frankie." She reached under there and pulled out a box. The box contained books. "Miss Mays bought me these. They're all my favorites."

I knelt beside her and looked at her books. She picked up the top one. Call of the Wild. "Remember this one?"

"Sure do," I said. That lump in my throat was making it hard to talk.

"Oh, this is my favorite story in the world," she handed me The Count of Monte Cristo. "Just because a person is born with nothing doesn't mean anything. Edmund Dantes was born poor. He was cheated and he still got his justice. The best part is when he is in prison for the crime he never committed and they're beating him and he sees that carving in the rock that says, 'God will give me justice.' That's the way I feel, too, sometimes. If there is a God, Frankie, don't you think He will make things work out fair just like in this story?"

"I do," I said. "I really do." She showed me the rest of her precious books, Little Women, My Side of the Mountain, Tales of Edgar Alan Poe, and some others. I heard her talking but I wasn't really listening. I was thinking about how she lived, how she did without all the things I took for granted, how she had endured three years of teasing from kids at school and had often gone without food and still, her eyes sparkled when she held a book in her hands.

"Frankie," she said, "why are you staring at me like that? Do you think I'm crazy or something?"

"No," I muttered. The lump in my throat had given way to a hurting in my chest, not one caused by broken ribs either. No, this was a kind of hurting that wouldn't show up if a doctor examined me. It was as if I was starving to be with Ellie even though I was sitting right beside her. I just wanted to pull her close to myself, close my eyes and take away every wrong thing that had ever been done to her. When I opened my mouth my words came out all shaky and in a rush. "I wish I could make things right for you and Mickey."

"Oh, Frankie," she said. "It's okay. We've got our plan." She smiled at me and her smile was like looking at a frozen pond on the coldest winter day and knowing that it was only a matter of time before the sun got warm enough to melt that ice and let all kinds of life come bursting out of the water. That was Ellie, a promise, a ray of sunshine that nothing had the power to stop. "I love you," I blurted out just like before. "I love you more than anything, Ellie McThacker." Then I leaned over and kissed her for a long time, even longer than I had kissed her in the woods and the next thing I know we were standing up then we were on the bed and all that time we were kissing. Who knows what else might have happened if somebody hadn't decided to bang on Ellie's front door.

"Ellie, you in there?" It sounded like Joe. "Ellie McThacker?"

"Wait here," Ellie said. She slid through the blanket-covered door.

I stood by the door, behind the blanket, listening. It was Joe's voice. "Ellie, Granny's in a fit, wants you over to the house right away."

"What's the matter?" I heard Ellie ask.

"Oh, Mickey's being ornery, says he's going up the ridge to find you because you ain't home yet."

"I swear my brother's retarded sometimes," Ellie huffed. "I just stopped over here to put some of my things away and do a little homework in peace and quiet."

"Well now, Ellie, you got to admit that things have been scary these days and Mickey's right about a person not being too careful, especially now that his boots have been stolen off the porch."

"I told him that it was probably just one of the dogs that packed em off."

"It's got him spooked, Ellie. Now, you best be getting on over to Granny's."

"All right, tell him I'm here. I'm safe and that I'll be right on over. I got something I have to do here. It shouldn't take me five minutes. Don't let Mickey out of the house and I'll be there."

"All right," Joe said. Then I heard Ellie close the door.

She came back into the bedroom. "I'm sorry, Frankie, but I have to go."

"It's all right," I said. "I do, too. I have things I have to do this afternoon. I'll see you tomorrow at school?"

"Yes," she said.

I kissed her one more time then we walked to the front door. We took our time walking up the road, holding hands and trying to stay far enough behind Joe that he wouldn't know we were back there.

"What's this about Mickey's boots getting stolen?" I asked.

"Oh, he had me put them out on the porch to air out last night about supper time, then when he went back out after dark to get them they were gone. I figured a dog got them, but Mickey swears up and down that somebody has stolen his boots. He really loves those boots."

At the end of the road I kissed Ellie bye then we parted ways. I headed toward Briar Ridge and she crossed the main road to go to Granny Flor's and prove to Mickey that she was all right.

As I passed the Jackson place, I saw Mr. Jackson sitting on the porch. He hollered at me and I stopped for a moment. We sat on the porch a few minutes and Mrs. Jackson brought us some coffee. Then I realized that it was past the normal time for me to be home and told him I had to go before my parents got worried. I said good-bye and thanked his wife for the drink.

When I got home Momma was on the couch, watching television as usual. "You're late," she said.

"I went down to see Mr. Jackson," I said.

"What on earth for?"

"I don't know. He's a nice old man and it seems like they're kind of lonely, living out there at the edge of the ridge all by themselves."

"Well, get your clothes changed and pack that bucket of slop down to the hogs, then go over to Eugene's and tell your daddy to be sure he gets here by five o'clock. I want to go to the woman's meeting up at the church and I need him to take me."

"I could take you," I said. "I can drive, too, you know."

"Now what are you going to do while I'm in the woman's meeting? You gonna sit out in the parking lot and talk to the old men like your daddy does?"

I shrugged. "I don't know. Maybe. Or I could go visit Brother Van Dyke, ask him some questions about seminary."

She looked at me like she suspected something then she said, "All right. Go tell your daddy that we're taking his truck."

Chapter Nineteen

I parked our truck at the church. Ladies were waddling across the gravel parking lot in pairs and groups of three. Most of them were plump with gray-blue hair piled on their heads, cut short and curled or else pinned under scarves or hats. A few of them were slender and a tad more youthful, but none of them were in any danger of setting records on speed or agility.

For the life of me I couldn't understand what Momma got out of these meetings with the blue-haired ladies in their sweaters and broaches. All I knew was that they took forever and a day to cross the parking lot then stand around on the porch, complaining about how the church men ought not to put their cigarettes out on the doorstep of the Lord's house. I knew that they talked about gardens, weather, grandkids and other stuff that lost my interest in under thirty seconds, until the pastor's wife came up to the church. Then they all went in together. I don't know what they did once there were inside and I wasn't about to ask. I was afraid Momma might really tell me and it might bore me so much that I'd die. I was pretty sure that if a person was bored long enough and strong enough, his heart would either explode or just stop beating and he'd drop dead right there on the spot just to liven things up.

After I saw Momma go inside I got out of the truck and walked across the graveyard to the parsonage. Brother Van Dyke met me at the door, wearing his sweater vest and house slippers again.

"Well, hello, Frankie. What brings you to my door tonight?"

"Momma," I said. "She wanted to go to the ladies' meeting so I thought I'd come over here for a minute."

"Well, I was just about to watch a western on the television. You're welcome to join me."

"I like westerns, but some of the ladies in the church think they're of the devil. I heard Momma say that once."

He smiled then picked his pipe up from an ashtray on the table. "Yes, it appears that we have some very opinionated ladies in the congregation."

We sat there, watching the western for a few minutes. I wondered what the characters would look like if they were in color like real people, wondered about the colors of their hair and their clothes. Then a commercial came on.

"I heard about your accident," Brother Van Dyke said. "I'm sorry you were injured while helping out a neighbor, but I'm sure it was a nice thing you were doing."

I lowered my eyes. I wanted to tell this man the truth about what had happened but Mickey had warned me not to trust anybody. How did I know I could trust Brother Van Dyke.

"You know, Frankie," he up and said, "things are not always what they seem and there's a lot more to everybody that meets the eye. Nobody's who they seem to be when you first meet them."

Goose bumps popped up on my arms. Miss Mays had said almost the exact same thing to me the day Rusty had tried to kill me and she had turned out to be Mickey's girlfriend. So, I wondered who Brother Van Dyke really was, his uncle? His long lost cousin?

"Wh…what makes you say that?" I stuttered.

He shrugged. "Oh, I don't know. People in this community. When I first came here it seemed like everything was so picturesque and innocent, but I tell you, Frankie, there's something sinister at work among the people of Briar Ridge, something that nobody talks about yet everybody knows."

I couldn't look at him.

"Oh, don't look so glum, Son. I don't mean you. I mean it's just a hush-hush community. It's hard to be a shepherd to people who want a puppet, not a leader."

Why was he telling me this? I was just a kid compared to him.

"I know you have considered going into the ministry," he said. "And I want you to know that it's not always easy. In fact, it's often very difficult. People will pretend to be one thing in front of you, hiding who they really are, because they somehow think you are going to pass judgment on them."

The show came back on and we watched it a while longer. It was about a gunslinger who came to a town that was hiding something crooked and it was the sheriff and the law that was behind it all. This renegade gun fighter, who just went around leaning up against buildings, lighting his cigarettes and staring at people from under the brim of his hat with beady eyes, took it upon himself to set things right and bring justice to the town.

During the next commercial break the pastor went into the kitchen and made us each a sandwich. We drank milk and ate our sandwiches during the next portion of the show, then he looked at brown and gold clock on top the television and said, "Meeting's over. Missus will be home in a minute. Don't tell her about that sandwich." He winked. "She doesn't like me to eat after eight o'clock."

"I better get going," I said. "Momma will be out." He followed me to the door.

"Have a good evening, Frankie," he said. I waved good night, went across the graveyard and saw Momma on the porch, talking to another lady. I got in the truck and waited another ten minutes or so, then we headed home.

As far as I know Miss Mays' brothers must have decided to stick around for awhile. Ellie said they took an apartment in town and were staying there. That next Saturday I worked for Meredith Goodin and they stopped in early to get gas. I waited on them up because Mrs. Goodin had gone up to her house to burn her garbage while the weather was fittin', which meant that the wind wasn't blowing as it usually did up on the ridge and it wasn't raining like it had been doing the night before.

I studied my teacher's kinfolk while I pumped their gas. Jerry got out with a scowl on his face, like he was figuring on something or trying to size me up. He leaned up against the store and just stared a hole plum through me. I could tell he was watching every move I made, even though he didn't so much as twitch or turn his head. He wasn't a big man by any means, but there was something cold and hard about him that made me think of him as a gun slinger from the Western I'd watched with Brother Van Dyke. It was a cool day and he was wearing a cream colored linen jacket. I wondered if he had a gun holster under that jacket. Then I shuddered and told myself not to watch anymore Westerns for awhile.

Martin Mays, got out of the car, put his hands on the back of his hips and leaned as far back as he could.

"Nice day, kid, don't you think?"

"Yes sir," I said. "It's a fine day."

"A might cool, wouldn't you say?"

"Just a little."

"Say, boy, do you all have those pickled boloney rolls in your store?"

"Yes, we do."

"Got eggs, too?"

I knew he meant pickled eggs. "We do."

"I'll have a slice of that boloney and some crackers. Jerry here, he'll have one of the eggs. We both want a drink, too."

I followed him in the store, picked up the big metal fork Mrs. Goodin kept on the counter, stuck it into a glass gallon jar which contained pickled bologna then sliced a big piece off the roll with a black handled knife she kept near the jar.

"You know the Dawsons?" he asked while I wrapped the bologna in waxed paper.

"I know who they are," I said.

"What do you know about them?"

I stuck the fork into the egg jar. "I know that they're mean." I speared and egg, brought it out and wrapped it.

"How do you know that?"

I figured Miss Mays must have him about what happened with Rusty

and he wasn't too happy about it. "People always say they're mean. Sometimes they come in the store here and they walk around like they could just take whatever they wanted to and nobody could do anything about it."

"I see," he said. "You don't know about them actually every bothering anybody though?"

I was suspicious for real now. I shrugged. "You should ask Miss Mays. She knows more about them than I do."

He smiled at me, not a happy smile, either, but a smile that was more of a look to let me know that he already knew more than I was saying and he already knew that I knew more than I was saying. I was uncomfortable around these men. In some ways they were just as scary as the Dawsons.

"That'll be four dollars for everything," I said.

He laid a five dollar bill on the counter. "Keep the change for yourself."

"Thanks," I said.

Mrs. Goodin came back about half an hour later and the day was uneventful with regular customers stopping by for gas and cigarettes. Then at lunch, a bunch of local farmers came in and ate thick sandwiches on the porch and in the store. They drank cold drinks, mostly orange sodas, and swapped tales. When quitting time came my dad drove up to the store, got gas, bought Momma some cigarettes and gave me a ride home.

Momma had supper ready and we had just sat down to eat when we heard an engine in the driveway. My dad jumped up and trotted into the living room. "Who the Sam Hill is that?" he hollered back toward the kitchen.

Momma and I went into the living room and I saw Mickey's car in the drive way about the same time that someone frantically banged on our door. My dad yanked the door open and there was Miss Mays. She looked like she had been crying. "I need to see Frankie," she said.

"What's the matter?" my daddy asked.

She shut her eyes and took a deep breath. "Udell Dawson has been murdered."

Chapter Twenty

"Murdered?" Daddy said. "What? How? Who?"

"His boys found him dead about two hours ago," she said. "I was in Swamp Holler. I had taken some books to one of my students there," she looked straight at me and I knew she was talking about Ellie and I knew that she was doing more than taking books to her. I knew that she was courting Mickey.

"I hadn't been there five minutes when the sheriff's car pulled into the driveway. The Dawson boys jumped out and came running into the house. They grabbed Mickey and dragged him out on the porch. They beat him while the sheriff stood…" she choked up. "They beat that boy while the sheriff stood right there and watched. Then he looked up and saw me and made them stop. Then he cuffed Mickey McThacker and arrested him on murder charges."

Momma started to say something but I cut her off. My heart was beating so hard that I thought it was going to explode. All I could think of was Ellie and how I knew that Mickey wouldn't kill anybody.

"He didn't do it," I blurted out.

197

Miss Mays shook her head and broke into tears. "Of course he didn't do it." I think that vote of confidence and the tears on Mickey's part threw my parents for a loop. They hadn't realized it was Mickey's car she was driving because they hadn't been up at the store all of the times I'd filled it up with gas.

"Where's Ellie?" At this point I no longer cared what anybody thought about Ellie and me. All I could think of was how hurt and scared and alone she must feel with Mickey in so much trouble with the law.

She looked toward the door. I brushed past her and ran out the door. I could hear my parents asking "What are you doing, Frankie? Where are you going?" but I kept running. I ran across our yard and reached the car just as Ellie got out. We went together like a couple of lodestones and I stood there holding Ellie. I think she was just too scared to talk or cry or anything and she had a right to be.

I didn't recall them following me outside, but everybody in the house did and they were there behind me while I held Ellie. Then Miss Mays laid her hand on my arm and said. "Frankie. Mickey needs your help right now."

"You hold on just a minute," Daddy said. "You ain't gettin my boy mixed up in this mess."

"You don't understand," she said. "He's already mixed up in it. He became mixed up the day he took on Rusty Dawson. Frankie will likely be called on as a witness and so will I. I may even be a suspect if word gets out that I threatened to shoot Rusty Dawson's head off.

"I need you folks to call my brothers." She reached into the vehicle and dug out a number. "This is Jerry's number. Call it. Tell him what's happened and tell him to meet me at the jail." She looked from Momma to Daddy. "I know you don't think highly of the McThackers but I also know that you're decent people and you wouldn't want an innocent man to pay for a crime he didn't commit."

"And how can you be so sure Mickey McThacker's innocent?" Momma asked.

"Because," she looked around as if scanning to be sure no one else could hear. "I was with him at the time of the murder."

"With him?" Momma said. "You mean delivering books?"

"No ma'am," she said. "I was delivering books when the sheriff came, but I have been with Mickey all day. He was with me when I bought the books."

"But why would the McThacker boy go with you to buy..."

"Oh for heaven's sake, Sarah Jean," my dad said, "can't you figure out anything? She's messing around with the McThacker boy."

"Sir, we're not messing around," she said. "Mickey and I are working together to make sure Ellie has a future. Mickey McThacker may be a moonshiner, but he's more honest than any man on this ridge."

Well, a pee ant could have knocked my momma over when she said that. Her face went white as milk. "But he's a moonshiner."

Ellie let go of me and stood straight as a locust tree. "He ain't a moonshiner no more. Me and Mickey just made the liquor so we could eat after…"

"You made liquor?" Momma said.

"We had to eat, ma'am. I don't suppose you know what it's like what with your fine white house and your cows and chickens, but it ain't everybody that's born so lucky. Anyhow Mickey was planning on sending me off to school and then when he knew I was okay, he was going to move to Lexington where Miss Mays' brother, Martin, was going to get him a fine job."

"Only trouble was," Miss Mays said, "the Dawsons have been running things down in Swamp Holler for half a century. They beat Joe Pablo within an inch of his life when he married Jewell

Eastridge, and the sheriff did nothing about it because Joe Pablo is a Mexican boy that doesn't have two pennies to rub together and the Dawsons paid him to look the other way. That's what they've done for years, paid their way out of trouble and threatened the ones they couldn't pay.

"When Mickey tried to quit, Udell Dawson and his boys didn't want to let him. They got sixty percent of his profits. They planned to take it out of his hide."

"They shot him," I said. "The man I helped that time in the woods was Mickey McThacker."

"Mickey McThacker?" Momma dabbed her face with her apron. "Oh, my word, what have you gotten us into, Frankie?"

Miss Mays brushed Momma's remark off and continued talking. "Dawsons have finally come up against somebody who's scarier, meaner and a whole heck of a lot smarter than they are. They've run into somebody they can't bully, intimidate or threaten and that is the person who has killed Udell Dawson. Smite the shepherd and the sheep will scatter. Only thing is that the person who did this is also smart enough to know that if he pins a murder on Mickey McThacker, no one will question it, after all, Mickey's just a bootlegger's kid, right? I mean you folks already believe he's bad."

"Well, he's a McThacker," my dad said.

Miss Mays cleared her throat. "So was Irene Falling Leaf. Have you told Frankie about her, Mr. Keilman?"

My dad's face turned red and Momma turned her back on my teacher.

"I'm taking Ellie to see her brother in jail," Miss Mays said. "Frankie, call my brothers, and then I suggest y'all have a heart to heart talk with your son and tell him the truth about who you are, what you've been and who he is. The time for secrets on Briar Ridge is over."

"You got no right coming here and saying this," Momma said. "Upsetting us, getting us involved in ugly things that are beneath us..."

"Beneath you?" Miss Mays said. "Go down to the Pablo graveyard in Swamp Holler's and tell that to Ellie's momma."

"Just who do you think you are?" Momma squawked.

"Someone who really cares about the families of her students. Believe it or not. Mrs. Keilman, it's time somebody in this community had the guts and the courage to stand up to the Dawsons. It's time somebody listened to the voice of the God you all claim to serve and stop bowing down at the altar of Elbert McAllister's money."

"You ain't got no call to be talking to us that way," Daddy said.

She motioned for Ellie to get back in the car. "Oh, Mr. Keilman, if you only knew. Please, if you care anything about Frankie, call my dad and tell him the truth or those who have conspired against Mickey may connect the dots back to you. Is that what you want? And you know that I'm telling the truth, don't you?" She stared at my dad and for a second I realized that those eyes of hers that had always stopped me cold in my tracks were the same as her brother's gunslinger stare.

My dad walked away, his shoulders slumped. He was like a whipped dog now and her sharp eyes and tongue had done the whipping.

I watched them leave. My momma's tongue got loose from whatever was holding it all of a sudden and she was going on something terrible about the shame I had brought on her by becoming associated with the McThackers. I just ran in the house, picked up the phone and called Miss Mays' brother, like she told me to. I could hear Momma outside hollering at Daddy to go inside and stop me from having anything else to do with white trash and riff raff, but Daddy just stood there like a tree stump, staring out at the hills behind Eugene's house.

For a minute I thought nobody was going to pick up the receiver but then a man said. "Hello."

"Is this Martin Mays?"

"Yes. Who is this? How'd you get this number?"

"Frankie Keilman," I could feel my voice quiver as it left my throat. "You know, the guy who pumps gas up at Goodin's Store?"

"Oh, yeah, I know who you are."

"Miss Mays, um, she gave me this number and told me to call you or your brother. Mickey McThacker has been arrested for the murder of Udell Dawson. His boys found him dead in his house and the sheriff came down to Swamp Holler and watched while the Dawson boys drug him out and beat him. Then when the sheriff saw your daughter, he made them stop and arrested Mickey. She said for you to meet her at the jail as soon as you can. She's on her way there now with Mickey's sister, Ellie."

He said something like, "Thank you. I'll get on it right away," but I wasn't really sure because I was shaking so much I couldn't focus. There was too much happening all at once and as I hung up the phone it hit me that Mickey may go to prison for the rest of his life and that Ellie would be a true orphan.

No sooner than I had the phone back on the hook, Momma wailed, "I can't believe what you've gone and got us all mixed up in, Frankie. I have worked so hard to build this family's name in the community and now you've just," she choked up as her tears became full blown. She hiccupped. "You've just wallowed our name in the mud, Frankie, just like an old hog. Ain't you got no respect for us, son. Don't you love us even a little bit?"

"Of course I love y'all," I said, "but I couldn't let Mickey McThacker lay there and die that day. What kind of a man does that?"

"If you hadn't been with that little holler whore in the first place," Momma wailed.

"Don't call Ellie that," I said. "She's a decent girl."

202

"Decent?" Momma said. "She's the daughter of Irene Falling Leaf. She's a dirty old Indian, Frankie."

"Shut up, Sarah Jean," I heard my dad say. I hadn't heard him come in. I turned and looked up. There he stood in the doorway, he wore the same look on his face that he always wore when Momma went off on one of her nagging fits.

"You old fool," Momma squawked. "You always did love Indians and Blacks and Mexicans more than your own kind. Don't you take up for them. It's your fault Frankie's turned out like he has. You destroyed our son."

My dad's nostrils flared, like a horse's does when it's hot from a long day of plowing. "Then I reckon it won't do no more harm to tell him the truth about everything, seeing as how I've already ruint our lives."

"You keep your mouth shut," Momma said.

"My mouth's been shut too long on account you," Daddy said. "You and me, Sarah Jean, we deserve to go to hell for all of the lies we told. That little teacher is right. This whole damn ridge ain't nothing but a nest of liars, snobs and hypocrites, singing praises to the Lord on Sunday morning and turning our backs on the suffering people in our own back yard every other day of the week. Well, I'm done lying to this kid. It's high time that I told Frankie the truth, about everything. I reckon he ought to know who we really are and who he is, too. They's been too many a secrets in this here family."

"No," Momma said. "You don't be telling nobody nothing." She picked up a magazine from the coffee table and threw it at him, then she flung plastic fruit right out of the bowl at him.

My dad ducked then motioned toward the door with his head. "Come on, son. Let's talk." A plastic banana hit him in the shoulder as he turned to go.

"Frankie," Momma screamed. "Don't you dare walk out that door with him. Don't you listen to nothing he tells you. It's all lies.

All lies. I have always been an upstanding woman with a good name."

But I kept walking. I knew I had to hear what Daddy was about to tell me, had to hear it no matter what.

Chapter Twenty-One

Momma followed us out onto the porch, yelling and screaming and cussing. I didn't even know my momma knew how to cuss, but she was doing it. She was screaming such filthy things at my dad that I reckon the devil himself couldn't cuss no better.

Once when I had been about seven Momma had told one of my aunts that she would rather see me dead than see me lose the respect of our family name. I remember sitting in the hen house and crying over that. A seven year old boy should never hear his momma say she'd rather see him dead than see him mess up. I can't remember what prompted her to say that, but she had said it, sure as the grass is green. I suppose I suspected every since that day but not voiced what I was now absolutely sure of, my momma was a raving lunatic. I walked away from her that night with a pit in my stomach so big you could've buried a horse in it.

We kept on walking. She followed us for a piece as we walked up the gravel road. She was hollering about how poorly she was and how she was too winded to follow us and that she might fall dead from shortness of breath before we got back, but we kept on walking. I hoped my momma wouldn't die from shortness of breath, but she had been dying of that since as far back as I could remember.

We walked down the road past Eugene's. Eugene was standing on the porch, lantern in his hand, looking back toward our house. "Sarah Jean's got the devil in her again," he said.

"Yep," my dad said.

"See," Eugene said. "That right there's why I never married. A man's better off dead than living with a she devil. Frankie, ye better be a learnin' from it, boy."

"Get on back in the house and mind your own business," my dad said. "Me and Frankie are just walkin'."

Eugene snorted. "Go on," but he didn't go back in his house. He stood on the porch watching us until we were out of sight. I didn't need to turn around to know that he was watching. I never heard his footsteps on the porch, never heard the screen door slam shut and besides that, I could feel his eyes on the back of my head. My dad and I kept on walking until we could no longer hear the sound of Momma's voice trailing up the road behind us.

Daddy took his metal flashlight out of his jacket and used it to light our way and we turned, heading in the direction of the old shack where I'd been stashing my artwork.

We were almost to the shack when Daddy started talking. "Ye've always nagged at me to tell you about how me and your momma come to know each other. Well, here's the story of it, Frankie, and you ain't gonna like it none too much, but I reckon the truth's got to be told sometime. A man deserves to know where he's come from and there's no denyin' it now. You've grown to be as good a man as anybody could've hoped you to be.

"Twenty odd years ago I was a soldier boy, returning from the war. There was a party up on Chelsea Ridge for all the returning soldiers. Me and some buddies of mine, we went. There was a girl there, prettiest damn girl I'd ever seen. Black hair, black eyes and a smile that'd melt your heart. She's friendly, too. Asked me to dance. Told me her name was Irene Falling Leaf.

"Turned out she was a half-Cherokee Indian what had moved up here to live with her sister. Irene was a young widow with a little boy. His name was Mickey. Yep, the very same Mickey that's been accused of murder tonight."

He paused for a minute as if that news were new to him. "Her husband had been killed in the war that I survived and she had only gone to the party that night in his honor. Make a long story short. She lived in Swamp Holler and I got to spending time with her. I had pretty much decided that I was going to marry her and help her raise that boy of hers..."

He stared off into space. I reckon he must have been thinking about all of the ugly things he'd said about Mickey McThacker . And me? I was scared to death that he was gonna up and say that Ellie was my sister or something like that.

He cleared his throat then went on, "My old man didn't want me having nothing to do with her. Threatened to cut me out of his will, oh, but I was stuck on her, Frankie."

"So what ever happened?" I asked.

"Your momma happened," he said. "I won't lie to you. I've never been a good man. I was a drunk. Still am a lot of the time. I was a bigger drinker back then than I am now, though. Reckon I was young. Reckon maybe I saw too much stuff in the war and liquor can make a man forget things. If there was a party anywhere in the county, I was there."

"Anyway, one night I got drunker than a skunk, so drunk I didn't know who I was, where I was or who I was with. I reckon my buddies thought it'd be funny to slip a little something extra in my drink and so they did. I woke up in Buck Jacob's old farm house with your momma. I didn't love her, Frankie. I didn't even really know her, but somebody had paid her to do what she did."

That stopped me in my tracks. My parents had met because Daddy was drunk and somebody paid Momma to sleep with him? No wonder Momma was screaming mad when we had left the house. No wonder she never wanted me to know the truth about her past. I felt like I was going to puke and grabbed hold of my stomach.

"Son, my old man knew I had a mind to marry Irene Falling Leaf and he didn't want me marrying no Indian from Swamp Holler. Our family had a name to uphold and your momma's family was looked up to. So to this day I believe my daddy paid her to do it just so I wouldn't marry Irene."

"Not long afterward your momma came to me and said she was expecting and that to protect both our family names we should get married. I thought she was carrying my baby, so I went to Irene and told her that I had to do what I had to do. I confessed all about getting drunk and waking up in that old house."

I had never seen my dad cry before, but I was sure that if there had been enough light in the woods I would have seen tears in his eyes, because his voice cracked in a way that I had heard only once and that was at my granny's funeral.

"I married her. Turned out we didn't even have a baby."

"You mean she lied?"

He shrugged. "Oh, I don't know. She said she lost the baby, on account of being poorly. So, I felt bad for her. The first few years of our marriage wasn't all that bad, Frankie. Before long she was expecting again and you came to be with us. I named you after the best president we ever had. Then I went to work as a state highway man, making pretty good money and getting in good with local politicians and the weeks just turned into years and before I knew what was happening, it was like Eugene says, I was with a woman that the Lord Jesus himself would have a hard time living with and nothing I did was good enough and the house that we built with

208

our own hands wasn't big enough. She was embarrassed by our truck, by the clothes I wore, by me."

"But you stayed together," I said. "You must care about each other a little bit."

"What do you want me to say, Frankie? That I love her?" I heard him take a deep breath. "I didn't stay for her, boy. I know I never said it before and I ain't good with words, but leaving her meant leaving the only thing I ever did right in my whole life.

"In the meantime Irene married Mooney McThacker and I suppose that lil gal Ellie was born to them about a year or so after we had you. Ellie ain't your sister or nothing like that. So don't be fretting over it. The big secret we been keeping from you ain't about Ellie. It's about your momma and," he stopped and took a deep breath, "I reckon it's mostly about you."

He handed me his flashlight, leaned against the shack, lit a cigarette and took a long deep draw off of it. This man talking to me was a stranger who had taken over the broken, empty, and angry person that used to be my dad. He flicked the newly formed ashes from the glowing tip of his cigarette. "Somewhere along the way I reckon I just gave up, quit caring about how I looked or what people thought. All I wanted was to get away from the house and the nagging. I thought a million times about running away, Frankie, about going to the city. Once, back before I went to the war, a man came through here and heard me picking my guitar and singing, offered me a job in Chicago.

"I should've took it, but people said that kind of music was of the devil and that if I signed that contract, I'd be signing away my own soul. "

"I didn't know," I said.

"I don't play no more," he said. "I ain't played to speak of since I met your momma. It ain't a Chicago honky tonk what stole my soul, Frankie. T'wouldn't the devil neither. It was a marriage license. I married your momma cause I wanted to protect a family name. I made a promise, Frankie, and a man's only as good as his word, but in tryin' to protect that name, I became a liar and a hypocrite. I should've left her when I found out the truth, but I didn't. I couldn't. Learning the truth didn't change the way I felt about you and I tried not to care for you, son, but ten years of loving a boy don't quit upon finding an old love letter to somebody else."

"What letter?" I shook so much that the light from the flashlight was dancing all over the wall of the old shack. There is an emotion that comes with finding out that your parents never loved each other and that your dad gave up a career in music to protect a family name he no longer believed in. It's a nameless emotion that leaves you numb and floating. That's the way it was for me by this point. Udell Dawson's death, Mickey's arrest, my mother's fit and now the revelations my dad was sharing with me was more than my mind could hold and I felt like my head was going to float off my body.

Then my dad up and said, "Frankie, your momma was unfaithful to me. She had a love affair with Udell Dawson that spanned about six years of our marriage. When I was away, working on the road, he'd come over. I found a letter and though I couldn't read, my sister could. She told me what was in the letter. She said your momma told Udell that she believed you were his boy, not mine."

I knew it was coming, but still it hit me so hard that I started backing up, trying to catch my breath. I needed room. I had the whole outside world, but I needed room to breathe. The pole that Rusty Dawson had hit me with did not do as much damage as the words my dad had just spoken.

"No," I said. "That's not true." I heard myself scream the words. "No, you just made that up. You're my dad. You have to be my dad."

He took a step toward me. "Listen to me, boy. It don't change nothin'. I raised you. Far as I'm concerned you're my boy."

"No," I said. "I'm not a Dawson. Don't you ever say that again. You hear? Never." Some things in a person's life stump him so bad that all he can do is just walk around in circles, jerking and flapping his arms, which is what I commenced to doing. I wanted to die right then and there. It wasn't real. It was some nightmare. I took off running. Maybe if I ran far enough and fast enough I'd fall down and wake up. I'd find myself in my bed and it'd still be the first day of school and there'd be milking to do and none of the craziness would have ever happened.

"Frankie, come back here," my dad was yelling and trying to run after me. But I didn't go back. I kept running as hard and as fast as I could through the woods, tree limbs swatting me in the face, catching my sleeves. I tripped, got up and kept running. I still had the flashlight in my hand but I wasn't paying attention to its light, I just ran. I came to the open field beyond Eugene's garden spot and kept running. I ran until I was completely out of breath and far from the house, until I ran straight into the creek about a mile down the holler from our house.

I stood there, freezing cold water up to my hips, a little silver flashlight in my hand and tears streaming down my face. I was a grown man and grown men weren't supposed to cry, but I did not feel like a grown man. I felt like a baby, a baby whose entire world had just been taken away. In that moment I realized that being the son of Ancil Keilman had been the single most important aspect of my whole life and now that was gone. I was nobody, a bastard child.

My momma was a glorified whore and my daddy wasn't even my daddy. My real dad was the meanest, most awful man who had ever walked Briar Ridge. Now he was dead and my best friend was being sent to prison for killing him. I folded at the knees and went under the cold water. I wanted to stop thinking, stop breathing, to die, but a Sunday school lesson about how suicides went to hell came back to my mind and I leaped up out of the water. It was a reflex, operated by fear of being in the torment I was experiencing forever without end. Maybe Hell was an eternity of nights like the one I was living. I couldn't take that chance.

I started walking again. I wasn't sure where I was going. I couldn't go home. I couldn't bear to see Momma's face. No wonder my dad laid out so often at night. He carried all of those horrible secrets in his heart and now, I was carrying them, too.

Chapter Twenty-Two

I guess I walked over an hour, wandering around like a mole in the sunshine until my feet brought me to Brother Van Dyke's house. I could hear Miss Mays telling me not to trust anyone, but at the moment, trusting this man seemed like the only thing I could do.

I banged on the door and he answered it. I must have looked like a drowned pup. "Frankie, son, what on earth has happened to you? Martha, honey, get this boy a dry towel."

I looked up and caught a glimpse of my reflection in their hall tree mirror. My face was covered in scratches and had blood all over it. Mrs. Van Dyke ran into the room with towels and Brother Van Dyke started drying me with them. That's when it happened. I broke. I broke so completely that I sat down on their floor and told them everything. I told them about Rusty Dawson trying to rape Liddie Grace, and about Miss Mays with a gun. I told them the truth about my busted ribs, about Udell Dawson being murdered, about Mickey being arrested." When I had told all I could tell, I sat there numb, staring at the legs on that hall tree. Blood dripped from my face and fell on my forearm but I lacked the energy to wipe it away.

My pastor squatted beside me and put his arm around my shoulder. "Frankie," he said, "the Bible says that the Lord is an ever present help in a time of trouble and I'd say this qualifies as a time of trouble. It says in Psalm 20 that He will answer us when we call on

Him and that He will save us with the saving strength of His right hand."

"My momma wanted me to be a preacher. What a joke," I choked up then and didn't say anything for a few minutes. "What would God want with me?"

"He is no respecter of persons, Frankie. His love for you has not changed."

"But Udell Dawson is my father."

"No, he's only the man who had an affair with your mother. The man who raised you, who stayed for your sake, who's out there looking for you right now, that man is your father."

"I don't know what to do next," I said.

"We're going to start by cleaning those scratches on your face," Mrs. Van Dyke said. "Then we are going to get you some dry clothes."

Brother Van Dyke stood. "The woman has spoken." He smiled at her and she smiled back.

While he doctored my face, she found some of his "old" things that he had outgrown, meaning he had gained so much weight that he could no longer wear them. She brought me a pair of tan slacks and a flannel shirt. I went into a bedroom and changed.

"Have a seat there on the couch," Brother Van Dyke said as I came out. I did. Martha Van Dyke brought me a cup of black coffee.

"I think," the preacher said, "that the right thing to do is to call your parents and tell them that I have seen you and that you are safe."

"I don't want to see them right now," I said. "I just can't. Not yet. Especially not her." I couldn't even bring myself to say 'Momma'.

"I understand," he said. "But I'm concerned about your...father. If he's not there, I will go find him."

"Okay," I said. "Could you take me down to Swamp Holler? I really need to talk to Ellie's folks. I feel like I owe them that."

He nodded. Thenhe picked up the phone.

I heard the phone ringing through the receiver. Then I heard my mother's voice on the other end. "Hello."

"Yes, Mrs. Keilman. This is Brother Van Dyke and I'm just calling to let you know that Frankie came by here and he wanted me to tell you that he's all right. He seemed quite upset about something but he wanted me to pass along to you that he is fine."

"Frankie...can you put him on the phone?" I shook my head. I wasn't going to talk to her, not even for the preacher's sake.

"No, ma'am. He just wanted me to tell you he's all right. Is your husband at home?"

"No," she said. "He's out in the truck looking for Frankie I suppose."

"All right. I'll meet up with him on the road. If he comes in, tell him Frankie's safe."

"Where'd Frankie go?" she asked.

"He asked me not to tell you," he said.

"If you're the man of God you claim to be then you'll tell me where my son is."

"I promised him, ma'am, and I can't break my word. Good-bye for now." He hung up and turned to me. "Let's go to Swamp Holler, but first I think we should pray."

So we bowed our heads and he prayed, "Lord, you are Frankie's help and your word promises that if we acknowledge you in all our ways then you will direct our paths and Frankie here, well, he's agreed to let me talk to you on his behalf. He's acknowledging you and we just thank you, Lord, that no matter how things look right now, everything is going to turn out the way it should." He said some other things, too, but I was too nervous to hear them all. Then he said, "amen."

I got in the station wagon with Brother Van Dyke. I had him drop me off on the side of the main highway at the head of Swamp Holler. I told him that it might be better if he didn't drive all way up to the house on account of I didn't want anybody asking questions. I wasn't ready to share about my family yet. I thanked him for his help then started up the lane which led to the little cluster of shacks where the Pablos and all their kin lived.

Half a dozen dogs ran out barking at me as I walked toward Joe's house, including the scrawny little mutt that had been there before. There was a light inside. I could see it through the half-covered window above the porch. I heard excited voices coming from inside and I knew the whole family was worked up over what was going on with Mickey. They had no idea who I really was and I wasn't about to tell them. All they needed to know right now was that I was with them, that I was there to help in any way I could.

When I stepped up on that porch my heart was beating so hard I thought it would knock a hole clean through my chest. I wanted to run but there was no place to go. I couldn't go home. I didn't know when I would be able to go home again. Joe Pablo answered the door. "Come on in, Frankie. What happened to your face?"

"Fell in the woods," I said. "It's not important right now."

He stepped back and I entered the house. Sadie Rose sat on the couch, along with Granny Flor and Jewell. Jim Elee stood in the bedroom doorway, leaning on the lentil, several more cousins and relatives stood around, solemn-faced, chewing tobacco and smoking cigarettes. Oscar Pablo sat against the wall with his chair leaning on its back legs. "Son, you ought not to be here," he said. "There's trouble brewing that you don't want to be mixed up in."

"Yes, sir," I know," I said, "But way I figure it, Mickey's my friend and I know he didn't kill anybody."

A silence fell over everyone and uneasiness hung in the air, then Sadie Rose got up from her seat on the couch. "Well, Frankie, ye might as well have some coffee while you're here."

She went into the kitchen and poured me a cup of coffee so strong that a spoon could have stood upright in it. The loud talking I'd heard from outside resumed.

"Lord, Lord," Granny Flor wailed. "Our poor Mickey. T'aint no way to get him out of this."

"It's just his word against the Dawson boys."

"What're we gonna do?" Jim Elee said. His eyes were red and it was obvious that he'd been crying over what was happening with Mickey. "Poor lil Ellie, they're liable to lock her up, too, on account of her part in the shining."

"Hush now," Jewell Eastridge said. "Nobody can prove that Ellie was involved in anything."

"Well, we're just going to have to tell that judge that Mickey didn't do it," Joe said.

"No judge around here's gonna listen to us, ain't no jury gonna try Mickey fair, neither. Which one of us are they gonna put up on the witness stand and believe," Jim Elee said.

"They'd believe me," Granny Flor spoke up.

"You're an old Mexican woman," Oscar said. "Do you have any idea how far an old Mexican woman's word would go?"

"Then let me testify," I blurted.

They all looked at me, coffee cups frozen in mid drink. Then Oscar put the legs of his chair on the floor. "You'd do that, son?"

"I would. I will," I said.

"But you're from Briar Ridge," Sadie Rose said. "Frankie, honey, we all preciate what you're trying to do but you ain't got no dog in this fight."

"Your dog is my dog," I said. Everybody kept staring at me then Granny Flor up and laughed. Then Joe laughed and Jewell, too. In spite of all of their problems and the terrible reality that Mickey might go to prison for a murder he didn't commit, the Pablo clan was laughing. Then I laughed, too. One of the little dark complexioned boys, a cousin, I figured, broke off a chew from his twist of tobacco and handed it to me. I looked around that room, white faces, brown faces, pink faces, all part of the same mixed up family, all with one concern, what would become of their Mickey and Ellie? I wished the whole world were like the Pablos. They didn't see color or skin shades. They only saw family and above all else, they were loyal to theirs. I almost cried then, wishing that it was Pablo blood flowing through my veins and not Dawson blood. I would take that secret to the grave with me. No one would ever know. I knew it was wrong to hate, but that night I did hate. I hated that I had Dawson in me.

"Your folks will never stand for it," Granny Flor said.

I looked at her deep wrinkled brown face and at the sincerity in her dark eyes. "I don't live there anymore," I said. "I've moved to a house across the woods from my cousin Eugene. My parents don't tell me what to do anymore." And in that moment I meant that, I had made up my mind in the span of time that it took me to make that statement. When I left the Pablos I would go home, gather my few belongings and go stay in the shack. Just then we heard a car pull up and everyone froze. I suppose we were afraid it was the law coming back. Oscar shot Joe a glance and both men went to the door.

"I'm looking for a kid named Frankie Keilman," I heard someone say, 'Is he here?'"

"That depends," Joe said. He took a puff off the cigarette he was holding. "Who are you and what do you want him?"

"Name's Mays," he said, "Martin Mays."

I sat my coffee on the stove tin and walked to the door with uncertainty. Joe and Oscar stepped aside and let me out.

"I'm Frankie."

He grinned. "There's the fella that pumped my gas. Would you consider riding up to the jail with me? Ellie's asking for you."

I looked back and Joe and Oscar. They gave me a nod, a go ahead. I walked over to the car. "How'd you know where to find me?"

He grinned. "A fat little preacher man called me."

"Brother Van Dyke?"

"Don't worry, kid. He's one of the good guys."

I got in the car with Mr. Mays. "Where's your brother?" I asked after he'd gotten in.

He started the car and drove out of sight from the house before he said, "At the jail with Mickey. They didn't want to appoint the boy a lawyer, but Jerry's taking the case."

"Jerry's a lawyer?"

"You might say that."

"And you?" I asked.

He nodded. "Senior partner."

"Are y'all gonna help Mickey?"

"We're going to do our best."

"Why? I mean why are you all helping the McThackers? You're not even from here."

"Well, it's a long story."

"Please, tell it to me," I said, "Right now nothing could shock or surprise me much."

He smiled, "All right. As you know Eadie, Miss Mays as you call her, came back here to take care of our great-aunt-Gertrude

219

who raised my daddy. So you are right to say that we're not from here, only we are from here in a roundabout way.

"My old man and McThacker had a deal going. You see after my daddy's family died in that house fire, Great-Aunt-Gertrude took him in and raised him as her own kid, but he was a troubled youngster and he fell in with the wrong crowd. To make a long story short, they would have killed my daddy if Mooney McThacker hadn't stepped in and stood up for him. Afterwards, Pops moved to Lexington, started a business, got married and raised three children, one teacher and two lawyers. He never forgot Mooney McThacker and the two of them remained tight for years. He helped McThacker establish a clientele in the city, but then one day McThacker stopped making deliveries and Mickey showed up, being driven by the Dawsons at the time. My old man knew something was up, but he didn't know what. Mickey's stories never held water.

"Time went on and Great-Aunt-Gertrude got down. A teaching job opened up at the Crooked Springs School so Eadie agreed to take that job so she could take care of Great-Aunt Gertrude. In the meantime, she got close to the little McThacker girl, and when she started telling us about Ellie and Mickey, well, we put two and two together. We decided to take a vacation down here and poke around. One thing about the Mays you need to know, Frankie, we always repay our debts. No matter how long it takes. My old man, sick as he now is, insists on getting to the truth about what happened to Mooney McThacker and now, well, Mooney's boy is in a heap of trouble. If Jerry and I can't bail him out, our dad is going to seriously regret all the years he worked to send us to school. He may even write us out of his will." He grinned, then added. "I've got to do this for my old man, kid. You understand?"

I nodded. I did understand.

"Good. I'm going to need you to tell me everything you know about Mickey, about Ellie, about Briar Ridge, about the Dawsons, about anything and everybody you know."

"I can start by telling you that Mickey didn't kill anybody."

"Good, but that doesn't prove anything. We need evidence, kid, and lots of it. The deck is stacked against Mickey just because of who he is. Jerry and I are going to need your help if we aim to bring Dawson's real murderer to light and prove Mickey innocent."

"I'll do whatever it takes," I said.

Chapter Twenty-Three

Ellie met us on the jail house steps. She jumped up when she saw me get out of the car. Martin Mays motioned for her to follow us and we turned and walked down the street a piece rather than going in the jail.

"Where we going?" I asked. "Mickey's back there."

"The jail has ears," he said. "I want to talk to you kids some place unnoticed." We rounded the corner and came upon Greely's Motel, a three story building that had stood behind the jail since the town was formed back in the early 1800s. Martin Mays took us up to a motel room, unlocked the door and let us in. A low bed, covered in a gold spread, sat along one wall and a chair with a small table sat near the draped window.

"Have a seat, kids." He motioned toward the bed. Ellie and I both sat down on the edge.

"You can't be seen with Mickey or Ellie in public," he said to me. "Life's got to go on like usual for you, Frankie, in order for my plans to work out right. You understand?"

"Not really," I said. Martin smiled and paced the floor with his hands in his pants pockets. Then the door opened and in walked

Miss Mays and Jerry. For the next hour or so they talked to me and Ellie. They told us things that made my blood run cold and they told me what I had to do in order to play my part in rescuing Mickey from the authorities.

My part included going back home, which I did at two o'clock in the morning when Martin Mays, wearing a full blown suit and tie, walked up the drive with me, knocked on the door and waited for my dad to answer.

Daddy opened the door, wearing his long johns so I know he had been in bed. Momma came into the room, wearing her curlers and house coat.

"Frankie," my dad said. "What's going on?"

"I'm Martin Mays. Mr. Keilman, I need to come with me."

"Oh, Lord, Ancil. It's the FBI. You're going to prison," Momma wailed.

"No, ma'am," Martin said, "we just need to talk in private. Frankie," he looked to me, "go on up to your room." I obeyed. I had given my word that I'd do whatever it took to save Mickey and that meant trusting Martin and Jerry Mays. In my room, I looked around. Nothing in that room was truly mine, only the clothes on the wall hooks and a big black Bible on the night stand. How could I have spent my entire life there and have nothing to call my own? I decided right then and there that as soon as it was daylight, I was moving in with Eugene until I could get my shack to where it was livable.

The next thing I knew I was waking up and the sun was beaming in through the window. I looked at the clock, ten o'clock. Neither of my parents had bothered to wake me. That meant Daddy and Eugene had long finished the milking. I didn't waste any time taking my few clothes off the hook and stuffing them into a pillow case. I rolled up my quilt and stacked it on top my pillow. That was it. All my worldly possessions, a pillow, a quilt and a pillow case with three pair pants, four shirts, some socks, underwear and a Bible in it. I was ready to live on my own.

I gathered my things and went downstairs. Momma was in the kitchen. I stood there at the foot of the stairs, watching her, because she hadn't seen me come down and with the radio playing, she hadn't heard me either. She sat at the table with a cup of coffee in front of her and a cigarette in her hand, which was resting on her forehead, like she was worried or had a headache. Her face was etched with lines. She took a puff off the cigarette and stared at nothing, then she puffed some more and moved her coffee around with her other hand.

Her whole life she had manipulated others and plotted to obtain a better lot for herself in life. Despite her ambitions, life had not given her the things she wanted, a fine house with gigantic columns, new furniture, fine clothes and a rich husband who worshipped her. My dad's property and money had long faded in comparison to the wealth of others like the McAllisters. For the first time I could remember I honestly felt sorry for Momma, not because she had such a rough life, but because she had wasted so many years pursuing a fantasy while letting the one man who could have, would have, loved her, whither and fade into a worn-out drunk. Momma had crushed Ancil Keilman's spirit.

Was I ever anything to her? Even my birth had been some sort of manipulative mind game. That's what life had been to her, a game. And I was an illegitimate token to be moved around and manipulated so that life would give her the things she wanted? Did she ever love me at all? I mean surely at some point she had held me and cuddled me, had fed me and bathed me.

She happened to look in my direction. "Frankie, I didn't see you standing there."

Then she looked at the pillow case full of clothes. "You going somewhere?"

"I'm leaving," I said.

225

She scoffed, "leaving? Where you gonna go? Down there to Swamp Holler to live with the Pablos and McThackers? Murderers, coloreds, gypsies, thieves...trash."

"I'll be eighteen before spring. I'll go where I wanna go."

"Just like your father," she spat. "You don't care about me or my needs. All you can think of is that little piece of filth..."

"Just like my father!" I hollered at her. "Filth. You should talk."

"Do you really think Udell Dawson is your daddy?" she snapped. "I wouldn't let that dirty piece of poop lay a hand on me. You don't know everything, Frankie." She took a puff off her cigarette. "McAllister paid me to write those letters, paid me to marry your dad and has been paying me for twenty years to keep my mouth shut."

"What?" I lost my footing and fell backwards. "Why?"

"Seems like your daddy thinks he knows something on Elbert McAllister that could cause a lot of stink for our family and his, too. So, McAllister slipped me some money and in return I agreed to say that I had an affair with Udell Dawson, fake a letter and remind your daddy every time he got drunk and threatened to tell something ridiculous on McAllister that the truth would come out and our family name would be ruint for life."

I must have looked as confused as I felt. Because she cackled a pathetic little laugh. "Yeah, that's right, son. I've done a lot for money, but Lord knows we needed it. Your daddy's farm don't make that much and what it does make, he drinks up. He's your real daddy all right. Can't you tell? You act just like him? All my hopes of you making something of yourself went out the window the moment you laid your eyes on that McThacker girl. What? Didn't you ever wonder why we never had more children? I'll tell you why. The day that McThacker woman died he blamed me for ruining his life and he's hated me ever since. Only reason we stayed together was you. And now, we don't have that." She put her cigarette out and looked at me. "Well, go on. Go live with Eugene if that's what you want."

I turned and walked out the front door, letting the screen slam shut behind me. I knew I would never live here again. If it makes me a sissy that I cried tears of anger that day, then I confess to being a sissy. I spent the whole afternoon working in my cabin. Eugene helped me. I didn't tell him everything. I just told him that I couldn't live with the fighting anymore and that was something he understood.

The next day I got up and went to work at Goodin's Store.

I was slicing pickle bologna for a customer, Mrs. Wattle, when the topic of Dawson's murder came up. Mrs. Wattle was an elderly woman with a lot of pull in the church and the school system, since her son was the superintendent.

"Lordy, Meredith, what's this world coming to," she said, "when an upstanding citizen is murdered right here on the ridge."

Upstanding? She had to be kidding. Dawson was a mean man and his boys were mean boys, but it didn't matter to these people, because he wasn't from Swamp Holler. He was still better than a McThacker in their eyes.

"I told Frankie here," Mrs. Goodin said, "that no good would come of that McThacker boy. Now mind you, I never cared much for Udell Dawson but to think that boy could murder him in cold blood like that, well, it's unthinkable."

I played ignorant. "So, have they found him guilty already?"

"Haven't you heard?" Mrs. Wattle said. "They found McThacker's boot prints all over the place around Dawson's house. Then they found the same boots sitting on McThacker's porch. If that isn't proof, what is?"

I cringed. I couldn't defend Mickey, not yet. I couldn't tell these two sweet little busybodies that I knew the truth about Mickey's boots.

I continued to work for Mrs. Goodin in the coming weeks. I had to walk to work but I didn't mind, and when the topic of Mickey McThacker and the murder came up as it often did, I would find a job to do outside, pump gas, wash windows, split wood, anything to keep me busy and to keep me from having to talk to people.

I also went back to school and so did Ellie. But word of Mickey's deed had spread all over the ridge and everybody was terrified of Ellie. Little kids ran from her when she walked into the school yard. Without Liddie Grace there to spur them on the teenage girls didn't have a thing to say to her. They simply glared at her with fear and hatred in their eyes and whispered as she walked by. Even Idy Jo was skittish and only gave Ellie a nod.

At lunch Ellie went to her old spot under the tree while the others gathered at the table. I rounded the corner and saw that Ellie by herself. I went over and took a seat beside her. We exchanged glances. "What are you doing?" she hissed.

"Acting normal," I said. "I always eat with you."

Harlan came over and tapped me on the shoulder. "I need to talk to you, Franklin." He used my real name so I knew something was bothering him.

I walked with him to the ball field. "Um, Frankie, look. Don't you know about her brother? He killed Rusty Dawson's old man."

"So, I heard," I said. "But she didn't kill anybody."

"She's one of them, Frankie. When you gonna realize that?"

"One of who?"

"Don't be ignorant," he said. "Daddy says that the McThackers and the Pablos, all of em, they're marauding Melungeons."

"What?" I said. I had never heard such terminology in my life.

"Daddy said he'd been cutting timber down in Hawkins, Tennessee, and came up on a bunch of people they called Melungeons. They all lived up in the hills and ran shine, just like Ellie's bunch. He said they's all colors and had peculiar ways. I'm telling you, Frankie, they steal and take what they want. He said they're like Gypsies or something and nobody knows where they came from or how they got here. These McThackers and Pablos, they're just like that, too. Nobody knows where they came from. They say they're Mexican, but part of them are black or Indian or something other. I know. I've seen em with my own eyes. Stay away from these people, Cousin."

"All colors you say?"

"That's right."

"Hmph," I said. "Well, at least we know they're not prejudices against white people, now don't we?"

"You make a joke out of it," he said, "but for once in your life you better be serious. I can't be hanging around you if you're gonna hang around her and neither can anybody else around here. I mean it was all right before but now…now there's been a man killed and things have changed."

The next day Ellie met me on my way to school. She stepped out from behind a tree near the same spot where I had saved Liddie Grace from Rusty Dawson. I nearly jumped out of my skin.

"Ellie, what on earth are you doing out here alone? It's dangerous for Mickey McThacker's sister to be anywhere alone right now."

She didn't answer. She just started bawling.

I put both my arms around her. "Ellie, what on earth is wrong." She cried a few more seconds then she pulled back.

"I've been asked to leave the school, Frankie. The sheriff and the superintendent came out to Granny Flor's last night looking for me. They said that I would have to go on homebound until this whole thing blows over and then they said they'd be sending somebody out to investigate and talk to my daddy. I told them he wasn't there, that he was working down in Georgia." Then I knew the reason for her tears. Mooney McThacker's death had never been reported and when they found out they would try to pin it on Mickey, too.

"Okay, here's what you do," I said. "If they come back, tell them your daddy's logging in Georgia and will be gone for months. Tell them you don't know how to reach him and that he's left you in Granny Flor's care. Don't you worry, Ellie. I'll talk to Miss Mays today and she'll know what to do. If she doesn't her brothers will." I walked Ellie back to the edge of Swamp Holler then returned to school, late.

At recess Harlan said, "You were awful late this morning."

"Eugene's hog got out," I said. "Took a while to pin him up." I felt a stab of guilt. I wasn't good at lying.

"Have you heard?"

"Heard what? I've been pinning a hog."

"Your little girlfriend, she's not coming back."

"I hate to hear it," I said. "I reckon life sure gets messy sometimes."

After school I stayed behind to help Miss Mays clean the room. When I was sure everyone was gone I told her about meeting Ellie in the woods and about what had happened.

"Hmph," she said. "Don't you fret, Frankie. I'm going to be Ellie's homebound teacher. I'll call the superintendent right away and put in a request to be allowed to deliver her books and lessons to her."

Next morning Miss Mays came around to mark one of my papers and wrote me a note on it that said, "Mission accomplished." I knew what she meant and nodded my approval. So it was that my teacher devised clever ways to get messages to me regarding Ellie and Mickey.

The next few weeks were lonely for me. At school I had to be aloof. I helped Miss Mays teach the little kids. I would take them into a back corner and give them their Spelling test. I taught the fourth graders how to do long division and stayed late every day to help Miss Mays clean the building and make sure that the fire was out. Any talking that I did was only to her and we would always make sure that nobody else was around. On more than one occasion she told me that Mickey's court date had been moved, put off.

At my cabin I was always alone. I worked to make sure there were no holes in the wall and managed to get the old well pump out back to working properly so that I could have water. Eugene had rigged me up a heat stove and whenever I had a spare moment I was chopping wood for the winter. I worked at the store on Saturdays and after work, I would walk up to Brother Van Dyke's just to watch westerns with him and drink coffee. We didn't talk anymore about my late night visit, but he always prayed with me before I left, asking the Lord to protect me and keep me from all harm. Then Mrs. Van Dyke would give me some fruit cake or ham or a jar of jelly. She said that just because I was a man on my own now, didn't mean that I couldn't enjoy home cooking.

On Sundays, while everyone on the ridge was at church, I would sneak down to Swamp Holler to see my friends. Mr. Mays had told me not to be seen with Ellie, but he hadn't said a word about me seeing her.

One warm afternoon in December we took a walk down the gravel road that ran along in front of Granny Flor's house, past the Pablo place and on out to the main highway. Then we turned and walked across the cornfield and came out at the bottom of a bluff. We decided to climb that bluff and by the time we got to the top we were ready to sit down and catch our breath. We flopped down under an old apple tree near the edge of another cornfield.

Ellie leaned back against the tree. "Sometimes when I close my eyes," she said, "I can see a place I ain't never been before. It's by an ocean somewhere and you know what, Frankie?"

Her voice sounded so far away, farther than the Great Wall of China or the jungles of Africa. There was magic in it. "No, what, Ellie?"

"I can see myself standing in a white room and the floor is made out of dark brown planks with knots all in them and there's a big old table with just a few dabs of paint left on it and an open window with a plain white curtain a blowin' in the wind and there's a door. That door's a standin' wide open, too. I reckon it must never rain in that place. Oh, and I can hear the ocean, just crashing against the shore somewhere close by. And you know what else? I'm happy there. I'm never afraid of the sheriff running in to arrest somebody or that somebody's going burn my house down. I just feel so peaceful. There are birds that fly over the ocean. It's a beautiful place and when I open my eyes I'm sad, because it's only in my mind."

"Maybe it's your kingdom by the sea," I said. "Can I come, too, Ellie?"

"Of course you can and we can live off fish and shells and eggs we find on a cliff somewhere."

We sat under that maple tree for a long time, not talking too much, because of all the hurt we were both feeling and because we were both imagining that place Ellie saw in her mind and I could see it, too. Oh, how I wanted to go there. As far as I could tell there wasn't a much better place to be and there wasn't much better to do when your heart felt like somebody had run it through a sausage grinder than to imagine a place where people were better off.

"I can see Mickey in that place," she finally said. "He's walking along the shore, done took his jacket off on account of it never gets cold there and it don't rain neither."

I laid my hand on top of hers. "No, it never rains there and it never gets cold and we'll stay there forever and ever."

"We'll be just like Sam Greely," she said.

232

I looked at Ellie all leaned back against that tree, the sun on her face and a breeze blowing her hair. "No, no we won't be just like Sam," I said.

She looked at me with a question in her eyes.

"Sam was alone. We'll be together."

"Frankie, I..."

"I love you, Ellie, more than anything or anybody in this whole wide world. We got something special. I knew that the day I walked you home after I ripped my britches. Ever since that day I haven't been able to see my future without you in it. Whether we end up on a desert island together or in the jungles of Africa or on a bluff overlooking Swamp Holler, I want to be with you."

Chapter Twenty-Four

Christmas came and went. I had no money so I drew pictures for Ellie and her family. I couldn't even do that for my folks though, because they saw no use in my drawings. So, for Daddy and Eugene I did one day of milking all by myself. For Momma, I came home and suffered through Christmas dinner. I was thankful when it was over. January was cold and uneventful. I stayed in my cabin, even when it snowed. I piled on extra quilts that I'd gotten from Eugene at night and kept a wood stove going all of the time. I spent every minute of my spare time cutting and chopping wood. I had always been thin, but now I had grown muscular from living on my own.

The last week of February, Liddie Grace McAllister came back to school. She told everyone that it was because her daddy figured that it was safe now, since Udell Dawson was dead and his boys were being watched so closely by the law. She carried on like always, even talking about that murdering McThacker's sister in loud, snobbish tones whenever I was near. But, whenever I looked at her, I couldn't even feel anger. All I could feel was pity. She had no idea about the real world or about the lives her daddy's money had destroyed.

March second was my eighteenth birthday. I couldn't even bear to go home for a birthday supper. I was chopping kindling that afternoon when I looked up and saw a light blue pick-up truck mowing its way up the overgrown path, knocking down underbrush as it came. I saw my dad sitting up high in that truck and wondered what was going on.

He cut the engine and got out. "Reckon if a boy's old enough to live on his own, he's old enough to have his own truck." He handed me a key. "Happy birthday, boy."

"What? How?"

"Sold my coon dogs."

His words stunned me. "What?"

He looked down, hands in his pockets. "No," I said, shoving the key in his pockets. "Daddy, they're your coon dogs. I can't...I won't..."

He pulled the key back out and handed it to me, "Aw, son, take it. I'm done with coon hunting. I'm getting old, Frankie."

I took the key. "I don't know what to say."

"Well, you could take your old man for a spin. See how she runs."

"Get in," I said. We rode up the ridge and talked about how good the motor sounded and about the engine.

When we got back to the cabin he said. "Your momma wants you to come down to the house for a birthday supper, you being eighteen and all."

I laid my hand on the steering wheel. "Daddy, I can't."

"A grudge is a heavy thing," he said. "It'll drag ye down until you're as bitter and unhappy as she is. I reckon the only hope for this family is you. One of these days me and your momma will be both be dead and gone and I wouldn't want you living them days with regret in your heart."

236

I stared at the dashboard. For all of these years I thought my dad was weak, that he just didn't have the gall to lay down the bottle or the gumption to stand up to Momma, but now I knew the truth. He had stayed with a woman who didn't love him in order to raise a boy who may or may not have really been his own and alcohol had become an escape route. My hands shook, so I sat on them. "I don't care what those letters said. You are my real dad and that's all there is to it. I love you, Daddy. I love you all the way to the moon and back."

He shuffled around a bit, uncomfortable, then he blurted in a nervous voice. "I'm proud of you, Frankie. Always have been." He zipped his jacket and straightened his hat. "You coming to supper?"

"What do I say to her?"

"How about 'good chicken'?"

I drove us back down to the house and we ate supper with Momma who had piled her red hair high up on her head, put on her Sunday dress and red lipstick. We had fried chicken and mashed potatoes with biscuits and gravy.

When I had finished I looked at my dad who looked at me and then I said, "Good chicken, Momma."

She lit a cigarette. "I baked you a cake, Frankie. Lemon with white icing, your favorite."

It wasn't really my favorite. I liked chocolate best. Then Momma got the birthday cake out of the refrigerator. It was a little lopsided and said happy birthday in red icing. I blew out eighteen candles and we ate lemon cake with black coffee.

We ate in uncomfortable silence. Afterwards Momma got up and started clearing away the dishes. "Won't you stay the night, Frankie?"

"No, I'll head back up the holler here in a bit."

"If you want to come home I won't bother your drawings no more, won't even go in your room and you can come and go as you please. It's been awful lonesome around here since you been gone."

"I can't do that, Momma. I'm a grown man now. I need to be living on my own now."

"So you do. Well, I reckon you ought to have some curtains on your window. There's a set of checkered ones in that basket behind the door and a couple little braided rugs, too. Do you have any chairs to sit in?"

"Eugene gave me a chair and I've got his old feather tick to sleep on. I've got a wood stove and plenty of wood around the cabin. I'm warm. I'm dry. I got a well out back and I heat bath water on the stove so most of the time I'm clean, too."

"You got a table to eat off of?"

"Me and Eugene made me one. It works just fine. One table, one chair. I live by myself. That's about all I need."

"Well, I just hate to think of you up there all by yourself."

I didn't know if she really missed me or if this was some sort of ploy to manipulate me. "I'll come home on Saturday night to eat supper. How's that?"

She nodded. "And on Sunday. Won't you come to church on Sunday?"

"I'm laying low right now, Momma. You know that. I can't go to church cause I can't bring my girlfriend."

"Girlfriend?"

"I love her, Momma."

"You love a McThacker?"

"Yes. I do."

"You gonna marry her?"

I shrugged. "I don't know. We both want to go to college."

"She's going to college?"

"Yes."

"How? She ain't got no money."

238

"We'll find a way. If we have to we'll take turns, but that's her dream and mine. We both want to go to school and then..." I paused. Would she revert back to the sharp-tongue lashings I was used to if I told her?

"What?"

"We want to travel."

She started to say something but I cut her off.

"I don't live here anymore. I'm eighteen years old. I love Ellie McThacker. And I'll marry whomever I choose, if I choose."

She turned back to the sink. "Well, don't worry about me. Suit yourself. I'll be all right."

"Yes, you will," I said.

"Do you love me, Frankie?"

I froze. Did I? "Momma, it's just that I'm grown now. Even a bird leaves the nest when it's grown."

"But do you love me?"

"Of course I do. You're my mother."

I saw my parents on the following two Saturdays and then on a Monday, a deputy's car found my cabin in the woods via my parents then Eugene. He delivered me a summons to court. Mickey was finally going to trial and I was being called in as a witness.

I rode into town with my parents because they had been summoned to court, too. Our town courthouse was a good ten miles from our home. It was an old red brick Scottish design that sat in the middle of town with a road going all the way around it. Along all the sides buildings had been built to form a perfect square. So, it was said to be in the center of the town square. The building had been there since around 1811 and people told the story that a slave woman was once tried for murder there and hanged on the oak tree that still stood in front of the building.

As we entered the courtroom that day I had butterflies the size of flying pigs in my stomach. I had gone home to clean up for this occasion and was wearing my Sunday clothes. I kept fooling around with my tie and combing my hair. I wasn't really worried about my hair, but it gave my hands something to do.

The room was large with white walls and row after row of wooden benches. Of course, there was a little fence-like deal that separated where the judge and lawyers and all the legal people were from the rest of us. I scanned that room and the faces that turned to see who had come in. All the Pablos, Ellie and Miss Mays sat up near the front on the left side while the Dawsons sat on the right and those Dawsons looked mad. They wanted Mickey to go to the electric chair. Behind them, a few rows back, was the McAllister family. My dad slid into a seat about three rows back from the Pablos.

It seemed like we just sat there in that weird, uncomfortable silence forever and a day before a man got up and said, "All rise." So we did. Then he said, "The honorable Judge Passmore presiding." And that's when the judge came in. He was elderly with white hair and glasses that made me think of a hoot owl. He wore a long black thing that looked like a graduation gown. Then we were all seated. Mickey McThacker's murder trial had begun.

Chapter Twenty-Five

The trial had gone on for some time with a recess here and there. Things didn't look good for Mickey. The prosecuting attorney, Hiram Dempsey, was a longtime friend of the sheriff and everybody knew it and both men were in big with Elbert McAllister. He had called Meredith Goodin to the stand who made it look like Mickey was always trying to steal from her and then he had called several other citizens of Briar Ridge who had testified to hearing Mickey threaten Udell in public.

Then he went over to the table and picked up Mickey's boots, the very boots that had been stolen from him. "Boy, are these your boots?"

"Yes," Mickey leaned forward, "um, yes sir. They are."

"And were you wearing these the night you murdered Udell Dawson?"

"Objection!" Jerry Mays shouted.

Mickey narrowed his eyes. "No, sir. I was not wearing those boots because I never killed Udell Dawson."

"Are you aware that boot prints matching yours, even down to the size and sole designs, were found all around Dawson's house?"

"Yes, sir, but my boots had been missing for some time, then the same night Dawson was killed they just turned up on my doorstep."

Mr. Dempsey laughed and then turned to the jury, shaking his head. His every body movement seemed to mock Mickey, as if he was trying not only to convict him of killing Udell Dawson, but to convince those folks that Mickey wasn't as good as other people. He whirled back around at Mickey. "You mean to tell me that somebody went to the trouble of finding his way down to Swamp Holler in the middle of the night, stealing your boots, wearing them to kill Udell Dawson, then brought them back to you with the mud from Udell's yard still on them and put them back on your doorstep?"

"Yes," Mickey said. "That's what I'm telling you."

A few of those people in the jury shook their heads like they thought Mickey was telling them the lie of the century.

Mr. Dempsey smiled and stuck his fingers through the belt loops on his pants. He reared back and stuck his chest out in obvious satisfaction then he turned to Jerry Mays. "Your witness, councilman."

Jerry stood. He looked too young to be a lawyer but he walked with all the confidence of a full blown gun-slinger as he approached that witness stand. "Mr. McThacker," he said, "you say that your boots were stolen. Can you tell us where you were when your boots were taken?"

Mickey nodded. "I was laid up with a bullet hole in my back."

"And how long were you 'laid up'?"

"Over four weeks."

"No further questions from the witness, your honor. If it pleases the court, I'd like to call Franklin Delano Keilman to the stand."

The judge gave his approval.

I felt like my heart had dropped down into my socks. My legs shook so badly that it was a miracle that I could walk to that

242

witness stand. The fellow with the Bible came over and I put my hand on it and swore to tell the truth, whole truth and nothing but the truth.

"Now, Frankie," Jerry Mays said. "Is it true that you are studying to enter the ministry?"

"Objection," Dempsey shouted. "Your honor, I don't see the relevance in this question."

Jerry spun around, arms out. "Your honor, I am merely trying to establish credibility."

"Objection sustained. Stick to only that which pertains to the case, Councilman."

Jerry turned back to me. "Frankie, can you tell the ladies and gentlemen of the jury what happened to you on the afternoon of September 27th as you walked home from school?"

"Yes, sir," my voice came out all squeaky. "I had just left school and was walking home, talking to Ellie McThacker, who is a classmate when all of a sudden Mickey McThacker came crawling out of the underbrush. He was shot in the back and bleeding."

"So you are saying that Mickey McThacker truly was shot in the back?"

"Yes, I saw it with my own eyes."

"Can you tell us what happened next?"

"Yessir, we got help from Mr. Jackson who hauled Mickey home in his car where I held him down while his granny picked a bullet out of his back. Then Jim Elee Pablo brought a doctor in, that man right over there." I pointed to the doctor.

At that time Jerry said he had no more questions and Dempsey was allowed to question me. He leaned over the rail and got real close to me.

"Now, Frankie," he said, "did you say that you were walking with Ellie McThacker?"

"I did."

"Is it true that the two of you have been going steady?"

I swallowed. I hadn't thought of it like that. "We walk home together," I said. "We talk about school and books we like to read."

"So you could say that you are very sympathetic to the McThacker point of view?"

"Objection," Jerry shouted. "Your honor, he's leading the witness."

"Objection sustained," the judge said.

"Very well," Dempsey said. "No further questions from the witness at this time.

Next, he called Granny Flor to the stand and tried to make it look like she had exaggerated about the seriousness of Mickey's wound, but when Jerry got the witness he questioned her in such a way that left no doubt that Granny knew a thing or two about bullet wounds.

After a recess Jerry called the doctor to the stand. He asked him if he had treated Mickey at home in September for a gunshot wound. The doctor, fidgeted and looked like he was scared half to death, but he said that he had.

"And how serious to you believe this wound to have been? Could it have been serious enough to require a month or longer healing time?"

"Oh, yes, I suppose it would," the doctor said.

"I submit to you, ladies and gentlemen of the jury that if Mickey McThacker was shot in late September that he would not have been capable of walking all the way from his home in Swamp Holler up the hills of Briar Ridge and murdering Udell Dawson less than a month later."

Court was adjourned for the day.

The next day Dempsey called all sorts of people to testify to the fact that Mickey ran liquor. He had more people testify that Mickey had threatened Udell Dawson on more than one occasion.

Jerry didn't seem to be rattled by any of it. He was the coolest, scariest individual I'd ever met in my life.

Then Jerry called me to the stand.

"Frankie," he said, "have you ever seen these boots before?" He pointed to Mickey's boots sitting on the table.

"Yes. Not long after Mickey was shot I walked Ellie home from school. She took me in her house to show me her book collection. I was in the bedroom, behind the quilt over the door when Joe Pablo hollered. Ellie went to talk to him. I heard him tell Ellie that Mickey was all worked up on account of his boots had been stolen off the porch."

Dempsey was allowed to question me after that. "Frankie," he said, "did your parents know you were at Ellie McThacker's house?"

"No, sir, they did not."

"So is it possible that you and Ellie were doing something more than looking at books?"

"Objection!" Jerry shouted.

"Objection overruled," the judge replied.

"It's possible," I said, "but it isn't true. I respect Ellie."

He snickered. "You're seventeen. You were alone with a girl. Admit it, you're in love and you were…"

"Objection!" Jerry hollered again. "He's trying to circumvent the evidence."

"Objection sustained. Stick to the facts, prosecutor."

"Is it possible that since you love her you would lie to protect her brother?" Dempsey shouted at me even though the judge was saying, "objection sustained."

He threw up his hands. "No further questions, your honor."

I looked at Ellie as I left that stand. She looked at me. Her eyes were full of hurt and fear and I felt like I could just dissolve and slide under a bench somewhere.

Next, Dempsey called Elbert McAllister to the stand. He testified that he had seen Mickey wave a gun at Udell three days before he was killed. He said that Mickey was wearing the boots when he did it.

Later during the day Jerry called Alice McAllister to the stand. She wore a hat with a little net that came down from the brim and she wore little white gloves and a dress with tight sleeves that came down just past her elbows. She looked just like a picture out of a fashion catalog, but the way she kept fidgeting with her handkerchief told me that even Alice McAllister could get rattled a bit. "Mrs. McAllister," Jerry said, "please tell the court what happened the afternoon that you and your husband drove Frankie Keilman to the hospital?"

She shot a glance at her husband, "Well, I don't rightly know. You see I heard a commotion out in the yard and ran out. Frankie and Liddie Grace were in the yard and the boy was hurt. I suppose he had fallen or something."

"You suppose? You mean he didn't tell you what had happened?"

"I can't really recall," she said.

"And you didn't think to ask him what was wrong?"

"Oh, I was so rattled. I just can't remember. That's all."

"Can't remember or won't remember?"

"Objection!" Dempsey shouted. "This has nothing to do with the case."

"Oh, but it does your honor," Jerry said. "I have a medical document right here." He picked up a piece of paper up from the table, "stating that Franklin Delano Keilman was treated and released for rib fractures, massive bruising and impact injuries concurrent with those likely obtained in a fight. Doesn't it seem likely that Mrs. McAllister, that anyone, would logically ask what had happened?"

"Objection overruled," the judge said.

Dempsey had no questions for Mrs. McAllister. I was called to the stand again and asked to recount what had happened between Liddie Grace and Rusty Dawson, which I did.

"And when you came to in the hospital who was there to greet you?" Jerry asked.

"My mom and dad and Mr. McAllister. But I didn't let them know I was awake right away. See, my mom and dad were arguing over something that had happened in the past, an old girlfriend or something like that, so I didn't want them to know I could hear them so I just laid there with my eyes closed. Then Mr. McAllister came in and he told my momma that he'd pay my way through school if she would promise to keep me quiet about what really happened. He didn't want word getting out that Rusty had tried…well, you know, to do things to Liddie Grace."

I suppose if Liddie Grace could've crawled under the pew, she would have.

Elbert McAllister jumped up, "That's a lie. It wasn't a Dawson that attacked my daughter, it was a McThacker, Mickey McThacker, a murderer and a rapist."

"Order!" the judge demanded. Rusty sat back down.

"No further questions, your honor," Jerry Mays said.

Then Dempsey questioned me. "Frankie, why were you taking a pie to the McAllister's in the first place?"

"Cause Liddie Grace was mad at me and I wanted to make up with her."

"Why was she mad at you?"

"Um, well, see, I wrote her a note that said I didn't want to go to the picnic with her. She got really mad at me on account of that. So, Momma said that she'd make a pie if I would go make up with her and ask her to the picnic. That's why I was taking a pie to her house, to ask her to go with me to the church picnic."

"Now, you say that Mr. McAllister offered to pay your momma if you'd keep quiet. Don't you think that was to protect his little girl's honor?"

"Objection," Jerry said. "Leading the witness."

"Objection sustained," the judge said.

"Did your parents comply?"

"Yes. I did, too, up to a point, but I couldn't live with the lie any more so I told someone the truth about everything."

"And who did you tell?"

"My preacher, Brother Van Dyke."

After I said that I could tell he was itching to call Brother Van Dyke to the stand and really dog him, but first it was Jerry's turn again and he called Liddie Grace to the stand.

"Miss McAllister, please tell the court what happened to you on the afternoon that Frankie Keilman brought your mother a pie."

Liddie fidgeted just like her momma had done. "Well, I was walking home when all of a sudden there was a big boy, a man, blocking the path and he attacked me."

She looked around and pointed straight at Mickey, "That man right there. He's the one that did it."

"I didn't do it!" Mickey shouted. "She's making that up."

"Order," the judge said.

There was a murmur.

"So if Frankie Keilman saw Rusty Dawson and you saw Mickey McThacker, one of you needs glasses, wouldn't you say?"

"Objection!" Dempsey shouted.

So then Miss Mays got called to the stand and she testified to seeing Rusty Dawson trying to kill me and she testified that she threatened to blow his head off with a sawed-off shot gun.

Then it was Dempsey's turn to question her.

"Please tell the court what happened on the day in question," he said.

She cleared her voice, "On the day in question Rusty Dawson enrolled in Crooked Springs School. I have the paperwork confirming his enrollment. Not only that but he also attacked Sandy Coltrain on the ball field and broke his nose. I have a medical report verifying that fact and sworn, signed statements from both of Sandy's parents as well as the testimony of every child who was in attendance that day, most specifically, Sandy Coltrain himself. I was on my way home from seeing to Sandy when I came upon Rusty Dawson attacking Frankie and Liddie Grace. I carry a weapon for protection because I walk home alone every day. I pulled the weapon, a sawed-off shotgun, out of my bag and threatened Dawson. He then ran into the woods and I proceeded to accompany Frankie and Liddie Grace back to the McAllister home where Alice and Elbert McAllister met us. Liddie Grace told them that it had been Rusty Dawson who attacked her. I don't know why they changed their stories."

"Perhaps they have not changed their stories, Miss Mays. Does it not stand to reason that since you are a sibling of the defending attorney that you would try to arrange your story to support his case?"

"Objection!" Jerry shouted.

"Objection overruled," the judge said.

"It is possible, but it's not true," she said. "I am telling the truth and so is Frankie."

"But just like you, ma'am, Frankie Keilman has reason to want to protect McThacker. Ladies and Gentlemen of the jury, please keep this in mind throughout the trial.After that Jerry called Mickey back up.

"Mickey," he said, "have you ever made liquor?"

The courtroom went stone cold silent.

Mickey looked at Ellie and there was hurt in his eyes. She stared back at him and gave him a little nod. "I have."

"Tell the court why you made liquor," Jerry Mays said. "Tell the court everything, Mr. McThacker."

Mickey looked over at the jury then he looked out at his family, "Because when I was little and Ellie was a baby, our momma died of a fever and our daddy, Mooney McThacker, he had to raise us. He was a moonshiner and sometimes, I had to help him."

"How did you help him?"

"I took care of Ellie and I did all of the cooking and wood chopping and stuff like that. I used to have to take him his supper when he was working the still."

"And where is your father now?" Jerry asked.

"One night I was coming to bring my daddy some supper and I was almost up to the still when I heard some men arguing. I got scared and hit down low in the bushes. It was dark but I could still see them on account of the moon was so bright and on account of Daddy had the fire burning."

"Who did you see that night?"

Mickey looked straight at McAllister. "I saw that man right yonder." He pointed at Liddie Grace's daddy. The room so quiet I could have heard a termite burb.

Jerry Mays laid his hand on the witness stand. "What happened next?"

"McAllister pulled out a gun and shot my daddy a whole bunch of times. Then he took off running." The room got wild, people hollering that Mickey was a liar. Even Liddie Grace and her momma were shouting. The judge made everybody get quiet again. "Are you saying that Elbert McAllister murdered your father?"

"I am," Mickey said.

McAllister jumped up, "You lying little son of a bitch."

Chapter Twenty-Six

"Elbert McAllister is not on trial here!" Dempsey was shouting.

"Can you substantiate these preposterous claims?" the judge asked. He looked so mad at Mickey that he could just bite his head plum off.

"If that fancy talk means can I prove it, then no I don't have any pictures of McAllister shooting my daddy but I know that it was him."

It was a madhouse in that courtroom for a little while. Mickey was hollering that McAllister killed his daddy and McAllister was calling Mickey a rapist, murderer and a liar and the Dawson boys were standing up yelling all sorts of cuss words and all of the Pablos and their kin were yelling. The court had to take a recess.

When we returned, the tension in that room was already thick enough to slice like pickled bologna when we walked in.

When Jerry got up he said, "Yesterday, Mickey McThacker claimed that Elbert McAllister killed his father and that he is buried in a thicket in Swamp Holler. At this time, I'd like to call Minister Jullain Van Dyke to the stand."

After the preacher was sworn in, Jerry started questioning him. "How long have you lived on Briar Ridge?"

"Less than one year," the minister replied.

"And do you have any special ties with anyone on the ridge other than the fact that you conduct services?"

"No sir. I conduct services at three separate churches in this county and there are some members of my congregations whose names I have yet to learn."

"I see. Is it true that you are also a photographer?"

"It is."

"And what do you usually photograph?"

"Wildlife, nature shots, that sort of thing, usually."

"But not always?"

Brother Van Dyke looked straight at me. "No, not always."

"Did you, in fact, photograph a moonshine still?"

He squirmed a bit. "Actually, I did. Only out of curiosity. I had never seen one before."

"Tell the court about the day you photographed the still."

"I was walking through the woods and came upon what appeared to be a lean-to. I decided to duck into and take a break, but lo and behold it turned out to be a still, so I did what any photographer would do. I photographed it."

"Why did you photograph it?"

"I had intended to maybe sell the picture to a magazine some day in the future."

"And did you develop this photo?"

"I did."

Martin handed Jerry a large envelope. Jerry took a picture from the envelope and allowed the ladies and gentlemen of the jury to view the picture.

"Why did you take only the one photograph if this was such an interesting subject that you hoped to sell?"

"I didn't take only one photograph. I took two. You see, I heard someone coming."

"Who did you hear?"

"I wasn't sure at the time so I got afraid and I hid behind two large boulders. I didn't recognize the voices so I turned and peeped through the crack behind the boulders and I snapped a photograph, just one. I don't know why I did it. I was scared half to death. I had accidentally walked up on a moonshine still and now I was listening to a conversation."

Jerry took another photograph from the envelope. "Ladies and gentlemen of the jury. You will see in this picture the exact same still which happens to be the McThacker still, however the two men in the photograph are Udell Dawson, the deceased and Elbert McAllister. Now why would Elbert McAllister be meeting Udell Dawson at the site of the McThacker still? It leaves one to question."

He turned the witness over to Dempsey. "Mr. Van Dyke, did you hear what these men said?"

"No, sir, there was a crow nearby making noise which is probably why they didn't hear my camera click."

"Then these two men could have met by happenstance?"

"Yes, I suppose they could. But it was odd that they would both be walking in the woods, in such an out of the way place."

"But you were there and you had no connection to the still." He turned to the judge. "No further questions, Your Honor."

I think that each time a witness left the stand my nervousness grew, anticipating that I was next.

Jerry stood and straightened his suit jacket. He rubbed his chin and stood stone still for a moment, like he was a cat preparing to pounce on something. Then he said, "I call Ancil Keilman to the witness stand." My dad rose, wearing a blue plaid pair of pants, a maroon and white striped shirt and a black tie. He adjusted his belt, took off his hat and approached the stand.

He took his oath and was ready to testify. He did not look at anyone. He stared at the floor. Then Jerry leaned on the rail. "Mr. Keilman, tell us what you know of Udell Dawson."

My dad cleared his throat. "Udell Dawson worked for." He took another breath. "I know that Udell Dawson worked for Elbert McAllister."

"Worked for him? You mean on his farm? Or tended his oil rigs?"

"No. He did other things for him."

"What do you mean other things?"

"Udell Dawson collected money from McThacker and gave a portion of it to McAllister."

"Now why would he do that?" Jerry asked.

"Because Elbert McAllister was holding it over Dawson. Dawson had killed a woman and only McAllister knew it. He had evidence of it and to keep him from turning in that evidence, Dawson was paying McAllister only he wasn't giving McAllister his own money, he was taking it from McThacker and later from his kids."

"That's a lie!" McAllister shouted. "I never took a dime from Dawson."

"No, it's not," Rusty Dawson shouted out. "It's not a lie. McAllister was taking money from our daddy."

The other boys pulled him down and I could hear them saying, "Shut up." The jury heard them, too, because they all looked that way.

"How do you know this to be the truth?" Jerry asked my dad.

"Because..." he looked back at me and Momma. "I used to sneak down to Swamp Holler to see McThacker's wife, to check up on her and the youngin's. I thought a lot of her. I was there one night when Dawson showed up and I heard him come to the door and threaten Irene and I heard him say that McAllister was wanting his money and that if McThacker didn't pay up then things were

254

going to start happening. A month later Irene died and as far as anyone knew the secret died with her, but I knew and McAllister, he always suspected that I knew."

Momma couldn't look at him. Her head was down, her shame complete. My dad was admitting openly that he had never stopped loving Irene Falling Leaf McThacker and that until she died he was still checking up on her.

"Just for the record, me and Irene, we weren't doing anything wrong," he said. "I just had to know she was okay from time to time."

"Thank you," Jerry said.

Dempsey couldn't find anything to cross examine my dad about. I suppose nobody could have. My dad had no reason to protect McThacker and no reason to lie about the McAllisters or the Dawsons. My dad was the last person on the ridge that anyone would expect to testify on behalf of the McThackers. But as he returned to his seat, I looked over and saw the look of pride on Granny Flor's face, pride and compassion. It was as if my dad's testimony had redeemed him in her eyes.

Next, Jerry Mays called my momma to the stand. As she stood to go, I grabbed her arm. "Momma, tell the truth," I said. "Please, for my sake, tell the truth." She looked at me for a second then headed to the stand.

I braced myself, not knowing what to expect from Momma.

She swore to tell the whole truth and nothing but the truth. She looked back at the McAllisters then at my dad and at me. She was taking her time. I suppose she was trying to decide on something. Jerry asked her if she knew anything about the things my dad had said and she began to talk.

"A long time ago I was paid by Elbert McAllister to pretend to have cheated on my husband and to say that my son was not really Ancil's. Elbert told me that Ancil could not be trusted and that if I didn't reign him in then he would ruin our name and any chance

Frankie would ever have of going to school and making something out of himself. He said that I cared anything at all about my boy's future then I'd do what he said to do. So I did it. I wrote a letter to Udell Dawson telling about our long and wonderful love affair, an affair that never happened and I did it because," she choked up and looked at me. "I did it because I was afraid of being alone and I didn't want anything to happen to Frankie."

"Objection," Dempsey said. "This has nothing to do with the trial."

"Your Honor," Jerry said, "it has everything to do with the trial."

"Objection overruled," the judge said. "Continue."

Jerry looked at the jury. "Ladies and gentlemen," he said, "young Mickey McThacker helped his father make moonshine at a still located just below Rainy Jackson's place where Swamp Holler and Briar Ridge join. Elbert McAllister was blackmailing Udell Dawson about a crime that he knew Dawson had committed years ago. McAllister believed that Ancil Keilman, because of his connection to the McThacker woman, had somehow become privy to the information, but he couldn't outright kill Ancil Keilman, it would cause too much of a stink so he found another way to keep him quiet. He used Mrs. Keilman's insecurities about her son's future to prod her into keeping her husband quiet, to even discrediting him if need be, in order to protect his own reputation and keep all questions at bay.

"To obtain the money to pay McAllister, Dawson was forcing the McThackers to give him sixty precent of their moonshine profits. When Mooney McThacker refused to continue doing so, Dawson told McAllister that McThacker had gone to the law and was about to expose everything so McAllister shot McThacker. He heard someone coming and ran."

"That's a lie!" McAllister shouted.

The judge ordered him to be quiet.

Jerry let Momma leave the stand.

"Now, you might ask how I can prove my statement. Well, I call to the stand Ellie McThacker." She walked like a turtle, shy and uncertain toward that stand. In her hands she clutched an old stained white purse that looked like it once belonged to a fine lady.

"Ellie," he began, "how old were you when your daddy came up missing?"

She shrugged. "I don't nine or ten maybe."

"Tell us what happened that night."

"Mickey went to take Daddy some supper. I had cooked us up some fry bread and jowl meat. Mickey was gone a long time. It was getting way past dark and I was scared cause I was all by myself at the house then Mickey came bursting through the door and he was crying. I had never known Mickey to cry, not even when a snake bit him that one time. I knew something was bad wrong. Daddy's dead," he said. Then right there on the witness stand, Ellie started to shake and was afraid she wouldn't be able to hold it together. Her voice cracked. "He took me…he took me out there in the woods and showed me out daddy, lying dead with blood all around, blood and bullets, cause that man shot him more than once and one of them bullets went clean through him. I don't know why I did it, but I…" she opened her purse and took out a bullet, a bullet that had killed her father.

Jerry Mays walked over to the table and picked up another envelope. He opened it and took out a bullet that was an exact match to Ellie's. "The same gun that killed Mooney McThacker is the gun that killed Udell Dawson. Ellie and Mickey McThacker did not kill their own father. They had no motive, but Udell Dawson had a motive and Elbert McAllister had a motive. Mooney McThacker wasn't going to give them any more money and Dawson rigged it so that McAllister thought Mooney was going to double cross them, then he used Mooney's own children to continue paying McAllister. When Mickey McThacker told

Dawson he'd do his own runs from now own, Dawson sent his boys down to threaten him which is what Frankie witnessed at Goodin's Store.

"Anyway, when McThacker stopped paying Dawson, McAllister wanted his money. Then Dawson enrolled Rusty in the school to make McAllister uncomfortable, but Rusty's young and his ambition got the better of him. He took it upon himself to rape McAllister's daughter in order to send him a message. However, he wasn't counting on Frankie Keilman and Eadie Mays to stumble into the picture. And when it all came down, McAllister ordered his wife and kid to lay the blame on Mickey, because you see by this time McAllister was fed up. The Dawsons weren't paying him and besides, by trying to rape Liddie Grace, they had brought too much attention on his otherwise perfect family reputation. No one in the county would ever suspect Elbert McAllister of extortion or murder."

"This is preposterous," McAllister said in a loud voice.

"Is it?" Jerry asked. "I submit one last piece of evidence." He opened an envelope and removed a gun. "The murder weapon," he said.

"Where did you get that?" McAllister shouted. "Where the hell did you get that?" He felt of his coat pocket, like he was looking for something.

Alice McAllister stood. "I gave it to them."

All of a sudden Elbert McAllister came across the seat. He lunged at his wife, knocking her clean out into the isle. I thought he was going to kill her right there in front of everybody. Liddie Grace was screaming and some men were trying to pull McAlllister off of her, but he was knocking people all over the place. A police officer that had been standing by raced over there and pulled a gun on him. "Stop," he said. And McAllister did. "Step away with your hands up."

Another police officer approached with a set of cuffs. He put them on McAllister and said, "I am placing you under arrest for disorderly conduct in a court of law, for the murder of Mooney McThacker and for the murder of Udell Dawson."

Chapter Twenty-Seven

The police led Elbert McAllister out of the courtroom that day while someone tended to his bleeding wife and frantic daughter. Some people who worked in the courthouse took Alice McAllister and Liddie Grace out of the building. They were both crying and hysterical. The Dawsons were yelling curses at him as he walked out the door. One of them said he hoped McAllister got the electric chair for what he had done. Then the door closed and Elbert McAllister was gone from our sight.

Then, in light of the proof that it had been McAllister who killed Udell Dawson, all the charges against Mickey were dropped. Jerry Mays had won the case. The Dawsons filed out almost unnoticed while the rest of us made sounds of relief. It was over. It was really over. Mickey was going home.

Right there in the courtroom the Pablos and McThackers started hugging each other and crying and patting Mickey on the back. Oscar, Joe, Jim Elee and most of the male cousins shook hands with the Mays brothers and the women were hugging Miss Mays and Ellie and they were kissing Mickey on the cheek.

When Mickey got close enough to Ellie he just reached out and grabbed her. Those two hugged long and hard, both of them crying. Then Mickey saw Eadie Mays standing there. He pulled her in and hugged her, too.

My momma and daddy weren't saying anything, but daddy looked like he had looked back years ago when he had to put one of our horses down. The thing was a nasty business and couldn't be helped, but it was over and life had to go on. He picked up his hat, smoothed the brim and put it on. Then he said, "Sarah Jean, let's go home. It's nigh on supper time." She nodded and they headed for the door. "Coming, Frankie?" Momma said.

I looked at Ellie's family one last time then started to leave, but stopped when somebody took hold of my jacket. "Don't you be a sneakin' outta here, boy." It was Granny Flor. "Ellie," she hollered. "Yer boyfriend's trying to run out on you."

Ellie looked up. "Where you going, Frankie?"

I smiled. "Nowhere I reckon."

Mickey let go of the girls and came over to me. He tussled my hair. "You're all right, sport. Kind of weird, but you're all right."

Ellie smiled like she could hear angels singing. "He's just a little touched is all, but he'll do won't he, Mickey?"

"Yeah, Ellie, he'll do."

I hugged Ellie right in front of my parents and everybody else.

As we all made our way out onto the courthouse lawn, Granny Flor invited all of us over for supper, but of course Momma said she was too poorly to be out so late, so she had Daddy take her on home, but I went to the Pablo's for supper.

There was laughing and talking and more back patting while we all hung around the Oscar Pablo's house. Cousins smoked on the porch and Sadie Rose made strong coffee. I stood on the porch, too. Ellie came up and put her hand in mind. I smiled at her. She smiled back. I felt like I could fly.

In the weeks that followed Momma and Daddy were quiet. There was no arguing, no bickering or belittling. I almost missed the way they had been. I continued living in my shed but I ate at home much of the time. Then one Sunday morning I went down to go to church with them. Daddy came out in a pair of blue plaid pants, a yellow striped shirt and a red spotted tie. He wore a straw hat. Momma said," You're not wearing that to church are you?"

"Why the Sam Hill not?" he said. "It fits don't it?"

I started grinning and I couldn't stop. Momma said. "What're you laughing at?"

"Nothing," I said. "Nothing at all." It's just that when the petty arguing started I knew they would stay together, that somehow there was an unspoken bond that they had come to share. The pettiness would continue, but the McAllisters, the Dawsons, would never be mentioned in that house again.

I was helping Mrs. Goodin at the store one Saturday in April when the McAllister vehicle pulled in for gas. Alice went in to pay Mrs. Goodin while I pumped. Liddie Grace got out.

"Bet you think bad of me, don't you?"

I looked up from where I was bent over putting the nozzle into the gas tank. Liddie was wearing a wool checkered coat and she still wore red ribbons in her dark hair, but all the giggles had gone out of her. For a moment I thought of how pretty she really was and I saw her the same way I had seen her the day Rusty Dawson attacked her, a young woman in trouble, only this time the trouble came from a bitterness growing inside.

"No, Liddie Grace. I don't think one bit bad of you."

"But my daddy murdered that man, murdered Ellie's daddy. You must think about that every time you look at me." She looked down. "I suppose that's all anybody's ever gonna see. He wasn't always mean, you know. He was my daddy. He did love me."

"He just made a bad choice. We're all capable of hurting people, Liddie Grace. And we're all capable of doing good. I reckon your daddy just put his love for money ahead of his love for his family and that took over him and consumed his life."

"But you don't hate me?"

"No, I don't hate you."

"We can't stay here," she said. "Momma and I. We're moving. People here will never let us forget. Soon as Momma walks out of that store Mrs. Goodin and everybody in there will start talking about us. They'll be whispering behind our backs before the screen door even closes. I know because before my daddy killed a man, I was one of them. This town, especially this ridge, will never let us live it down."

"Where will you go?"

"Back to Atlanta," she said. "We've got a lot of family there."

They had family on Briar Ridge, too, but those family members would likely distance themselves from them. Some of them would probably move to other locations within the county or the state.

"I'm gonna miss you, Frankie," she said. "I really did always like you."

I hung up the gas hose. "I know."

Her mom came out of the store and she turned to get in the car. "Liddie Grace," I said. She turned. "I just want you to know that I won't forget you. You'll always be the girl that I ripped my pants for."

She smiled.

"It's gonna be all right, Liddie Grace. You're gonna be all right."

"See ya, Frankie," she said. She got in the car. Her mom glared at me from over her shoulder then they drove away. I watched their car until it was just a speck on the horizon. I didn't see Liddie Grace anymore after that. I suppose they moved to Atlanta.

When May came Miss Mays was told that she would not be rehired for her position as teacher at Crooked Springs School. It had become common knowledge that she was courting Mickey

McThacker. Of course, that wasn't the reason she was given by the school board, but everyone knew. She didn't care. Miss Mays stopped wearing her hair up after that and stopped wearing those long skirts. She took to wearing her hair like girls on the television and to wearing shorter skirts. She even wore make-up and when she did, she looked better than a country music star.

People talked at the store. They talked about the McAllisters and whatever became of them. They talked about Gertrude Mays' great niece and how she was openly courting the McThacker boy from Swamp Holler and what was the world coming to when a pretty well-to-do blonde girl like her would take to wearing miniskirts and courting a moonshiner's boy, but mostly they talked about that Ellie McThacker and how she had been accepted to Berea College on a science scholarship and how she had made the highest grades of anyone in the entire school, or the county for that matter. Some said the system was rigged, because nobody from Swamp Holler was naturally smart. Others said nothing would come of it.

I went to Ellie and Mickey's house on a Saturday after work. It was May. The swampland was alive with vivid colors. Blooming white trees and dark green canopies of leaves covered the hills that encircled the holler. Blue and purple wildflowers bloomed all along the swamp road. I drove slow taking it all in. When I pulled into the drive, I smiled. There sat Miss Mays and Mickey on the porch, brazenly courting as the folks over at the store would say. Miss Mays was wearing a short paisley print dress and white boots. She had her hair puffed and wore a white band in it to match her boots. Mickey was sitting on a big block of wood he had rolled onto the porch. He wore a white t-shirt with his cigarettes rolled up in one sleeve. His dark tan arms were lean and muscled and he wore his hair slicked back.

"Hey, Ellie," Mickey hollered. "Get your nose out of that book and come out. Your feller's here."

He smiled at me. "Behave yourself. If you get my sister in trouble I'll kill you."

I acted like I was going to kick the block of wood out from under him. He got up and pretended to rough me up, scuffing my hair.

Ellie came out. She was wearing a pair of pants. I had never seen her in pants, but sure as the world, she was wearing them. Her long brown hair was parted in the middle and she sported pony tails. She still wore her boy shoes. I came to the conclusion that maybe Ellie just liked that pair of shoes.

"Let's go for a walk," she said then took my hand, pulling me toward the road. "Maybe go over to see Joe and Jewell. They're having a baby you know."

"No, I didn't know. Gee whiz, seems like so much has happened and we're all suddenly so old."

"Jewell's same age as me," Ellie said. "I'm not ready for that yet."

"We've got the rest of our lives," I said.

"Anyway, they're going to name the baby Jerry Wayne if it's a boy. After Mickey's new brother-in-law, because it was Jerry that kept Mickey out of jail. And the Wayne is after Mickey Wayne. Joe says since Mickey got shot in the butt he deserves to at least have a kid named after him."

I laughed.

"I like the pants," I said. I plucked a purple flower from beside the road and stuck it behind her ear. "You look like you're ready to go on an adventure now."

"My sister-in-law to be bought them for me," she said.

"So Miss Mays and Mickey are getting married?"

"Yep, last week of July. I reckon Eadie's daddy is throwing them a big wedding. Mickey's already got a job lined up in Lexington. He'll start first of August, working on a big horse farm."

"So are you moving to Lexington?" I was a little afraid she was going to say yes, but I hid it.

"Only for one week then I'm off to school. You know I got accepted into Berea?"

"I know. I'm proud of you."

"Frankie, this means we're not going to be seeing each other for a while come August."

I nodded. "I suppose it would if..."

"If what?"

"If I hadn't also applied to Berea."

She stopped dead in her tracks. "But I thought you were going to Asbury to be a minister."

I shrugged. "Maybe God didn't create every man to stand behind a pulpit. Maybe He made some of us to draw and to sing…" I laughed. "Maybe he made some of us touched and He did it on purpose."

"You're going to Berea?"

"I am. I'm going to pursue a career in the arts, Ellie. And do you know what else?"

"What?" she asked.

"We've still got the summer."

She pulled a weed from beside the road and ran it through her fingers. "That we do." I took the weed and made a complete circle around her finger with it.

"I know we are young, but when our college days are done and I go off on my grand adventures to see…"

"The Great Wall of China?" she said.

"And the jungles of Africa," I added.

"And you get sick from malaria and need a doctor to nurse you back to health."

"Exactly," I said. "Well, it had better be you there beside me cause anybody else would just let me die or be eaten by a lion. I want our future to be together."

"I'll be there," she said.

"Promise?"

"As sure as Mickey's butt was sore from that bullet," she said. "I'm good at keeping my promises."

"Yeah, I know," I said I put my arm around her and held her close as we walked across the highway and down the path.

ABOUT THE AUTHOR

Darlene Franklin Campbell is an award-winning poet and novelist from southern Kentucky. She is also a first grade teacher and visual artist. Her other works include *I Listened, Momma*, *Uncommon Clay* and *Looking for Pork Chop McQuade*. Darlene donates portions of her royalties to aid in the fight against cancer and to fund efforts aimed at halting mountaintop removal. She holds an M.A. from Lindsey Wilson College and has done other post grad work at Western Kentucky University. She is proud of her Appalachian heritage and writes about the region and its people, not as an outsider looking in with romantic notions, but as one who has risen up out of the Kentucky soil, like a tree, with roots going four hundred years deep, touching long-gone Scotch Irish settlers, Native American bloodlines and Melungeon legends. In her spare time, Darlene is an avid disciple of martial arts and enjoys spending time with friends, family and nature.